Kelly Elliott is a *New York Times* and *USA Today* bestselling contemporary romance author. Since finishing her bestselling Wanted series, Kelly continues to spread her wings while remaining true to her roots and giving readers stories rich with hot protective men, strong women and beautiful surroundings.

Kelly has been passionate about writing since she was fifteen. After years of filling journals with stories, she finally followed her dream and published her first novel, *Wanted*, in November of 2012.

Kelly lives in central Texas with her husband, daughter, and two pups. When she's not writing, Kelly enjoys reading and spending time with her family. She is down to earth and very in touch with her readers, both on social media and at signings.

Visit Kelly Elliott online:

www.kellyelliottauthor.com
@author_kelly
www.facebook.com/KellyElliottAuthor/

COWBOYS & ANGELS
Book 4

NEW YORK TIMES & USA TODAY BESTSELLING AUTHOR

KELLY ELLIOTT

piatkus

PIATKUS

First published in Great Britain in 2018 by Piatkus

1 3 5 7 9 10 8 6 4 2

A CIP catalogue record for this book
is available from the British Library.

ISBN 978-0-349-41846-9

Printed and bound in Great Britain by
Clays Ltd, St Ives plc

Cover photo and designer: Sara Eirew Photography
Editor: Cori McCarthy, Yellowbird Editing
Proofer: Amy Rose Capetta, Yellowbird Editing
Developmental/Proofer: Elaine York, Allusion Graphics
Interior Designer: JT Formatting

Papers used by Piatkus are from well-managed forests
and other responsible sources.

Piatkus
An imprint of
Little, Brown Book Group
Carmelite House
50 Victoria Embankment
London EC4Y 0DZ

An Hachette UK Company
www.hachette.co.uk

www.littlebrown.co.uk

This book is dedicated to those who have lost love ... only to find it again.

Aunt Vi

John and Melanie Parker

Waylynn   Tripp   Steed and Paxton   Mitchell and Corina   Cord   Trevor   Amelia and Wade

Chloe   Gage

Love Again

A Note to Readers

Love Again is book four in the Cowboys and Angels series. The books in this series are not stand-alone books. Stories intertwine between books and continued to grow within each book. If you have picked up this book and have not read *Lost Love, Love Profound, and Tempting Love,* I strongly suggest that you read them in order.

For a list of characters in the series as well as other fun extras, please visit the series website: www.cowboysandangelsseries.com

PROLOGUE

Waylynn

Summer

I didn't hear a word that the interior designer was saying. I was focused on the way Jonathon looked in those Wranglers. And his boots. And the freaking black cowboy hat that made his grey eyes stand out. I swallowed hard.

Jesus… could this guy get any hotter?

Jonathon caught my stare from across the room. When he smiled my panties nearly disintegrated. The man had never even touched me, and yet one look from him and I was damn near panting.

Yes, he could *get hotter. Christ Almighty.*

Before I could stop myself, my tongue ran over my dry lips. Jonathon's brows rose and his boyishly handsome smile turned into a sexy-as-hell grin. When his eyes smoldered, my breath hitched.

I wiped my brow. *Shit, is it hot in here?*

Jonathon knew where my dirty little mind had taken me, and I was pretty damn sure his was going in the same direction. I closed my eyes and tried not to picture anything sexy, but failed. Me…up against the wall with him buried deep inside me, giving me a long overdue orgasm.

"Waylynn? Waylynn?" Ann's voice pulled me from my naughty thoughts.

Popping my eyes open, I cleared my throat. "What? Huh?"

With a sweet smile, Ann repeated the question I had totally tuned out.

"The color scheme. Are you good with it?"

I frowned. What in the heck was she talking about? Color scheme? "Umm."

The young woman waited patiently, while I stood there with my mouth open like an idiot.

"Color scheme?" I asked with a slight smile.

Ann laughed. "Did you even hear a word I said?"

My eyes darted to Jonathon. He was leaning against a desk in the middle of the room. It was the only piece of furniture that had been left by the previous owners of this space. His arms were now crossed over his massive chest, and he wore a shit-eating grin. Did the man know how freaking handsome he was? That sex appeal dripped off of him?

He winked, and I had to lock my knees to keep from falling.

Bastard.

He knew exactly where my mind had gone, because his was there as well.

Turning back to the interior decorator, I replied, "I'm so sorry. Jonathon was distracting me."

One quick glance back and Jonathon's smile vanished, replaced by a shocked expression. "Me?" he asked.

I nodded. "Yes. You."

Ann was now staring at Jonathon. I could see by the look in her eyes and the way she chewed her lip that she was having similar thoughts. It was obvious by the way she was trying *not* to look in his direction while she talked. She was probably the same age as he was, and that pissed me off. Then again, I had to remind myself that Jonathon hadn't been staring at Ann. He'd been staring at me.

"What did I do?" Jonathon asked.

I wanted to say that his hotness was making my panties wet, and the throbbing between my legs was making it hard to think, but I decided it was best to avoid the truth.

"That desk you're leaning on. I keep wondering why the previous owner left it?"

Jonathon looked down at the desk as Ann asked, "Do you want to keep the desk? It would be beautiful refinished."

I shrugged. "I'm not sure."

Jonathon walked around it. "I'm sure we could put this to good use. I can come up with an idea or two."

His head lifted and his eyes caught mine. I swore they turned as dark as the night sky. I swallowed, trying to ignore the pulse between my legs.

"Yes, I'm positive we can come up with a few ideas. Maybe you can even use the desk in your office," Ann added.

I forced myself to look away and focus on Ann. "Yeah, maybe. Okay, so the color scheme?"

Clapping her hands, Ann started into the soft greens and blues. I had to stay focused on her lips, avoiding the temptation to look at the stud cowboy who was now walking around the room behind us.

"You've made a note of the wood floors I want in the studios?" I asked. Ann nodded and looked over to Jonathon.

He held up his folder and gave it a little shake. "I've got it all in here."

"Now, Waylynn, do you want a window covering in your office for privacy?" Ann asked.

Why I turned and looked at Jonathon was beyond me. The left side of his mouth rose, and if I had been turned on before, now I was practically dead.

With a grin, I replied, "Yes. You never know when you might have that certain someone stop by and give you a quickie against the wall."

Jonathon laughed while he shook his head and walked to the area that would be for the parents while they waited for their kids.

Ann stared with her mouth gaping. "Oh, um, I wasn't really thinking for that purpose, but okay!"

It was time to wrap this shit up. The sexual tension in this room couldn't get any heavier.

"Is that it for now?" I asked, as I gave Ann pleading eyes that were begging her to say yes.

Flipping through her notes, she frowned. "I think so. As we get closer I'll bring in some fabrics for the chairs as well as some paint samples." Ann walked over to Jonathon and placed her hand on his arm, smiling. "Jonathon? You'll keep me updated on how things are moving along?"

He nodded.

"You have my cell number still?"

Still? Well, that's interesting.

"I have it written down somewhere."

Ann frowned slightly before plastering on a fake smile. "I'm sure you'll be able to find it this evening." She turned my way. "I'm so excited to be working with you, Waylynn. I've heard you're an amazing dancer. You certainly have the legs for it!"

Peeking down, I looked at the long dress I had on that nearly went to the floor. When I looked back up at her, Ann's face was flushed.

"Well, I mean, I watched a few videos from when you were a Rockette. You were amazing."

I laughed. "For a second there, I thought things were about to get awkward, wondering how you knew what my legs looked like!"

Ann let out a loud laugh. "Oh, no! Ha! Well, I'll be going."

Following Ann toward the front door, she stopped short and nearly caused me to run into her back.

"Jonathon, are you coming?" she called over her shoulder.

"No, I've got a few things to discuss with Waylynn."

Ann shook my hand. "Thank you for giving me the job. I know I don't have as much experience, so I appreciate you taking a chance on me."

"It's going to look beautiful. Thank you, Ann."

I followed her to the door and waved as she headed down the street to her parked car.

Spinning on my heel, I took a deep breath and walked into the building. I stopped when I saw Jonathon had moved the desk.

"What are you doing?" I asked.

He was measuring the desk. "I figure this will be about the middle of your office after the changes."

I walked closer. My brows rose as I attempted to keep my cool and not let my raging libido take control.

"And why are you putting it there?" I asked, coming to a stop in front of him.

He smiled and my knees wobbled. When his hands began to lift my skirt, my heart nearly jumped out of my damn chest. Before I knew it, I was in his arms, my legs wrapped around his body, and he was setting me on the desk.

"If I'm reading this wrong, tell me now, Waylynn, but I'm pretty sure you want the same things that I want."

His mouth was on my neck while his hand slipped inside my panties.

I couldn't think; I was so overcome with desire. "I do. God, I want this...and you."

His hands were everywhere on my body, causing me to go temporarily insane. This was wrong. He was six years younger than me. He was Cord's best friend.

"Tell me what you want, Waylynn. Tell me, and I'll do it, baby."

My mind was screaming at me to stop while my body was screaming for more.

With shaking hands, I unbuckled his belt and made haste getting his jeans down. I hadn't been with another man since before Jack. What in the hell was I thinking?

His mouth found its way to my ear where he whispered, "Tell me, baby."

There was no use fighting it. I wanted Jonathon Turner more than I had ever wanted any other man. Pulling my earlobe into his mouth, he let out a groan as he pushed his fingers inside of me.

Finally finding my voice, I panted, "I need to come, Jonathon."

He pulled back and stared into my eyes. His smile nearly had me coming, never mind the fact that his fingers were massaging my insides. "Fast or slow? I'm about to lose control, Waylynn."

I returned the smile. "Lose every ounce. I'm all yours."

CHAPTER 1

Waylynn

November

I stepped into my office and tossed the paint samples onto my desk. Ann was going to be the damn death of me. Who in the hell knew there were so many shades of green?

I moaned and dropped my head back. At least I could lose my shit in here if I needed to. The clear windows were covered with brown paper, giving me a sense of privacy. Of course, the paper would be replaced by shades in due time. Once the studio was finished, and we were open, I'd have a view of the main dance floor from my office. I'd never be able to let the instructors oversee the dancers completely; dancing was in my soul. This was my dream come true.

I faced the window that looked out to the small courtyard. I smiled, thinking about how fun it would be to take the little ones outside and practice our stretches.

"Waylynn?"

His voice sent tingles through my entire body. Taking a deep breath, I turned to face Jonathon.

"Hey," I said, leaning against the windowsill.

He stepped inside my office. "I need to talk to you."

I was never one to be nervous or scared around men, but being in the same room with Jonathon Turner scared the living daylights out of me. It also pissed me off knowing how much power this man held over me.

"About?"

He shut the door and stood with his cowboy hat in hand. I tried not to let my eyes scan his perfect body. He was toned beyond belief. Those three mile runs he ran every day kept the man in shape. Not to mention the nightly trips to the gym I knew he took because we always crossed paths, him coming in just as I left my yoga class.

"I can't stop thinking about you," he said.

My breath stalled in my throat. "I've already told you, Jonathon. This can't work."

He took a few steps closer, and I stayed as still as I could. My fingers itched to touch him.

"Then why did you seem pissed off that I brought a date to Steed and Mitchell's birthday party a few weeks back?"

"I wasn't upset," I lied.

Jonathon took two long strides forward, standing in my space. His large, fit body inches from mine. I had to force myself to breathe.

"Can you honestly look me in the eyes and tell me you don't feel anything?"

Lifting my chin, I kept my face neutral. "Feelings aren't the issue here, the calendar is. I'm too old for you."

He laughed. "Fuck that, Waylynn. You're scared and you're using age as an excuse. Look at me and tell me you didn't feel anything when we were together."

My chest rose and fell with each labored breath. Goosebumps broke out across my body as I thought about that afternoon months ago. My eyes closed as I remembered Jonathon moving deliciously fast and hard as he fucked me on the desk and then against the wall in my dance studio. It was raw. Passionate. Spontaneous, and hot as hell. And, yes...I *had* felt something. I felt something every time this man was close, a feeling I'd never experienced before, but I couldn't admit that to him.

I smiled. "Two amazing orgasms...that's what I felt, Jonathon."

He leaned in closer, the smell of his cologne tangling with my libido. Shit. I needed him to step back before I lost control and begged him to take me right then and there.

He twirled a piece of my blonde hair between his fingers. "I know that wasn't all you felt. I saw it in your eyes then. I see it now."

I turned my head. "I'm six years older than you, Jonathon. I want things you can't possibly give me."

He huffed. "How do you know I don't want the same things?"

With a harsh laugh, I stared him down. "I want to get married, and I want kids. At least three. Can you honestly look me in the eyes and say you want that at this point in your life?"

"Yes!" he said, cupping my face in his strong hands. "Waylynn, I'm not twenty fucking years old, I'm almost twenty-seven, and I want those things, too. I'm not saying let's run off and get married tomorrow, but why won't you give us a chance? I don't care that you're older than me."

My heart was racing. "You want kids? What, like when you're thirty-five, or something?"

He closed his eyes and shook his head before opening them and pinning me with his intense stare. "You can't push me away with that. I can honestly tell you if it were up to me, I'd already be settled with a wife and kids. But no one has made me want to even think it's a possibility...until you."

My body trembled. "It…it could never work."

"Why? And stop saying because you're older than me."

Memories of Jack flooded my mind all at once. Everything from him telling me I'd never make it in New York to him sitting with his lover at the restaurant. Was I ready to open my heart again? "It just wouldn't."

Jonathon pressed his body into mine, sending a rush of desire through my veins. His lips were inches from mine. The wall I had built was beginning to crumble piece by piece. I needed to be stronger.

When his lips brushed across mine, I gasped.

His hand moved up my dress, slowly sliding it up as he pushed his hard-on into me. I gripped his strong arms to keep my legs from giving out.

Damn it. What does this man do to me?

"Please, don't push me away. I want you in more ways than just fucking you against a wall. Give me—hell, give *us*—a chance to show you that we can make this work."

Electricity zapped through my body. I was about to break.

Maybe we could fuck one more time and that would satisfy the itch I had for Jonathon Turner. His fingers brushed across my panties and I squeezed his arms.

One. More. Time.

I knew that wouldn't be enough. I needed more. I *wanted* more.

I opened my mouth to tell him to take me…when the perfect moment came to an immediate halt with the knock on my office door.

I pushed Jonathon away and dragged in a deep breath as I fixed my dress.

Jonathon walked to the other side of my desk, his hat positioned in front of his jeans to hide the bulge in his pants.

"Come…come in."

Shit. My voice was shaky.

The door opened, and Cord walked into my office. He smiled with raised eyebrows when he saw me, which made me even shakier. I was still leaning against the windowsill, trying like hell to act like my panties weren't soaking wet from the proximity of his best friend.

"What's up, big sis? I saw your car parked out front and thought maybe you'd like to go to lunch?"

My eyes darted to Jonathon.

Cord turned. "Hey! I was hoping I'd see you here. Was I interrupting anything?"

"No," I said.

"Yes," Jonathon said.

Cord bounced his gaze between the two of us. "No. Yes. Which is it?"

Jonathon grinned. "I mean, no, it's fine. I needed to find out if Waylynn had picked out which flooring she wanted."

My head was spinning. I had already told him that months ago. "Birch is fine," I softly said. Jonathon nodded.

"Listen, I know this is last minute, but a few of us are heading to Vegas tonight for the weekend. I'm taking a few days off from the bar. We're each renting our own room in case of potential hookups." Cord wiggled his brows while I looked away and I rolled my eyes.

Jonathon looked at me. "I can't go. I've got to install the light fixtures in the ballet room."

Our eyes met, and I knew what he was doing.

"You can't take the weekend off, dude? I mean, it's Vegas. Flights are wide open so getting a ticket won't be a problem."

Jonathon continued to stare at me. I regretted my next set of words before they even came out of my mouth.

"The lights can wait, and Cord's right. It's the weekend and you know what they say, 'what happens in Vegas, stays in Vegas'."

Jonathon narrowed his eyes at me.

Cord clapped his hands. "Awesome, then you're free to go. What do you say?"

The look on Jonathon's face about killed me. He looked hurt, and I hated being the person who made him feel that way.

Placing his hat on his head, Jonathon faced Cord. He plastered on a fake smile. "Sounds like a plan. I could use a little bit of fun. It's been awhile since I've had any. Count me in."

My heart dropped to my stomach, and I had to grip onto the windowsill to keep myself upright. It took everything I had not to show any reaction to Jonathon's words. They hurt more than he could know, but then again, I deserved it.

Making his way toward the door, Jonathon cleared his throat. "I've got to run if I'm heading out with y'all."

Cord gave him a light slap on the back. "You won't regret it." He leaned in closer and said, "I promise."

Before leaving my office, Jonathon looked back, tipped his hat and said, "Waylynn." It was meant to sound like a goodbye, but I knew what he was doing. He was giving me one more chance to stop him.

My heart was fighting with my head. I swallowed hard, trying to convince myself I was about to do the right thing by letting him go. "Enjoy Vegas, Jonathon," I replied, trying to keep my voice even.

His eyes turned dark, his face cold. "I will."

His words felt like a knife straight into my chest.

Jonathon looked at Cord. "Maybe I'll even get lucky this weekend. Hell, maybe I'll find myself a girlfriend. Someone to marry and have three kids with."

Cord laughed. "Jesus, dude, we're going to Vegas, not church. Hey, let me walk you out, I'll fill you in a bit more on the plans."

Glancing over his shoulder, Cord called out, "Be right back, Waylynn."

I forced a smile and nodded before I turned away from them both. Tears filled my eyes as I stared at the large pecan tree that was blowing in the wind.

The courtyard matched the feeling in my heart.

Empty.

CHAPTER 2

Waylynn

Cord's returning footsteps pulled me from my trance. "Hey, you ready for lunch?" he asked.

"Yep."

"You want to go down to Lilly's?"

"Sounds good to me," I replied.

I shut and locked the door to the dance studio. I knew Jonathon wouldn't be coming back this evening so there would be no reason I would need to come back either. Especially now that he had plans to leave for Vegas with Cord.

We walked in silence toward Lilly's place. My mind raced. Should I call Jonathon? Ask him not to go to Vegas? How unfair would that be, especially after I had told him I wasn't interested in a relationship.

"What's on your mind, sis?"

My head snapped up to Cord.

"What?'"

Cord drew his brows in. "You're preoccupied. Everything okay?"

"Yeah," I answered, making sure my voice sounded even. "I've got a lot on my mind with the dance studio."

"I can understand. It takes a lot to start a business. I remember what it was like when I opened the bar. You sure it isn't anything else?"

We stopped walking and stared at one another. For a brief moment I wanted to tell him about Jonathon. Come clean about all of it, but I stopped myself.

"I'm positive. Stop worrying, little brother, okay?"

His dimpled smile made me grin. "Okay, then let's get some food before I have to get back to the bar. I need to make sure everything is in order before I leave tonight."

I wrapped my arm up in Cord's. "Who are you leaving in charge?"

"Trevor."

"I don't think you have to worry. Trevor knows how to run that bar better than you."

Cord chuckled. "Yeah, you're probably right."

"I'm surprised Trevor isn't going with y'all."

"Well, it's last minute. We only decided to go earlier today. I hope Jonathon can get on the plane. I tried calling him earlier, but he must have had his phone on silent."

The bell on the front door of Lilly's rang as we walked in. A quick glance around showed that Cord and I practically had the place to ourselves. In the back corner, a group of teenagers sat in a booth, laughing loudly.

"Oh, to be young again," I mumbled while Cord laughed.

"Ain't that the truth."

After we sat down, Lucy made her way over to us.

"How's it going, y'all?" she asked, setting two waters in front of us.

"It's going good. How are things?" Cord asked as he winked at the young woman and her cheeks pinked. Cord seemed oblivious to her reaction, leaving me to wonder if my brothers had any clue about their gifts with women.

With a shrug, Lucy answered, "It's been slow today."

"Where's your mother?" I asked.

"She took the day off and headed into San Antonio. Said she needed a spa day."

With a smile, I replied, "Good for her!"

"What can I get ya?"

Cord grabbed the small menu on the table that listed the specials. After looking it over he said, "Club sandwich for me, with a Coke."

After jotting down Cord's order, Lucy glanced my way. "I'll have the same thing."

"Perfect! I'll get the sodas right out."

When she walked off, Cord stared me down as I took a drink of water. I wasn't prepared for what came out of his mouth next.

"So, when are you going to tell me who you were getting it on with when old lady Hopkins walked into your dance studio?" I choked on the water and Cord laughed. "Afraid the guy will get his ass beat?"

Ugh. When will everyone forget that Mrs. Hopkins walked into the studio when Jonathon and I were getting it on?

"Wh-why is it so important for everyone to know my business?"

Cord shrugged. "I don't know. Just trying to figure out who it is. Brother's duty."

"Why? So y'all can harass him?"

He flashed me an evil grin. "Maybe."

Lucy walked over and set our sodas on the table before heading back toward the kitchen. The interruption allowed me to compose my response to my nosey brother.

"Well, it doesn't matter. It was only a one-time thing."

Leaning forward, he said, "As long as it wasn't Jonathon. Then I'd really have to kick some ass."

When he sat back in his seat, he laughed again. I prayed that my face didn't tell all of my dirty little secrets.

What in the hell? Did he know *it was Jonathon? Was he kidding around or being serious?*

Shit! Shit! Shit!

Cord's phone went off, and he pulled it from his pocket. He smiled and looked back up at me. "Speak of the devil. Looks like Jonathon got the plane ticket for Vegas."

I forced a smile. "Y'all don't get into trouble, Cord. You've got too much to lose if you do something stupid."

He scoffed. "Please, I'm not twenty-one, Waylynn. We're going to have a bit of fun, that's all. And if I happen to meet a girl who wants to hook up, then all the better."

Rolling my eyes, I said, "Seriously, y'all are going to hook up with random women?"

"No. We're going to gamble, and if we're really lucky, we'll hook up with a random woman…or three."

I snarled. "Pig."

"Says the girl who was caught doing the nasty by a poor old woman."

"That was different. It wasn't a random guy."

Cord's brows lifted. "Ahh, you've given me a clue."

I smiled. "You'd love to know, wouldn't you?" I asked, keeping my voice calm and clear.

He shrugged. "Like you said, sis, it's your business. Not mine. As long as he treats you good and doesn't hurt you. Not like that asshole you were married to."

"Like I told you, we're not an item. Maybe it wasn't a random guy, but it was a random thing."

"So you keep saying. By the look in your eyes right now, I'd say you're not happy with that."

I swallowed hard. "What?"

"You want something more than a one-time hook-up There's nothing wrong with wanting a relationship, Waylynn. I'm sure you're ready to settle down and pop out a kid or two."

"Well, I don't think this guy is ready for the whole white picket fence dream of mine. There's an age difference."

Cord rolled his eyes. "Who cares if he's older or younger? As long as he makes you happy, that's all that matters."

Letting out a sigh, I took a drink of my Coke. "Like I said, we're not together, so…"

Lucy brought our sandwiches. "Here y'all go. Anything else?"

Glancing at the waitress, Cord flashed his dimples and another wink. "Thanks, Lucy."

Her cheeks heated again. "Sure thing, Cord."

When Cord focused back on me, he picked up his sandwich and took a bite, then started talking. "I'll tell you the type of guy you need."

I rolled my eyes. "Do you always talk with your mouth full?"

He nodded.

"And you hope to pick up a woman—or three—with those manners? Tell me, Oh Great One, who is the type of guy I need?" I took a bite of my sandwich.

"You need someone hard working, but not married to his job. Someone who knows how to treat a lady and won't step out on you. A guy who wants the same things as you. Marriage and kids."

Nodding, I lifted my Coke to my lips. Maybe my brother did know what I wanted.

"Someone like Jonathon."

The drink slipped from my hands and crashed on the table, spilling everywhere.

Cord jumped back. "Shit, Waylynn. What happened?"

I sat there stunned for solid seconds while Cord wiped the spilled drink. I hadn't even noticed it had been running off the table and into my lap.

"Damn, I'm sorry. It slipped from my hands." I tried to help him clean up while Lucy rushed over with a rag.

"I'm sorry, Lucy."

"No worries. I'll get you another one."

Sitting down, I stared at Cord. "Why would you pick him as an example?"

Cord stared like I had lost my mind. "Why Mitchell?" He shrugged. "I don't know. I guess because he's devoted to making Corina happy. I could have said Steed."

"Mitchell? You said 'Mitchell'?"

With a tilt of his head, he asked, "Who did you think I said?"

I shook my head. "Um, I don't know. I guess I didn't hear you when I dropped the drink."

"You sure you're okay?"

Putting on the fake smile I had mastered long ago, I replied, "I think I need a spa day myself!"

We both laughed. The rest of lunch was filled with small talk. My heart had finally settled to a normal pace by the time we stood and walked outside.

"Thanks for lunch, Cord."

Leaning over, he kissed me on the forehead. "My pleasure. We need to do it more often, especially with the dance studio across the square now. I better run. Love you, sis."

I nodded. "Let me know when y'all get to Vegas…and stay out of trouble! Love you too!"

"What's that you say? I can't hear you, Waylynn."

Laughing, Cord turned and started toward his bar, Cord's Place. Right as he crossed the street, I cried out, "Be good!"

He spun around and shouted, "Where's the fun in that?"

Dropping the car keys on the kitchen island, I let out a long groan, opened the refrigerator, and reached in for a bottle of Great Northern beer. Amelia had turned me on to it after her little fling with Liam in New York. Finding the beer outside of the bright lights and big city of New York was a pain in the ass, but well worth it.

I twisted the cap off and leaned against the counter, looking around the guest house that I now called home. It was quiet. Too quiet.

Pulling out my phone, I hit Amelia's number.

She answered on the first ring. "Hey, Waylynn. What's up?"

"I'm bored and it's too quiet in my house."

Amelia chuckled. "Get a pet."

"I don't like cats or dogs."

"Get a turtle."

I laughed. "A turtle?"

"Yeah, you're always pulling over on the highway to save them. Next time just bring Michelangelo home."

"Michelangelo?" What the hell was she talking about?

"You know, the ninja turtles," she said, laughing like it was the funniest thing ever.

Pursing my lips, I looked up at the ceiling. "Maybe I will get a turtle. I've always wanted one."

"See, there ya go."

"Yeah, but that's not going to bring life into this place."

"Then get a pig."

"A pig? Can you be serious? I have a real problem here."

Amelia sighed. "Your problem is not being able to admit that you want to be with Jonathon. If you let things flow naturally between you two, you'd be having him in your place right now, and he'd probably be making you cry out his name in every room of your house."

I closed my eyes and sighed. "Nope. He's on his way to Vegas with Cord. Their plan is to gamble, drink, and hook up with random women."

"What? I mean, Cord I get, but Jonathon was down for that?"

I stayed silent longer than I should have as I made my way into the living room.

"What did you do, Waylynn?"

A groaned as I flopped onto the sofa. "I might have twisted his arm and forced him to go."

"Oh, no! What happened?"

Leaning my head back, I closed my eyes. "I don't know what I'm doing, Meli. I want to try this with him, but I'm sure it wouldn't work. I want a family, and he's younger than me. And there are already rumors flying around town about me. I don't think I can handle more gossip."

"First off, screw the rumors. The people in this town are either bored or jealous. And how do you know he isn't ready to settle down? Cord mentioned Jonathon dated a girl from Uvalda for a couple of years. He was ready to get serious, but she wasn't. He broke things off with her about a year ago."

My heart dropped at the idea of Jonathon wanting that with another woman. "Really? What was her name?"

"I don't know. Some girl he met at Cord's place. She still shows up every now and then, Trevor said."

"And why were you and Trevor talking about Jonathon?"

"It was a few nights back, Jonathon was at Cord's Place and I casually brought him up to Trevor."

"Ugh! Amelia, I don't want anyone to put two and two together."

She let out a frustrated sigh. "Jesus, Waylynn. I doubt it would make a difference. They already know you bumped uglies with someone. Might as well let them know who."

"Cord asked me earlier today. I nearly told him."

"What made you stop?"

"Do you not remember our brothers beating up Wade?"

Amelia chuckled. "They didn't exactly beat him up, but I get what you're saying. Listen, I was worried about what Trevor might do, and that actually turned out better than I thought it would."

"I don't know. I've driven around for hours thinking about it. Maybe I could convince Jonathon to keep it on the down low...I mean, *if* we gave this a go."

"You really want to sneak around, Waylynn?"

I blew out a frustrated breath. "No."

When my phone beeped, I pulled it away from my ear and saw an incoming text from Cord. I hit speaker and pulled up the text.

"Looks like they made it to Vegas," I said as I opened the attachment.

"Yeah, I got a text too."

When the picture loaded I felt sick to my stomach. "I'm heading to bed. I suddenly got really tired. Talk to you tomorrow."

"Waylynn," Amelia whispered. I knew she had opened the attachment.

"Night, baby sis. We'll talk tomorrow."

I hit End before she could say anything. The picture Cord had sent popped back up on my phone with the text *we made it*. It was a selfie of him at the casino. Behind him were Dustin, Tom, and Jonathon. There was a blonde smiling and hanging on Cord with her head thrown back, laughing. My stomach tightened as I looked at Jonathon. A brunette had her arms wrapped around his neck.

Swallowing hard, I texted Cord back.

Me: *Didn't take long for the buzzards to start swarming.*

Cord answered almost immediately.

Cord: *No shit! They were on us the second we walked into the casino.*

Anger pulsed through my veins. Jonathon was like all the other guys. All they cared about was crawling between some whore's legs.

I thought back to the day I was with Jonathon. I was no better than the girl hanging on his neck.

Me: *Have fun with the Vegas bunnies. Wrap your stick.*

Cord: *Always, big sis! Always!*

I erased the message and tossed my phone onto the coffee table before I dragged myself to the shower. The faster I got into bed, the better.

CHAPTER 3

Jonathon

The brunette was hanging on me like her life depended on it. With the amount of alcohol on her breath, she probably couldn't stand on her own, and I worried that if a spark was lit anywhere near her, the whole place would go up in flames.

She was *that* drunk.

Reaching up, I pulled her off me. Dustin and Tom were already talking to the girl's friends. The blonde next to Cord was waiting while he texted.

The blonde grabbed Cord's arm. "You boys want to go up to our room? I'm thinking we can have a bit of fun."

He looked up at her and smiled. "As fun as that sounds, I think we're gonna gamble for a bit, sweetheart."

She pouted and her little drunk friend was back to clawing up my body.

"I bet you have a big dick!" she shouted.

I pushed her away. "You'll never find out, darlin'."

Her smile faded, and she attempted to put her hands on her hips. "Why…why not? You think you're too good for us, cowboy?"

"First off, you're so drunk you can't stand straight, and secondly, I'm not interested in a hook-up with someone who won't remember my name in the morning."

Her eyes slid over to Dustin who was also attempting to ditch the chick who was talking dirty to him.

"Listen, ladies, as much fun as a big ol' orgy sounds, we're not interested. We just got here, and we want to get a little gambling in," Cord said.

The blonde pushed Cord back as hard as she could, and it only made her stumble. Cord grabbed her while Tom went in search of security.

We finally got the four girls away from us and left them with the security guys, and made our way back into the casino.

Tom slapped Cord's back as we sat down at a blackjack table. "Jesus Christ. I like pussy, don't get me wrong, but those girls were crazy drunk! One grabbed my dick, and I swear to God, she wanted to rip it off my body. Can you imagine getting a hand job from her?"

We laughed and placed our bets. It didn't take long before Dustin and Tom wondered off to another table.

The cocktail waitress set my Bud Light in front of me. The second it hit my lips, Cord asked, "How are things going with the dance studio? Waylynn's not giving you too much trouble, is she?"

I paused before taking a drink. "Things are good, and no, she isn't giving me any trouble."

He nodded. "Good."

He flipped a chip back and forth between his fingers.

"What's really on your mind, Cord?"

He let out a chuckle. "I need you to find something out for me."

"You asking me to spy on your sister?"

He shrugged. "I guess. If you want to look at it like that."

"I'm not spying on Waylynn. You want to know something, ask her."

"I've tried. She's hung up on someone and won't admit it. I can tell she likes the guy."

My heart froze. "What makes you think that?"

He turned and looked at me. "She's my sister. I see it in her eyes, and she seems miserable. There's a reason she's pushing this guy away, and I want to know what that reason is because I'm not buying her excuses."

I cleared my throat before speaking. "You ever think it might be her business?"

His brows rose. "My family *is* my business. I want to know if this guy used her for a quick fuck and moved on. So I can kill him."

Dragging my eyes away from his, I stared at the dealer and tapped the table after looking at my cards.

"I don't think your sister is the type of woman to let some guy use her like that."

He didn't respond at first. "No, neither do I. But she's tight-lipped. The only thing she told me was that there was an age difference, and she didn't think he was the white picket fence type of guy. If he's anything like that asshole she married, I'm stepping in."

"Well, I respect your sister, Cord, and I'm working for her. I won't be your spy." The dealer swept up our losing cards.

Cord sighed. "Yeah, I guess it is pretty shitty to ask you." He turned and faced me. He let his gaze linger before he asked, "Do you know who it is?"

Fuck. Just come clean with him. Tell him the truth.

Forcing a smile, I shook my head when I remembered Waylynn making me promise not to tell anyone. "Nah, I don't know who it is."

"Another round of cards, gentleman?" the dealer asked.

Cord grinned. "Let's hit the Craps table. I'm feeling lucky."

I let out the breath I had been holding. Standing to follow my best friend, I pushed down the bile that was sitting at the base of my throat. I hated lying to him, but if I was going to try to make this work with Waylynn, I needed to at least have a shot before Cord put my ass in the hospital.

By the time we got back to our rooms, it was three in the morning and I was exhausted. I tried calling Waylynn three times, and my text asking her to call me went ignored.

After a quick shower to get the smell of smoke and alcohol off of me, I made my way to the king-size bed. Dustin, Tom, and Cord had each picked up a girl and had taken them back to their rooms. The last thing I was interested in right now was a mindless hook-up. I'd never been the type of guy who cared about that anyway.

Sitting down, I reached for my phone.

Nothing.

I tried one more time.

Me: *I know you're asleep, but please call me when you get up. I don't care what time it is.*

As I went to put my phone down, it went off.

Waylynn: *What's wrong? The brunette didn't do it for you?*

I stared at her response for a good minute. What in the fuck was she talking about?

Me: *What's that supposed to mean?*

Waylynn: *Please do us both a favor and go back to treating me like the woman you work for and not the woman you want to fuck.*

Me: *You mean more than that to me, and what the fuck did you mean about a brunette?*

Waylynn: *You honestly think I'm going to believe you were all good little boys and went back to your rooms alone?*

Anger pulsed through me.

Me: *Not all of us, but I did. I've been trying to get a hold of you all night, Waylynn. You think I've been fucking a girl while texting and calling you?*

Waylynn: *I don't know. You have proven you can multitask.*

I hit her number. It rang about six times before she answered. "I'm not in the mood for this."

"Then why in the hell did you answer?"

She sighed. "I don't know. What do you want?"

"I want you, Waylynn Parker, and I'm not going to give up on us."

"Us? What *us*? We fucked one time, Jonathon! That doesn't make *us* anything."

"Cord asked me to find out who you're hung up on."

The line fell silent for the longest time.

"Hello? Waylynn, are you still there?"

I heard a shaky breath before she asked, "Did you agree to?"

"No! Of course I didn't. I told him I respected you too much to spy on you and that it wasn't any of his business."

"That little fuck! I'm going to twist his balls and hang them up to dry in the middle of the pasture for the crows to peck at!"

Moving my balls to the side, I said, "Jesus, woman. That visual hurts me."

"It's the truth. I'm going to kill him. Thank you for not saying anything."

"He seems to think you're hung up on this mystery man. Are you?"

She remained silent. "Who was the girl hanging all over you in the picture Cord sent?"

My brows pulled together. "What? When did he send a picture?"

"When y'all first got there. You asshats had women hanging on you."

It hit me then who she was talking about. "Oh, Christ. Are you talking about the ones who attacked us the moment we set foot in the casino? Yeah, we had to get security to come get them. That brunette you're talking about was so drunk she could hardly stand."

Waylynn took a few seconds before she responded. "Cord isn't with one, is he?"

I laughed. "No. He's smarter than that."

"If he was smart, his ass wouldn't be with any girl. Ugh. Men are so...so...so. Ugh!"

"Tell me how you really feel, babe."

"Don't call me that."

"Why?"

"Because it pisses me off."

"What doesn't piss you off, Waylynn?"

"I'm hanging up on you, asshat!"

I laughed. Damn, this woman drove me insane. "Waylynn, before you hang up, will you let me say something?"

"You have twenty seconds starting now."

Taking in a breath, I closed my eyes and said, "I didn't mean what I said when I walked out of your office earlier."

"Which part?"

"All of it. I'm not interested in being with anyone but you."

Waylynn's breath caught. If I was standing in the same room as her right now I would be able to see the wheels spinning in her head.

"Call me when you get back. We'll talk."

My heart leaped. "I'm catching a flight first thing tomorrow morning."

Laughing, she replied, "Stay and have fun. Besides, I need someone to watch over my brother. I have a feeling that boy is trying to sow his wild oats. Something in the water in Oak Springs is making all my brothers fall in love."

It wasn't just the Parker brothers falling in love.

"I promise," I said. "I'll keep an eye on him."

"It's late, I better go."

For the first time in weeks I felt like Waylynn was giving this—giving us—a chance. She'd only agreed to talk to me, but I knew that was all I needed to make her see we deserved a try.

"Sleep good, Waylynn."

Her voice dropped to a slight whisper. "You too, Jonathon. Night."

I closed my eyes and softly said, "Night."

When the line went dead I blew out a breath and sat on the edge of the bed. Thank fuck. Lacing my fingers through my hair, I tossed my phone and headed toward the bathroom, pulling my shirt off in the process. An idea hit me, and I backtracked to the bed.

Reaching for my phone, I took a selfie and pulled up Waylynn's name.

Me: *You know, we could always have a bit of phone sex. What happens in Vegas stays in Vegas.*

After attaching the photo, I hit send.

It didn't take long to get a response.

Waylynn: *What are you…seventeen? No!*

Me: *Come on. I'll show you mine if you show me yours*

Waylynn: *What exactly are you wanting me to show you, Mr. Turner?*

My dick instantly went hard.

Me: *You could show me your pinky at this point. I'm pretty sure my hand is going to be getting a work out while thinking about you. I thought a picture might make it a little better.*

Waylynn: *So you want me to send you a picture of myself that you can jack off to? Is that what you're asking?*

Me: *You said it…not me.*

When a photo attachment appeared on my phone, I held my breath. Holy shit. She sent a picture. The second it loaded, my mouth dropped open.

"What in the fuck?"

Me: *A turtle?*

Waylynn: *Night, Turner. Sweet dreams.*

Me: *My dick is now limp as the noodles at a bad Vegas buffet. Thanks a lot.*

Waylynn: *Note to self. Turtles make Jonathon unable to copulate.*

Me: *You slay me. Night, Parker.*

Setting my phone down, I let out a chuckle as I headed to the shower. Oh, yeah. Waylynn Parker was going to be a handful, and I couldn't fucking wait.

CHAPTER 4

Waylynn

I woke up anxious the day after I talked to Jonathon. I needed an outlet for these emotions, and I knew exactly what I had to do.

"How am I supposed to ride you if you won't cooperate with me?"

Nothing.

No reaction at all.

I'd lost my touch.

With a sigh, I tried again. "Come on, boy. I want to ride you."

My bay horse, Copper, stood in his stall, staring me down like I was some sort of disease.

"No? You're not in the mood?"

Copper bobbed his beautiful head up and down.

I let out a groan as I shut the stall door. "Fine. But I'll have you know, if I said that to any other man, they would be all over it!"

Copper nickered and went about eating his hay. With a sigh, I placed my hands on my hips. "You're really hurt my feelings, boy. I was looking forward to a good run in an open pasture."

"Do you always make a habit of guilting your horse?"

I didn't bother to look at my brother, Mitchell. I let out a huff and put my saddle up. "He hates me."

"No, he doesn't. Copper's never been a fan of cold weather."

I shook my head as my brother took the saddle and made his way to another stall.

"Mitchell, these horses are spoiled. They are in a climate-controlled barn, for Christ's sake. You're telling me that little prick doesn't want to go outside because it's sixty degrees out?"

He faced me. "Yep. That's exactly what I'm saying. If you want to ride, I can give you a damn good horse to ride who likes the crisp fall weather."

I brushed it off with a wave of my hand. "Never mind. I don't feel like riding now. Nice to know I have a pussy for a horse."

Mitchell grinned and headed to the tack room to put up my saddle. He shut the door and draped his arm over my shoulders.

"Talk to me, Waylynn."

"It's nothing. I only wanted to get out for a bit."

"I've got an idea, if you feel like hanging out with me for a bit."

Smiling, I nodded. "I'd love to, Mitch."

We were soon sitting in the Mule, driving out through the west pasture. "Where are we going?" I asked.

"You'll see," he replied with a crooked smile.

"You do know that pretty boy smile doesn't work with me, Mitchell Parker."

He laughed. "Pretty boy smile?"

"Yeah. All my brothers have the same one. You got it from Daddy."

"Is that so?"

"Yep. You smile, show your dimples, and maybe give a wink, and any girl does as you wish. It doesn't work on kin, just so you know."

"I never thought it worked on you or Amelia. Both of you are too damn stubborn. It does, however, work on our mother. And you have the same smile, big sister."

Grinning, I looked over the passing fields. It didn't take me long to figure out where Mitchell was taking us. "The tree house!"

He chuckled. "Yep."

"Oh, my gosh. I haven't been there in forever. How do you know it's even still standing?"

"Steed showed it to Chloe. He replaced a few boards and made it sturdy again. He said Chloe loves it. She wants to furnish it!"

Tripp, Steed, and Mitchell had built a tree house when I was around twelve. At first they said I wasn't allowed in, but after I promised to supply them with chocolate chip cookies for an entire year, I was allowed to use it. We dragged beanbags, a table, and Lord knows what else into that thing. As the years went on and we got older, it became our own private getaway and not so much the fort it once was. It was the place we went when we were upset with our parents, or when the football team lost, or when our hearts had been broken for the first time. I couldn't count on my hands how many times I had sat up there with my brothers or friends and cried, laughed, and screamed.

We remained silent as Mitchell drove through the pastures and up to the giant live oak that still served as the foundation for our tree house. When we got out and looked up, we said the same thing.

"It's so small."

I made my way to the ladder and climbed. I could hardly stand up straight as I made my way to the middle of the tree house and sat down.

"Wow. Boy, does this bring back memories," I said.

Mitchell followed my lead and sat down. "I know. Now it's been passed down to the next generation."

"Yep."

I pulled my knees to my chest and stared at my younger brother. I was happy for him and Corina, but the ache in my chest was heavy. Their baby news made me jealous.

"Want to talk about it?"

Lifting my eyes to his, I asked, "Talk about what?"

He tilted his head. "I know you're happy for us, but I saw something in your eyes on Thanksgiving when we announced the baby."

"I *am* happy for y'all. It's just hard to watch my younger siblings settle down and have kids. It's something I dreamed for a long time, and I feel like Jack robbed me of it."

Mitchell reached for my hand. "Waylynn, you do know you're not an old lady and you have plenty of time to have kids."

"At the rate I'm going, Mitch, I'll be in my forties when I get settled and have kids."

He laughed. "I don't think so."

I shrugged.

"No one has caught your eye?"

Looking away, I stared at a doll's crib Steed must have brought up for Chloe. My heart physically hurt.

"I'll take that as a yes."

"I'm not sure it can work between us."

"Why not?"

Looking at him, I replied, "Because there are obstacles."

His brows pulled together. "Like?"

I stretched my legs out and put my hands behind me on the floor as I laughed.

"Well, for one, he's younger than me."

"So? As long as you aren't robbing the cradle, what's a few years?"

"He's also friends with one of my brothers."

Mitchell laughed. "That *could* be a problem, but any guy you date is going to have to deal with your brothers, and this is Oak Springs. Everyone knows everyone!"

I giggled. "That's true!"

He bumped my leg with his shoe. "Is it the guy you were with when old lady Hopkins walked in?"

Heat danced across my cheeks. "Maybe."

Mitchell tilted his head and stared at me. "You see it going anywhere?"

"I think I want it to, but I'm not sure. I'm gun-shy after Jack."

He left the conversation to dangle. "Corina being pregnant doesn't make anything easier... This hit you harder than you're admitting."

My chest tightened. "I feel like it's never going to happen for me, but I'm okay and I love that you're concerned. I just need to get a few things in my life figured out is all."

"Like where this thing is going with the younger dude?"

"That's complicated."

"Why is it complicated?"

I laughed and stood. "Trust me. It is. You ready to head back?"

"You don't want to talk about it?"

I took his hand in mine. "This is something I need to figure out on my own. I'm still trying to deal with the rumors about why I divorced. The last thing I want is to add fuel to this town's constant gossip fire."

"I get it, sis. I do...but at some point you need to live for yourself and not for everyone else. Jack was a prime example of that, and look how that turned out."

I knew he was being truthful. It hurt, but every word was exactly what I needed to hear.

Mitchell stood, and we headed back down the ladder.

The ride back to the barn was quiet. I was left to my own thoughts, my own decisions. It had been so long since I could make my own decisions about my love life, and here I was, on the precipice of running or jumping headfirst into a relationship. Mitchell's words replayed in my head. Things with Jonathon were complicated, but was that only because I was making them that way?

We'd only been together the one time, but the endless flirtation and sexual tension promised that he wanted more. He had even admitted it. So, why did that scare me? Wasn't that what I wanted in a man? The truth was, I was worried what people would think about me dating a man younger than me. And I couldn't get that out of my head...

Reflecting on that, I realized I was allowing this town and its people to make my decisions for me. I'd simply replaced Jack with them...exchanging one prison warden for another.

By the time we got to the barn I had settled it out. I'd let things go naturally with Jonathon and me. That spark we felt together might be purely sexual and burn out before we could start an actual relationship. A few more times in bed with each other might give us both some fun and release, and then we could both move on.

Or it might feed the fire Jonathon Turner ignited the moment he caught my eye from across the room. Jesus, I was going to be literally and figuratively fucked no matter what decision I made.

"Penny for your thoughts," Mitchell said, drawing me out of my own head as he parked the Mule outside the main barn.

Smiling, I replied, "Sorry. Thinking about the dance studio. Too many decisions still need to be made."

He looked at me like he knew I was a damn liar. "I bet."

We started toward the two vehicles we had driven down to the barn. "Will you be at dinner this week? You know how much Mom and Dad love having us all there."

"Mom said Thursday, right?"

He nodded.

My phone buzzed in my pocket. When I pulled it out, I saw a text from Jonathon.

Jonathon: *I found this and thought of you.*

The picture of a stuffed turtle appeared on the screen and I couldn't hide the smile on my face.

Me: *Pick up a stranger in Vegas?*

Jonathon: *She was cheap. Like you told me, what happens in Vegas stays in Vegas.*

This time I let a chuckle slip out.

When I glanced up, Mitchell was leaning against his truck. He motioned toward my phone with his head. "That him?"

I nodded. "It is."

"Well, the guy can't be all that bad if he makes you smile like that."

My chest squeezed.

Mitchell held up his hands. "It's complicated. I know. I'll see you around, sis. And for sure at dinner this week, right?"

"I'll be there."

Mitchell kissed me on the forehead, turned back to his truck, and climbed in. After starting the engine, he rolled his window down.

"I love you, sis."

My heart melted. "I love you too, Mitchell."

He drove off toward our folks' house and an emptiness settled into my chest. Maybe it was more jealousy that I couldn't admit to myself.

Closing my eyes, I wrapped my arms around my stomach and breathed a deep breath, slowly letting it out along with my negative emotions. When I opened my eyes, the sun began to lower in the sky. It was breathtaking.

"A new beginning," I whispered. And maybe that beginning was Jonathon.

CHAPTER 5

Waylynn

I stood in my bedroom and stared out the window. The morning sun shone through the clouds and caused the dew on the grass to glisten. It was one of the most peaceful things I'd ever seen. I closed my eyes and took a deep breath.

Jonathon had sent me a text late last night. He wanted to talk, and yet all I wanted to do was hide.

Ugh. Pull yourself together, Waylynn Parker.

Feeling melancholy and a tad anxious, I mumbled, "What is this day going to bring?"

"Shopping!"

Screaming, I grabbed the first thing I could find and threw it at the intruder.

"Ouch!" Amelia said as she, Corina, and Paxton all laughed.

Clutching my chest, I shot them a dirty look. "You scared the shit out of me! What are y'all doing here?"

Amelia walked into the room and headed to my closet. She started flipping through my clothes.

"Seeing if you wanted to go into town. There are a few cute boutiques that opened up on the square."

Paxton sat on my bed. "I can't believe how much growth our little town has seen."

I rolled my eyes. "I'd have the dance studio nearly done if that old bat hadn't tried to shut me down before I even got started."

Amelia grabbed a black dress and held it up. "Oh my! Can I borrow this for a date night with Wade? Holy crap, it is sexy as hell."

Sighing, I plopped on the bed next to Paxton. "Sure, Lord knows I won't be wearing it anytime soon."

"You haven't decided on Jonathon yet?" Corina asked, leaning against the dresser.

"I told him I'd talk to him when he got back."

"Are you going to give it a try?" Amelia asked.

Chewing my lip, I looked around at all three of them. "I think I want to."

They jumped up and started screaming. Their infectious excitement made me smile because I knew these three would have my back, no matter what.

"Wait!" I shouted as I stood and held up my hands. "I said, *I think*. I haven't said I was going to. There is a lot that could go wrong."

Paxton scowled. "Like what? You get caught doing the deed in public? *Again?* Waylynn, why are you so scared?"

Dragging in a deep breath, I walked to the table next to my bed and opened the drawer. I pulled out the Oak Springs newspaper and handed it to Paxton. "That's one of the reasons. The other reason is that I want to have a baby. Sooner rather than later."

"How do you know Jonathon doesn't want that as well?" Corina asked.

I stared at the floor. "We've fucked one time. I hardly think he is ready to settle down and start popping out kids."

Paxton shook her head. "Why are you in such a rush, Waylynn? You're only thirty-two! You've got plenty of time for kids. And you sort of need 'help' in order to get pregnant. What man is going to turn down sex with you?"

How could I make them understand? I'd been dreaming of a family since I was a little girl. That was the one promise Jack held over me because he knew how desperately I wanted it, and he knew he could eventually wear me down, which he did.

"That's the thing...I went to a sperm bank in San Antonio. To see what I'd need to do to get pregnant on my own."

"What?" all three of them said at once.

"Waylynn! Why would you go through something like that without telling us?" Amelia asked.

Something like anger rushed through me. Maybe anger mixed with jealousy. Whatever it was, it was about to show its ugly head.

"Because, Amelia, I wasted my time on a husband who strung me along year after year with promises of starting a family, only to emotionally beat me down to the point where I gave up. Because I don't have a man warming my bed every night like y'all do, or kids running around my house chasing goats! Or a baby in my stomach. I don't have any of that, and goddamn it, it's all I've ever dreamed about, and for some reason God won't let me have it!"

All three of them stared like I had finally snapped. Maybe I had. Tears threatened to spill but my anger kept them at bay.

"Don't look at me like that. Don't the three of you dare look at me like that! You have no idea what my life has been like. All those years I plastered on a smile for everyone and pretended everything was okay when I knew deep down that my rotten husband was cheating on me. A husband who wanted a trophy wife at his side for his functions. Every time I told him I wanted kids, he would take me on a trip to Paris or Italy. Shower me with attention and jewelry and romantic evenings and I fell for it...each and every single time. What does that say about me? That I can be tricked with a shower of gifts and affection? That I'm willing to give up my dreams for a man?"

The tears finally won out. One blink and they trailed down my face. "Hell, he couldn't let me get pregnant. It would ruin his perfect image! The powerful millionaire and his Barbie doll wife. But he... got his whore pregnant and splashed it all over the *New York Times* how excited he is to have a baby."

"What?" Corina asked, grabbing my hands. She pulled me back onto the bed. "He's going to have a baby?"

I nodded while the sob I was trying to hold back came out. Corina pulled me into her arms and I forced myself not to cry harder.

"What a cocksucker!" Amelia gasped.

"Bethany Lenard wrote this?" Paxton asked. She was reading the article that was written in the *Oak Gazette that I had handed her earlier.*

I cleared my throat and nodded. "Yeah, I guess. I have no clue who she is, but she certainly likes to talk shit about my ex-husband."

Amelia took the article. "She's Jonathon's ex-girlfriend. She sometimes writes guest articles because she's friends with Kenzie Lewis, who works for the *Gazette*."

Pinching my brows together, I asked, "Wait, isn't that who Jonathon brought to Steed and Mitchell's birthday part?"

Paxton nodded. "It looks like Bethany has a little bit of a jealous streak."

"What does the article say?" Corina asked.

"It basically says that Waylynn is a washed-up dancer who couldn't make it happen in New York so she hooked up with a rich guy who ended up cheating on her, causing her to come back to Oak Springs with her tail between her legs."

I stared at Paxton. "Wow. Thanks for that great summary, Paxton."

She frowned. "Sorry. I can't believe I didn't see that article sooner."

Amelia tossed the newspaper down. "Holy shit. What a C-word!"

Laughing, I dropped onto my bed. "She wrote that right after I hired Jonathon to help with the dance studio. It was before we'd even hooked up. I don't even know her!"

Corina was now reading the article. "I mean, they put it on a page where it could easily be missed. Probably on purpose. Waylynn, if your parents saw this they would have laid into the *Gazette*."

"They did see it. Mom brought it to my attention. I asked them not to make a big deal and draw more negativity to our family."

Amelia huffed. "Why? Oh, my gosh, Waylynn. Why would you let them write this trash about you?"

Sitting back up, I looked at my baby sister. "Meli, I've had worse things written about me when I was in New York and when I was with Jack. *A lot* meaner, as well. I figured rumors would fly when I came back."

"Sure, rumors, but to put it in the newspaper? I have lost respect for the *Gazette*. They're not a rag magazine." Amelia placed her hands on her hips, her cute nose turning red the more pissed she got. "I'm writing a letter to the editor. They can't get away with this."

Corina clapped her hands. "I love when you get fired up!"

Amelia let an evil little smirk play across her face. "Fired up? Oh, you haven't seen fired up until you've seen a Parker women pissed off. And I am pissed *off*."

Paxton started herding Amelia toward the door. "Well, before you burst into flames of vengefulness and write an article, can we hit up the stores in town before I have to relieve Steed from daddy duty?"

I sat up. "Let me change into something else, and I'll be ready to head out."

The three women retreated out of my bedroom so I could change. After slipping on a pair of jeans and a long sleeve T-shirt with the name of the ranch on it, I put my sneakers on and was ready to go. My phone beeped and I couldn't ignore the small pull in my stomach when I saw his name.

Jonathon: *I'll be home tomorrow. Can we meet for dinner?*

My fingers trembled as I came up with my response. Even a text message from this man got me worked up.

Me: *Where? I don't want it anywhere public.*

Jonathon: *Waylynn, I'm the contractor on the build out of your dance studio, I hardly think it would be scandalous if we met for dinner in a public place.*

Smiling, I chewed on my lip. *Should I be flirty or play it cool? Fuck that. Flirty it is.*

Me: *Well, what if we decide you need to do some hammering? I don't plan on wearing any safety gear to this dinner. And by safety gear, I mean panties.*

Jonathon: *Christ, woman. Now I'm gonna have to jack off before we go to dinner.*

Me: *I would say I'm sorry, but I'm not. Enjoy your dinner!*

Jonathon: *The only dinner I'm going to enjoy is the one with you tomorrow.*

Me: *Am I on the menu?*

Jonathon: *Fucking hell... You're gonna be the death of me, Waylynn Parker.*

Me: *Gosh, I hope not. I'm looking forward to dessert tomorrow night. Gotta run...*

I slipped my phone into the back pocket of my jeans and headed to the living room to meet the girls. The idea of seeing Jonathon and the hopes of what would come after dinner lifted my spirits. I walked into the living and clapped my hands.

"Come on, ladies. I'm in the mood to do some Christmas shopping!"

CHAPTER 6

jonathon

Cord talked non-stop on the flight back home. All I could think about was burying my dick in Waylynn, which filled me with nothing but guilt. My best friend had no idea I was falling for his sister, and I sat next to him like a pussy and didn't say a word.

Truth be told, if Waylynn hadn't asked me not to say anything, I'd have already told Cord I had feelings for her. Of course, I knew Cord and his brothers. They would expect me to get their blessings first, but fuck that. Waylynn was a grown woman who didn't need anyone's permission.

I sighed. The whole situation still bothered me. I didn't like keeping secrets from Cord.

"Did you hear a word I just said, Turner?"

"What was that?"

"Dude, I've been going on and on and you're not even listening."

I smiled. "Sorry, hangover from last night."

Cord smiled. "Last night was fun. Dude, I can't believe you didn't hook up with that redhead. Hell, she was practically dry humping you."

Shaking my head, I replied, "Not into that kind of thing."

"Yeah, I guess you never were. You're still not hung up on Liz, are you?"

"Liz?" I asked with a laugh. "Hell no."

Liz was the girl I had thought might be the one. We had dated for a few years. I was ready to take it to the next step...at the same time that she was ready to date other people. It was clear we had two very different ideas about where the relationship was going.

"You back with Bethany, then?"

"No. I knew bringing her to the party was a bad idea, but I needed a date."

Cord nodded. "Nothing there? Y'all not rekindling the spark?"

I laughed. "Again, hell no. Bethany only cares about two things in life. Her and her clothes. And shoes. And make-up."

"That's four things, bro."

"Yeah, well, bottom line is Bethany only cares about Bethany and who would be the perfect guy to bow down to her and shower her with gifts."

Roaring with laughter, Cord said, "Damn. I always knew she was superficial. I never did understand what you saw in her, Jon."

"Neither did I. She wasn't even good in bed."

"Well, there must be someone back home because you didn't even look at a chick this weekend."

I stared at him. My head was screaming to tell him. I couldn't take it. I couldn't lie to him any more.

"Cord, let me ask you something."

"Okay, ask away."

"What would you do if I told you I was falling for Waylynn?"

Cord's smile faded, and he looked away for a brief moment before turning back. "Are you?"

I glanced down for a few seconds to gather the strength to answer.

"I am."

His jaw tightened. Okay, maybe I should have told him when I had a place to escape to...not strapped in at thirty-thousand feet in the air while sitting next to him.

Smart going, Turner.

"How long?"

"If I'm being honest, the moment I met her in the dance studio for our first consultation."

I couldn't help but notice his hands balling up.

"Were you the one fucking her when old lady Hopkins walked into the studio? And don't you dare lie to me, Turner."

No longer able to look into his eyes, I turned away.

"You *asshole*. I swear to God if I wasn't on a plane right now I'd kick your ass. That's my sister!"

"I know who the hell she is, Cord," I whispered. "I'm sorry if you feel like I betrayed you."

"Betrayed me? You slept with my sister! My sister who happens to be a lot older than you!"

"Her age has nothing to do with this."

"You're goddamn right. She's my sister!" Cord shouted. It didn't take the flight attendant long to come over to us.

Her eyes bounced between the two of us. "Gentlemen, do we have a problem here?"

"I need to move my seat before I kill this prick."

Her eyes widened in shock.

"I sort of just told him I slept with his sister," I said with a half shrug.

"I see. Well, there is an empty seat in first class, why don't you take it, sir," the flight attendant said to me.

"Wait! Why does he get the first-class seat? He slept with my sister! There are rules against this sort of thing."

She frowned and leaned closer to Cord. "There are also rules for threatening to murder someone on an airplane. And there are rules for when you sleep with a woman and sneak out in the middle of the night."

Cord looked harder at the flight attendant. "Have we?" He pointed between the two of them.

Nodding, she replied in the same hushed tone. "On your last trip to Vegas, Cord Parker."

Cord closed his eyes and mumbled, "Ah, hell, I thought you looked familiar."

Motioning for me to head to first class, she got one last jab in as she placed her mouth against Cord's ear. I didn't hear what she said, but Cord's face turned white as a ghost. When I looked back, he shot me a go-to-hell look.

"You can take a seat here, sir," the flight attendant said when she caught up with me in the first class cabin. "I'll get your carry-on in a moment. Would you like something to drink?"

I smiled. "Um, no thanks. I appreciate you breaking that up, and I'm really sorry about the whole one-night stand thing with Cord."

She smirked. "I wouldn't tell him this, but he was worth it." And with a wink, she headed up the galley.

Cord, Dustin, and Tom made their way to my truck. I was guessing Cord was cursing himself for not driving.

Dustin hit me on the shoulder, "Dude, he's ready to tear your head off."

Tom laughed his ass off as Cord opened the back door and threw his bag in. "What, now you don't want to sit in the front, Parker?"

"Fuck you, Tom. It wasn't your sister he screwed."

The hour and a half drive back to Oak Springs felt like an eight-hour drive. I dropped Dustin and Tom off first and then took Cord back to his place. When I pulled up, I got out of the truck and followed him to the back stairs.

"You keep following me, Turner, and I can't promise you won't be facing a gun at the top of the stairs."

I sighed and kept going. "Will you just talk to me, Cord? Please."

After unlocking his door, he pushed it open. "You have ten minutes, and after that, I'm fucking beating your ass."

"What if I finish in five? Do I get a five-minute head start?"

He narrowed his brows. "If it only takes you five fucking minutes to explain why you went around my back and slept with my sister, then no. I still get to kick your ass."

I raised my hands. "Fair enough."

Following Cord into his place, I waited for him to tell me to start. He walked into the kitchen, reached into the refrigerator and grabbed two beers. "Your time has already started, asshat."

"Well, hell, you could have told me I was on the clock."

"You're wasting more time."

Reaching for the beer, I nodded. "Right."

I took a long drink, let out a gust of air, and sat on the sofa.

"It was wrong to approach your sister without telling you how I felt about her. At the same time, though, we're all adults here, Cord. You can't keep your sister from being with someone."

He grunted.

"The attraction was clearly mutual, and I fought it. Honestly, I did. But your sister is so damn amazing. She's smart and funny and that mouth makes me laugh every single day."

A slight smile appeared on his face before he went back to a stony expression.

"She's determined to have everything exactly the way she wants it, and there is something incredibly sexy about that. She's happy in her own skin. Do you have any idea how freaking refreshing that is in a woman?"

He raised his brows and took a drink of his beer.

"When I'm around her, I feel like I can't get enough of her smile or laugh. I follow her like the seasons follow one another. I felt something the first time her eyes captured mine. I don't know how to explain it, Cord. I feel something I've never in my life felt before. She's been pushing me away, telling me it won't work because of our age difference, and small town gossip…and because of you. But I'm not buying it, and I'm telling you right now, I'm not walking away if she gives us a chance. To hell what you or anyone in town thinks. Waylynn is going to have to tell me to leave her alone. No one else."

Cord sat in silence for a few minutes as he let my words sink in. I knew Cord Parker. He was my closest friend, and if anyone would treat his sister right, he knew it was me.

"When you say you're falling for her, do you mean you're falling in love with her?"

"I don't know. I know I've never felt like this before. Every second of the day I'm awake, she consumes my thoughts."

He chuckled. "Sounds like a Parker woman."

"I would never hurt her, Cord. You know that's true."

With a nod, he replied, "I do. And I know if my sister was going to fall for someone, I sure as hell would rather it be you than some fucker from New York who ends up taking all her dreams away from her."

"Jack didn't take her dreams away, Cord. He wasn't the right guy to make them come true. I am."

Leaning forward, Cord's arms rested on his knees. "You think you're the guy who can make my sister happy?"

"I'd sure as hell like to have a shot. I care about her, and I want to see where this could go, but I can't do that unless she knows you gave me your blessing."

He finished his beer and set it on the table. Standing, he took a few deep breaths in and out before looking at me.

I stood and faced him, eye to eye.

"I want you to know I'm pissed you went behind my back and slept with my sister."

"Oh, trust me, that's been fully noted."

He shot me a dirty look. "And I want you to promise right now, gentleman to gentleman, best friend to best friend, that you will not hurt my sister."

"I promise you, Cord."

Nodding, he shook his head. "You know I still have to beat your ass."

"You can try."

"And I'm gonna have to tell my brothers, and you may want to avoid Tripp. He and Waylynn are close, and I'm pretty sure he's gonna wanna rip your dick off and shove it down your throat."

"I'd imagine he'd have to find someone to do that for him. You know, the whole keeping his name clean and all that shit."

Cord nodded and pointed to me. "That's right. The whole mayor thing."

"Yep."

Slapping his hands together, we walked closer to each other.

"Do I get to pick where the first shot goes?"

Laughing, Cord said, "This isn't you making a move on the hot chick first or losing at a bet. I get first call."

My hands lifted. "You're going for my face, aren't you?"

I braced myself as Cord smiled, his fist coming at me.

CHAPTER 7

Waylynn

I pulled up in the parking lot of Lane's Grill. It was new to Oak Springs and had only been open a few weeks. Jonathon had overseen the remodeling of the place and wanted to try it out.

"Waylynn Parker? Is that you?"

Glancing at the side entrance, I smiled when I saw Laney Sanderson. "Oh, my gosh, Laney! How are you?"

She ran over and pulled me into her arms.

"I thought you were in Chicago!" I said.

"And I thought you were in New York City!"

We both laughed.

"Turns out I was married to a cheating bastard who recently got his twenty-year-old girlfriend pregnant. So, I moved home and am opening a dance studio."

"Gurl, I raise your cheating bastard with a cheating bastard whom I found out already has two kids under the age of five from one whore, and has knocked up the latest girlfriend...*with twins*. I moved back home and opened up Lane's Grill."

My mouth hung open. "You win that hand!" Turning, I looked at the old historic barn and it hit me. "Lane's Grill. How stupid of me not to put two and two together. Laney! You opened your own restaurant!"

She nodded with excitement. "After years of managing restaurants in Chicago, I decided it was time to follow the dream. Once I found out the jerk was cheating, I packed up the kids and we headed home. Mom and Dad are helping, of course. I couldn't do it without them. They're happy just to have me and the kids here in Texas."

I couldn't hold back a big smile for my old high school best friend. "Chris and Jessica, how old are they now?"

"Six."

"Wow! Time is flying by. I hate that we lost touch like we did."

Laney shrugged. "It happens, right? But what are the odds we would both end up back here in Oak Springs?"

"As divorcees!" I added.

Her smile faded a bit. "Did y'all end up having any kids of your own?"

"No. Turns out that was a blessing, though. I was able to have a clean cut from the man."

Laney grumbled. "I had to fight to get full custody and move away. He tried every trick in the book, but in the end, the judge agreed with me."

We stood for a few moments in silence. It had been years since we'd seen each other. Both of us had dreams we wanted to pursue, and the fact that we were standing in Oak Springs hit me hard.

"Well, I better get inside. I'm meeting my...um...ahh... contractor. He actually did the remodel of your restaurant."

"Jonathon Turner?" Laney asked.

"Yes. He suggested we come here for dinner. I'm glad he did. It was so nice seeing you again, Laney."

She wrapped me in for a hug. "You, too, Waylynn. Let's plan a night out to catch up and not talk about the damn exes."

I handed her my phone, and she handed me hers. After we exchanged numbers, she led me into the restaurant. The inside was beautiful. Rustic, to match the outside. The original wood beams were left exposed, and a giant floor-to-ceiling fireplace had been added with an iron sign above it that read,

"Did y'all have reservations, Waylynn?"

"Yes, they're under my name."

The hostess smiled as she grabbed two menus. "Please, follow me."

I followed the hostess toward the fireplace. A table was set for two right next to the crackling fire. It was incredibly romantic for a business dinner.

I looked around and saw people I knew. A few nodded and said hello, to which I replied. It was a godsend that our little table was set back from prying ears.

"Would you like a glass of wine? We carry all Texas wines."

"Any pinot grigio, please."

She smiled. "Grape Creek Vineyards has the best. Glass or bottle?"

I glanced around again. One or two people were still watching me. Then I caught sight of Jonathon. I was positive my eyes nearly popped out of my head at his black eye and swollen lip.

"Oh, Lord. Better make it a bottle."

"Yes, ma'am. I'll let your server know."

She turned to leave and ran right into Jonathon. That caused enough commotion to make everyone look yet again. All I wanted to do was slide down in my chair and hide, especially when the good-looking bastard had the nerve to kiss me on the cheek! I was so shocked to see his beaten-up face, I didn't even bother to pull away.

"Christ Almighty, Jonathon! What happened to your face?"

He reached for the water and took a long drink. "Well, I'm afraid that story is going to make you mad, so why don't we save it for last."

I narrowed my eyes. He and his friends had probably gotten into a fight in Vegas. Men.

"Well, you look simply awful."

"Thanks, Waylynn."

Leaning closer, I whispered, "You know what I mean. You look like something the dog dragged in. Why didn't you cancel dinner? Everyone is staring at us."

He picked up the menu and glanced around. "No one is staring at us, but if you keep making a fuss, they will."

With a huff, I grabbed the menu. My gaze kept drifting over his face. A strange pain in my chest hit me each time. All I wanted to do was take him home and put a bag of peas on his eye. Isn't that what you did for black eyes?

"You need a bag of peas."

Jonathon looked at me. "I beg your pardon?"

"For your eye."

He laughed and shook his head before he went back to the menu.

"Why was that so funny?" I asked.

A young lady appeared in front of us.

"Good evening. My name is…" She paused. "Jonathon? What in the world happened?"

The way she grabbed his chin and forced his head up told me they knew each other.

"Hey there, Evie. I'm fine, can you please let go of my face?"

A spark of jealousy raced through my veins. Who in the hell was Evie? And where in the hell did this jealousy bullshit come from?

The waitress let go of him. "Mom is going to crap her pants when she finds out you were in a fight."

"Mom?" I asked.

Evie turned to me, a huge smile spread over her face. "Waylynn?"

My eyes widened. "Do we know each other?"

The girl practically jumped. "Oh, my gawd! It's so great to finally meet you!"

I turned my focus on Jonathon, who sat there with a stupid smile. I looked back at Evie. "Um, it's a pleasure meeting you, but I'm afraid you have me at a disadvantage. I didn't realize Jonathon had a younger sister."

Evie laughed. "There're six of us."

"Six?"

How in the hell did I not know he came from a big family?

"Jonathon is the oldest. Then there is me, I'm twenty-two, then Hollie, she's eighteen. Dalton is ten, Hope is eight, and Rip is the baby. He's six. Well, about to be seven."

"Wow!" I said with a laugh. "I didn't know you had so many siblings."

"Blended family!" Evie said. "Our father died when we were younger, and mom married Rip senior. Dalton is from Rip's first marriage, and Hope and Rip are from this marriage."

Jonathon cleared his throat. "Now that you've filled Waylynn in on the family history, can we get some drinks?"

Another waitress brought over the bottle of wine.

"I went ahead and ordered some wine," I mumbled as I waited for the girl to open the shit up so I could down a glass.

"Do y'all know what you want to eat or should I give you a few minutes?"

When the waitress handed me the sample of wine, I downed it. She tried to hide her chuckle but failed. "Yep, it's good. Now pour me a big glass."

"I think we need a few minutes, Evie," Jonathon said.

"Sure! No problem. I'll leave you lovebirds alone."

I choked on the wine as Evie spun walked to another table. Setting the glass down, I glared at Jonathon. "What in the hell was that?"

He shrugged. "Evie being hopeful, that's all."

"Hopeful of what?"

With a knock-my-panties-right-off-of-me smile, he replied, "Us."

Leaning closer, I whispered, "You say that like we're an item."

He poured a glass of wine and held it up. "I hope by the end of dinner we are."

My eyes closed. "You drive me insane, Turner."

With a grunt, he put the wine glass down. "No, you drive me insane. It was your flirty little text that had me in my hotel room with my hand around my cock."

A lady behind us cleared her throat.

"Shut up!" I whispered loudly.

Frustration bubbled inside every time I looked at him. Was sexual frustration what got him in that fight? A small part of me hoped it had been.

"You told your family about me?" I asked, changing the subject.

Jonathon half shrugged. "I might have mentioned you at a family dinner."

"What did you say?"

A mischievous smile played across his face. "Well, I didn't tell them I got caught fucking one of my clients."

My stomach dropped. "Stop being crass," I said before adding in a lower voice, "Save that shit for the bedroom."

His brows rose. "You like the dirty talk, do you?"

It was my turn to shrug. "I don't know. I've never experienced a man talking dirty to me in bed before."

"Is that a challenge, Waylynn?"

Taking a sip of my wine, I replied, "Do you want it to be?"

He leaned forward, his eyes full of hope. "Do *you* want it to be? I think you already know how much I want you."

My teeth dug into my lip as I let the corner of my mouth rise into a slight smile. "I mean, it would be a shame for me to have gone panty-less for nothing."

Jonathon hooked my chair with his foot and pulled me closer. When his hand touched my leg, I let out a gasp. "A little jumpy there, babe?"

"Don't call me *babe*." I looked around the restaurant. Not a single person was looking in our direction. The long black tablecloth was hiding the fact that Jonathon's fingers were moving up the inside of my thigh.

"Spread your legs open…babe."

My mind fought my body, and my damn body won out. My legs slowly spread open as I picked up my wine and took a sip. When his fingers brushed over my folds, I sucked in a breath.

We were sitting entirely too close for this to be considered a business dinner. If anyone in my family walked in, they would know this was a date. Hell…if anyone in the room looked over, they would know this was a date. And how in the hell was he doing this with his sister about to walk up at any moment!

Moving his lips to my ear, Jonathon whispered, "Are you wet for me?"

Lifting my chin, I kept the wine in front of my mouth. "Why don't you find out?"

I spread my legs wider, my dress riding up my lap. Jonathon pushed a finger inside and let out a low growl that rumbled through my entire body, straight to where his hand was. I'd never had an orgasm from a simple touch before...until now.

"Oh, God," I whispered as I gripped his arm with my free hand. My body trembled as the orgasm rushed through me.

"Sensitive tonight?"

Pushing his hand away, I set my glass down and adjusted the dress.

"It's been awhile," I bit back, causing him to laugh. When he pushed his two fingers into his mouth I nearly died with embarrassment.

"Mmm...preview of dessert."

"Y'all ready to order?"

I let out a small yelp. Evie had scared the living daylights out of me. Swallowing hard, I tried to talk but nothing came out.

"I think I'll have the surf and turf. Can I also get a Caesar salad?"

Evie wrote down Jonathon's order. When had he even picked out his meal?

"Waylynn?"

I picked up the menu and scanned it. "I'll have the um...toasted pecan crusted chicken."

"Ohh! That's one of my favorites!" Evie added. "I'll bring some warm bread with the salads."

My cheeks still felt hot from our little escapade. How was it this man could make me so weak I would let him get me off at a damn restaurant?

"That wasn't appropriate, Jonathon Turner."

He chuckled slightly. "Were you thinking of how Miss Manners would handle a situation like that when your legs were spreading, Waylynn Parker?"

I shot him the finger quickly. "It was a moment of weakness." Rubbing my temples, I tried to erase the headache that was slowly building. "I agreed to have dinner with you to talk about a possible future, not for you to...you know."

"No, tell me, Waylynn. I want to hear it from that pretty mouth of yours."

Dropping my shoulders, I stared. "Can we be serious now? Yes, that was fun, *really* fun, but please can we talk."

Jonathon reached for my hand and gave it a gentle squeeze. "Yes. I'm sorry I let things get out of control." He leaned back in the chair, motioning for me to start.

I knew he wasn't really sorry, and neither was I.

I dragged in a deep breath, and slowly let it out.

Here we go...

CHAPTER 8

Jonathon

I waited for Waylynn to start talking. She sat there wringing her hands as she looked everywhere but at me. At the rate she was going, our dinner would be out before she even said a word.

"Tell me why the idea of *us* scares you so much."

Her eyes shot over to me. After a few seconds of gnawing her lip, she spoke. "When I moved back home, rumors started circulating about my failed marriage. I've never given much thought to what people said about me before, but that was in New York where I could pass a person every second and probably never see them again. Here, at home, I see these people all the time. I'm fixin' to start a business where peoples' kids will come to me to learn to dance. I just don't want to be known as the washed-up dancer who is dating…"

"A construction worker?"

Her eyes widened. "You're not a construction worker. You own your own business. And even if you were, that doesn't matter to me."

I folded my arms over my chest. "Then what matters?"

Her eyes landed on my chest, and she slowly ran her tongue over her bottom lip. I couldn't believe her stupid-ass ex had let her go. His loss was my gain.

"Your age."

"I don't care about it. My family doesn't care either."

"Well, I'm not sure how mine will feel."

Leaning forward again, I placed my finger on her chin and brought her gaze to mine. "Do they want you to be happy?"

"Of course they do."

"Do you think you could be happy with me, Waylynn?"

Her teeth sank into her lip again, turning it white. *Fuck, that is hot as hell.*

"Do you?" I asked again.

"Yes."

"Then who gives a shit about what other people think? Let me love you like you deserve to be loved. Give me a chance to prove that we can make this work."

A wide smile spread over her face. Leaning closer, I brushed my lips across hers. It hurt like hell with the busted lip Cord had given me, but my girl was kissing me back. In public. I wasn't about to stop.

When I dropped her chin and sat back, her eyes were ablaze. "I give you until tomorrow morning before one of my brothers hear about this."

"It doesn't matter, because now that I've got you, I'm not letting you go, Parker."

The brilliance of her grin made my heart soar. "Please, don't," she whispered.

I needed to tell her about Cord. The longer I put it off, the worse it would be.

Evie walked up with our salads.

Draping the napkin over my lap, I thanked my sister for the salad and casually dropped the bomb.

"Besides, after the beating Cord gave me when I told him about us, I can't let you go 'cuz I promised him I'd never hurt you."

From the corner of my eye I saw her fork freeze at her lips. I was fixin' to feel the wrath of one pissed-off Parker woman, and I thought I was mentally prepared.

Boy, was I wrong.

I unlocked the door and watched Waylynn march through it. She threw her purse onto the table and faced me. Her hands went to her hips and her blue eyes locked on me with intense fire.

Oh. Shit.

"Brace yourself, Turner. I'm about to go all female crazy on your ass."

Lifting my hands, I took a step back. "Before you get all Parker crazy, let me explain."

"Explain? You want me to give you a chance to explain? You're fixin' to have another black eye to match the one my brother gave you."

"Waylynn, I couldn't lie to him. Earlier in the weekend, he asked me if I knew who you were crushing on, and I lied. I get why you didn't want him to know, but can you at least look at it from my perspective? He's my best friend. He's like a brother to me, and I didn't feel right lyin' about you and me."

She drew in a deep breath through her nose and slowly exhaled. Even though her expression softened, there was no way I was letting my guard down. I was smarter than that.

"I'm going to guess he was rather pissed off."

"Yes. At first. When we were on the plane."

Her eyes widened. "You told him on the plane? In an enclosed area with no escape? Are you crazy, Jonathon?"

I chuckled. "I actually thought it was the safest place, truth be told. The flight attendant separated us, speaking of, remind me to tell you about how she knew Cord."

Waylynn's brows pulled tight, figuring out their "connection" without me even vocalizing it.

"Anyway, by the time we got back to his place he had cooled off."

Pointing to my face, she smiled. "That's your definition of cooled off?"

"It could be worse."

With a shrug, she agreed. "That's true. Keep going."

I motioned for her to sit on the sofa while I took the chair across from it.

"Well, he gave me the chance to explain things. I told him it was wrong to act on my feelings for you before I talked to him about it, but that we're adults and your brothers don't have a say in whom you're dating."

Waylynn grinned and leaned back. "What else did you say in this moment of insanity?"

The corners of my mouth rose as I continued. "I told him how I feel about you. How I love your smile and laughter. This feeling I have for you is unlike anything I've ever experienced before, and I can't even begin to put it into words. I told him I'm falling for you, Waylynn, and I do not intend on sitting back and not fighting for you. I want to see where this will go, because when I close my eyes at night I see a future that I've longed for, and you're the woman in my dreams."

She swallowed hard. "You said that to him?"

"I did."

When she pulled her lip between her teeth, my dick jumped to attention. Damn, she did that a lot.

"Do I get brownie points for standing up to a Parker?"

"Maybe. What did he say after you said that?"

"That if anyone was going to date his sister, he'd rather it be someone he trusted with his life. And he may or may not have threatened my life if I ever hurt you."

Her smile grew bigger. "Sounds like Cord."

"He's a teddy bear. It's Tripp I'm worried about."

Waylynn let out a laugh. "How about if I let Tripp know. Lord knows what he'll do to you."

Now it was my turn to swallow hard. "That makes me feel tons better. Your brothers are going to give me an ulcer."

Slowly standing, she made her way over to me, lifting her dress higher as she walked.

"I bet I can make you feel better. Help relieve those bumps and bruises…"

My heart slammed against my chest, beating so fucking fast. If I didn't know better, I'd have thought this was my first time having sex.

"After all, I am still without my panties."

I let a slow grin move across my face. "You're going to keep me on my toes. Aren't you, Parker?"

Her tongue slid across her bee-stung lips as she crawled onto my lap. "I'm sure as hell going to try. Do you know what I'm going to do first?"

My head slowly shook as I let my eyes drop to her chest. I was itching to put one of her nipples in my mouth and hear her moan.

"Fuck," I groaned as she moved against my dick.

She chuckled as her lips moved over my neck, dropping kisses along the way. "You wish. No, the first thing I'm going to do is show you what happens when you go against what I ask."

I was dizzy with desire. Need. Want. Waylynn Parker had a way of making my body completely surrender.

Her words finally hit me, and I pulled back to look into her eyes.

"What?"

Lacing her fingers through my hair, she pressed her lips to mine. Our tongues danced in harmony, and we each let out a long, soft moan while she pressed harder against my cock.

Just as my hands were moving to grab her ass, she broke the kiss and climbed off of me. With her head tilted and sporting an adorable grin, she said, "Enjoy your evening, Turner."

She turned, grabbed her purse, and started for my front door.

What in the hell just happened?

I flew up and nearly tripped over my own damn feet trying to get to the door. Before she could open it, I placed my hand on it. Still breathing heavy from her kiss, I asked, "Where are you going? I thought we were gonna…"

"Fuck?" she blurted out.

Jamming my hand through my hair, I closed my eyes and tried to clear my thoughts.

"Yes. No! Waylynn, I thought we were going to be together tonight."

She tapped her finger on my nose. "Aww, you're so cute. I did say we would talk, but then you told my brother about us sleeping together when I specifically asked you not to…and without even giving me a heads up."

My jaw dropped open. "So, you're…um…"

"Leaving. Yep." She popped her *p* and winked. "We can try the whole talking thing tomorrow."

Her eyes drifted down to my still rock-hard dick. With a shrug she snapped her gaze back up at me. "Pity you're going to have to take care of that all alone."

Reaching up on her toes, she gave me a hasty kiss then opened the door. When it closed, the only thing I could do was laugh. I rubbed the back of my neck and made my way into the kitchen for a beer. "Lesson one? Don't piss Waylynn off. Retaliation is a bitch."

CHAPTER 9

Waylynn

The sound of my feet hitting the ground and the feel of cold morning air in my lungs were the exact things I needed to clear my head. After last night, I'd been desperate for a release and no matter how hard I tried to make myself come, it had been no use. I finally gave up and fell asleep at two in the morning.

An early morning run was the one thing I could count on to get out built-up energy and frustration. A truck came up behind me, and I stopped and turned around. Smiling, I waved as my father's truck pulled up.

"Hello there, young lady."

Catching my breath, I leaned my hands on my knees. I hadn't realized how fast and hard I'd been running. "Hey…Daddy."

"Hitting the dirt road early this morning, aren't you?"

I blew out a deep breath. "Needed to clear my head."

With a nod, he motioned for me to hop in the truck. "Come with me. We can catch up on things."

I loved spending alone time with my father. Even when I was little, having his full attention was something I loved, and so did my brothers and sister. The Parker kids jumped at the opportunity when it came around, which was often. Our father made sure his children knew how much he loved us.

I jogged around to the front of the truck and climbed up in the cab of the Ford F-250.

He put it in drive and started down the main ranch road. "How are things going with the studio?"

Grinning like a silly fool, I answered, "Wonderful! Now that we're on schedule and things are moving smoothly, we should be open in mid-January."

"That's wonderful, sweet pea. I'm so very proud of you for following your dreams."

My heart ached slightly. "Well, most of them anyway. A part of me wishes I hadn't wasted all those years on Jack and kept dancing in New York. Who knows where I would have ended up."

"Well, I know you wouldn't be here right now, and call me greedy, but I do like having you close to home." He squeezed my hand.

"I love being home, Daddy. Honestly, I do. And opening a dance studio in Oak Springs is a dream, so it's win-win no matter what. I'm just doing it a little sooner than I thought."

"That's my girl," he said, giving my hand another slight squeeze.

We drove along in silence for a minute or two before he dropped a bomb. "So, Jonathon Turner, huh?"

I sighed heavily and faced him. "News still travels fast among the Parker men, huh?"

He laughed. "First thing this morning I got a call from Tripp, asking what I thought about my daughter dating a man younger than her."

Anger rushed over me. "How dare he! Why is it okay for men to date younger women, but God forbid a woman date a younger man! I'm going to string Tripp's balls up in the town square with a sign that says *vote for someone else*!"

My father let out a roar of laughter. "You are so much like your mother, it is unreal. Now, calm down, sweet pea. I told Tripp he needed to take a seat and rethink what he just said. I asked him if it were another woman, would he have an issue? He said no. But you're not any woman, you're his sister."

Okay, I had to admit, that one got me in the heart. I had no doubt that my brothers loved me and cared about me.

"Thank you for that, Daddy."

"Waylynn, I think what your brothers think about your dating situation should be the last thing on your list of give-a-fucks."

I chuckled. "You're right on that one."

He pulled over and turned the truck off. "Let's go for a walk, shall we?"

I warmed as yesteryears with my father flooded my memory. One of my favorite things to do was walk along the Frio River with him, skipping rocks and just talking about things.

"I'd love to go for a walk! We haven't done this in forever!"

His face lit up. "The last time was right before you married Jack, I believe."

"I should have listened to your advice when you said you didn't think Jack was the right man for me."

He stared ahead, his arm draped over my shoulder. "Some things you have to learn on your own, sweet pea."

We walked for a few feet in silence. "And what is your advice for me today?"

"Are you asking for it?" he asked as we stopped and faced each other.

"I'm assuming you want to give me some if you tracked me down and invited me for a walk."

He chuckled. "Nonsense. I don't need a reason to spend time with my beautiful daughter. But now that you mention it, I will give you my two cents, for what it is worth."

I held my breath and waited. My father's opinion had always mattered and the one time I chose to ignore it was the time I'd needed it most. But now—now I was scared he would tell me that he thought me dating Jonathon was a bad idea. That it would only bring heartache to both of us if we started up a relationship with all the rumors it would inspire. My heart didn't want to hear that advice. Not one bit.

"First, I think you need to figure out what is scaring you about a relationship with Jonathon."

A lump formed in my throat, and for a brief moment it was hard to talk. How in the world could my father know this? Hadn't he found out about Jonathon and me only this morning?

"Are you a mind reader now, Dad? What makes you think something is scaring me?"

He took my hand, and we walked down the path to the river. It was the same path we had walked hundreds of times, but this time something was different.

"You know all those years you wore that pretty smile of yours, your mother and I knew you weren't happy. We knew you weren't going to give up on your marriage because we raised you to fight for the things you want. And it didn't take me long to figure out there was something between you and Jonathon. I think I knew when I saw the two of you together for the first time."

My mind drifted back. "When did you see us together?"

"Well, you weren't together romantically, but it was the way you looked at each other the day your mother and I stopped by the dance studio. I've known that young man since he was in diapers, and the way he was looking at my daughter was screaming 'I've got a thing for her'."

I hit him lightly on the stomach. "Daddy!"

"It was confirmed at the boys' birthday party. You plastered on a smile, but boy howdy, you were throwing darts at the poor girl on Jonathon's arm."

"I was not!" I said, scrunching my nose and stomping my foot. I was acting like a five-year-old, which made my father laugh.

"Same old Waylynn."

"I was not throwing darts at her."

He lifted his brow.

"Fine, so maybe I glanced their way a time or two. I still don't get how you figure I'm scared."

After leading us over to a rock, my father and I sat down.

"It wasn't hard to put it together, Waylynn Parker. I have been around the block a time or two. That boy owns his own construction company and has men to do the work but seems to be the only one working on your job. Plus, the little incident with old lady Hopkins."

My cheeks burned, and I looked away. "I thought we agreed to never bring that up, Daddy."

"I never agreed to it."

Sighing, I turned to face him again. "Fine. So you pieced it together long before you officially found out. Only tells me my hiding skills are not up to par like they were when I was younger."

"Even way back then, Waylynn, your mother and I knew more than we let on."

His revelation had me combing through years of things best left hidden, praying that he didn't know too much.

He bumped my shoulder. "Talk to me, sweet pea."

I watched as the water rolled over boulders both big and small. "I'm conflicted on a few things."

"Want to talk about them?"

"You'll think I'm a royal bitch if I tell you."

He chuckled. "Try me."

Taking in a deep breath, I slowly let it out. "For starters, I'm extremely jealous that Steed and Mitchell are parents and soon-to-be parents. How wrong is that?"

His blue eyes met mine. "Why is that wrong?"

"Didn't you hear me?"

"I heard you. Do you love your brothers?"

My eyes widened. "Of course I do, Daddy!"

"And Chloe and Gage?"

"Yes! And I'll love Mitchell and Corina's baby the same!"

Squeezing my hand, he bent over to meet me eye to eye. "It's okay to want a family, Waylynn. It's okay to be a little jealous when you see your younger siblings getting what you thought you'd already have by now."

My heart nearly burst when my father said that. "Yes! That's exactly it. I thought by now I'd be in a little house with a fence around the yard and a few kids running about. Instead, I'm divorced, living back at home, and about to start dating a younger man! What are people going to think?"

"And there is your other issue. The age difference."

I stared down at the ground. "I want to start a family, and before you tell me I'm still young enough, I need to tell you I've already been to a sperm bank in San Antonio. To see if I want to become a parent all on my own."

The look on my father's face was one I would never forget.

Shock.

Pure shock.

CHAPTER 10

Waylynn

"What?" My father sat on the rock, his face devoid of all color.

"I only went to ask some questions, to see if it might be the best option for me."

"Waylynn, bringing a child into this world is hard when there are two parents. I can't imagine going at it alone, but your mother and I would help you if this is what you want."

Sighing, I gazed over the river. "I guess it felt like it was never going to happen otherwise. But now, this thing with Jonathon has me rethinking my entire plan. The last thing I would want to do is make him feel like I only wanted him as a baby maker. He knows I want to start a family. It was one of my excuses when I initially pushed him away."

"And how does he feel about kids?"

I grinned. "He wants to have kids someday."

"Well, that's a step in the right direction, and darling, you are still young. So, is the main concern the age difference?"

I shrugged. "I guess, and the idea of starting all over again with someone is terrifying. Jack also told me he wanted kids and look where that got me!"

My father scoffed. "Jack is an asshole. I don't see Jonathon playing around with your emotions like that."

Tears filled my eyes because I knew he was right.

"Daddy, we've only been on one real date, not counting the countless hours of flirting we've done. Is it to soon to feel something...different?"

He gently smiled. "By different, do you mean different from Jack?"

"Not just that. I've never felt this way with any man before. I was honestly head over heels in love with Jack. At least, I thought I was. Maybe he just swept me off my feet with all the trips to Paris and London, and I was blinded by the gifts and attention he showered me with. That makes me feel shallow."

"Nonsense. You were young. He promised you the moon and stars and didn't follow through."

I dragged in a deep breath and exhaled. "This feeling I have for Jonathon...it's so different that it's confusing. It's almost like I don't remember life before he was in it. How can that be? We only just started dating! Not to mention I should be focused on the dance studio and opening up my own business. Throwing a relationship into the mix with the potential of *not* achieving my dreams...again...has me scared."

"I understand those concerns. They are valid. But does the intensity of your feelings for him spook you?"

Chewing on my lip, I nodded.

"Yes, more than it should."

"I wouldn't necessarily say that. You've been hurt, Waylynn. To open your heart up to be hurt again is a risk. But I believe it is a risk worth taking."

"Even if my brothers don't see it that way?"

Tossing his head back to laugh, my father cried out, "Even if! I say go for it, sweet pea. Live your life, Waylynn, and don't worry about what the people of this town think. I mean, if I worried about what everyone in this town said about Aunt Vi, I'd never show my face."

Hitting him on the arm, I scolded him. "Daddy! That is your sister!"

He stood. "The stories about my sister... I could fill your head with hundreds of them and each one would make you blush. Let's save those toe curlers for another time."

My hand in his, we made our way down to the riverbank.

"Waylynn, darling, don't be in such a rush for kids. I know your younger siblings are starting to settle, but it will happen, I promise. Sometimes God has other plans for us and things don't happen the way we think they should."

I picked up a rock and tossed it across the river. "I know I need to be patient and check these jealous feelings, and focus on the happiness of seeing my siblings growing our family." Facing my father, my eyes teared up again.

"Daddy, I really am happy for Steed, Mitchell, and Amelia. I hope you don't think I'm self-centered."

He wrapped me in his arms and held me tightly. "Oh, sweet pea, I could never think that about you. Just take a deep breath and let life happen."

Closing my eyes, I let my father's advice settle in.

Let life happen...

I stood outside Jonathon's door, still dressed in my running clothes, taking deep breaths. With a shaking hand, I lifted it and went to knock, but the door quickly opened.

"Waylynn, what are you doing here?"

"Thought you might want to have that talk, and maybe pick up where we left off last night."

His eyes brightened. "Yeah?"

With a slight grin, I nodded. "I wanted to catch you before you left for work."

"If I invite you in, I'm afraid I'll miss my meeting, and I don't want to piss off this person. I've seen how she gets when she's angry."

Oh, his meeting was with me.

"Maybe I could give her a call, explain how stupid I've been by pushing you away and not admitting that I'm falling for you. I can almost guarantee she'll understand."

My body trembled when he brushed a strand of my hair back from my face. His grey eyes danced with possibilities.

"I don't know. She's kind of a bitch."

Laughing, I hit him on the chest. "She is not! She simply knows what she wants."

"Does she?" he asked, his brows lifted.

"Yes," I replied and my voice shook with excitement.

Cupping my face, Jonathon stared into my eyes as if he was looking into my soul. I heard cars driving by behind us, but I didn't care who saw us or what they thought. I was finished worrying about what the people of Oak Springs thought about my choices.

"And what does she want?" he asked, his voice so low and husky that warmth flooded through my body.

My gaze flitted across his face before landing on his eyes. Each breath was shallow as I said the words my heart had been begging to release. "You. Us. This."

Jonathon leaned over and brushed his lips across mine, whispering, "Finally."

Sliding his hand behind my neck, we kissed and the world fell away. My body felt like it was floating above me. The kiss was slow and soft as our breaths mingled. Moving my hands to his body, I drew him in, until we were pressed together, and I could feel his heart beating against my own. Jonathon moved his mouth down to my neck, his hot breath making my skin feel like it was on fire with each softly pressed kiss. In that moment I knew I would forever be addicted to Jonathon's kisses. To his touch.

"Waylynn," he said, prolonging each letter as if he was burning it into his memory.

I would never forget the intensity of his voice, the desire I heard in it.

"Make love to me, Jonathon. Please."

He moved quickly, swept me up into his arms. "My neighbor, Karen, is watching us."

"So?" I replied, running my fingers into his hair.

"She's your brother Tripp's secretary."

With a smile, I turned and faced her. She was slowly walking down the steps of her house.

"Oh, this is going to be fun."

Lifting my hand, I waved and shouted, "Hey Karen! Tell my brother I said hi!"

She smiled and replied, "Will do! Have fun, you two!"

Jonathon and I laughed and walked into his house. He kicked the door shut with the heel of his boot.

He pulled me down the hallway and into his bedroom. I wanted to look around since I hadn't really gotten to last night, but my focus was on him, on this moment, on where we were headed both literally and figuratively.

Jonathon cupped my face again. "I'm going to make love to you all day, but…"

"But?" I asked.

"But first I get to pay you back for leaving me in the state you did last night."

My lower lip jutted out. "But I'm so horny."

"Is that so?"

"So. Very. Horny."

"Then I better take care of that."

I smiled. "I always knew you were handy with your tools."

He pulled his shirt over his head. Licking my lips, I let my eyes travel over his perfectly fit body. His chest was massive and toned, and the veins popping out down his arms were a huge turn on.

Jesus have mercy on me.

Jonathon took a step closer, his hand moving under my T-shirt to my back. A couple of flicks and my bra was off. I dropped my head back as he moved his fingers over my body. Pushing my bra and shirt over my breasts, he pinched one nipple as he leaned down and brought the other into his mouth.

"Oh, God. Yes!" I hissed as the energy in his mouth rushed through my body. I could already feel the buildup of my much-needed release. My fingers went into his dark hair, pulling and tugging to spur him on.

A warm hand made its way up my leg, tickling the skin along my thigh as he slowly worked it into my panties. His boot pushed my feet apart to spread my legs, and the moment he plunged his fingers in, I cried out his name.

"Jonathon!"

My orgasm rolled through my body as I felt myself clench around his fingers. Closing my eyes, I let myself sink into the euphoria and soon found I was in Jonathon's arms. He was carrying me to the bed. Quick hands pulled the rest of my clothes off. I watched as Jonathon kicked off his boots and then pulled his jeans off. His thick, long, shaft sprung free, and I couldn't help but lick my lips. I wanted it in my mouth, but I wanted it inside of me more.

Jonathon pulled open the drawer at the side of his bed and ripped open a box of condoms. He tossed a few on the bed and crawled over me. His mouth crushed mine as we kissed deeply, passionately, until my lips felt raw from his stubble.

Framing my head with his hands, his gaze pierced mine. "I want to taste you… I'm going to taste you before this day is over, but first, I need to be inside of you. I am going to die if I don't feel you wrapped around my cock."

I smiled as I ran my foot up and down his leg. "What are you waiting for, Mr. Turner?"

His hand slipped between my legs, and when he pushed two fingers in, a low growl came from the back of his throat. "I'd say you're ready."

All I could do was nod. I was more than ready. My body felt like it was going to combust, every molecule *on fire*.

Jonathon reached for a condom, ripped it out, and rolled it on. My stomach flipped with excitement. I wasn't sure why I was nervous. We'd already been together, so it wasn't our first time. Yet, it felt like it was our first time.

Ever so slowly he pushed inside of me. Inch by delicious inch. My back arched as my body begged for more of him.

"Christ Almighty," he whispered, burying his face into my neck. When he was finally fully seated, he paused. Wrapping my arms around him, I pulled him even closer as I dug my heels into his lower back.

"You feel so good, Waylynn."

Slowly, he moved. In and out. With each movement, my body felt like it was being lifted higher and higher. His hand moved ever so softly over my skin, leaving a trail of fire. Jonathon's mouth found mine again. His lips felt softer, the kiss so gentle it nearly brought me to tears.

The next words from his mouth burned deep in my heart.

"You're mine, Waylynn. Forever mine."

CHAPTER 11

jonathon

I always looked forward to Poker night. But not tonight. All I wanted was to be in bed with Waylynn wrapped in my arms. Since she'd showed up at my place the other morning, the last few nights we had done just that. Never mind the fucking hot sex in her office yesterday, and the countless other places we had sex over the course of the last three days. I couldn't help smiling when I thought about it. Sex with Waylynn was addictive. I'd never in my life wanted a woman so damn much. I'd thought it was the chase that was driving this insane desire, but it wasn't. Every time I finished making love to her, I wanted her again, which was evident from our nonstop fuck sessions.

Once in the kitchen at the dance studio, once in my truck on the way to the flooring store in San Antonio. On her desk at the studio…twice. And countless times in my bed at home. Hell, Monday we had spent the entire day getting to know what the other person liked. Waylynn seemed to melt when I placed my mouth against her ear and spoke. Even something as simple as placing my hand on her lower back to lead her into a room had led to her dragging me into the restroom at the restaurant last night and fucking her on the sink. For someone who didn't want our relationship to go public, she sure didn't mind us walking out of the ladies' restroom together, sporting that just-fucked look.

But tonight was guys' night. Waylynn said she was exhausted and needed to soak in a hot bath…and a part of me was jealous. My dick was certainly thanking me for the reprieve. Even he needed a night off.

I knocked on Cord's door. It opened and Cord flashed me a smile. "Right on time, as usual."

I handed him the normal entry fee of a six-pack of beer, and he motioned me in. After a few steps I glanced to my left and stopped walking.

My eyes closed and I mumbled, "Oh fuck."

"Well, if it isn't Jonathon Turner."

There they were. A lineup of Parker brothers. None of them smiling. I held out my hand as I walked up to each of them.

"How's it going, Steed?"

He simply nodded. I moved to Trevor. "Trev, how's it going?"

"I've had better days."

My smile faded, but I knew better than to show fear. "Sorry to hear about that."

Next came Mitchell. He was no longer a cop, which was not a good thing for me. He had been one of the only Parker brother you could count on to not get crazy because of his job. Well, actually him and Tripp. Now that Mitchell worked on his daddy's ranch, I had a feeling he had some pent-up steam to let out, and I was the first punching bag available to him.

I turned slightly and saw Tripp. He was leaning against the bar that Cord had on the other side of the living room.

I couldn't get Cord's warning about Tripp out of my head, but I forced my feet to take me over to him.

"Tripp, great seeing you again."

He grunted as he reached for my hand. His handshake was the firmest of all. When he dropped my hand, he let an evil smile play across his face.

"Karen said she saw Waylynn heading into your house."

Awww, hell. Here we go.

"Yes, that's true."

"And according to my sources," Mitchell added. "She didn't come out of your house until late afternoon."

My eyes darted around the room. I noticed for the first time that Cord only had one exit in this damn place. How had I never noticed that before?

"Um, that's right."

I looked past the bar to the balcony. It faced Main Street. If I ran, I could call for help. Surely someone would help me...wouldn't they?

"You want to tell us what she was doing that whole time in your house?" Cord asked, taking a seat in his oversized, brown leather chair.

Glancing around, I focused on Cord. They'd all shit if they knew how many times she'd been back to my house. "Are you sure you want me to answer?"

"You afraid to answer?" Trevor piped in.

"No. If you want to hear how your sister and I spent the day, I'll tell ya."

"NO!" all five of them said at once. It was a small victory, and probably one that was going to lead to another black eye and busted lip.

Pushing off the bar, Tripp hit me on the back and headed over to the other sofa. "We've got some...things...we need to discuss with you."

The front door opened, and Wade walked in. I let out the breath I'd been holding.

"Please, tell me you're my backup?" I said, desperation in my voice. Wade glanced around the room and then back to me.

"Sorry, dude. I'm only here to make sure things don't...you know." He shrugged as he pointed to the five men sitting in the living room staring at me like I had a death wish hanging over my head.

"No, Wade. I really don't know."

"Go ahead. Fill him in," Cord said.

Wade took a seat at one of the barstools at Cord's kitchen island. "I'm here to make sure they don't go too far with you." He sliced his hand across his throat.

I swallowed hard and looked back at the balcony. "It might actually be worth the broken leg if I just run and jump right now. Save y'all the trouble."

Steed laughed. "What fun would that be, Jon?"

With a sigh, I threw my hands up in surrender. "Fine. Let's do this." I closed my eyes and scrunched up my face while I waited for the first punch.

"What are you doing, asshole?" Cord asked.

Opening one eye, I looked at him sitting there. "I figured y'all were here to beat my ass, so I was getting ready for it."

"So, you'd actually let each of us hit you? Why?" Tripp asked.

With a half shrug, I replied, "If that's what y'all feel like you need to do. There's nothing you could do or say to make me stop seeing Waylynn, so we might as well get this all said and done with."

They looked at each other and then back to me.

Trevor stood up and cracked his knuckles. "Alright, then, if that's how you want to do it, let's just get to it. You want it in the face, gut, or dick."

"Dick?" I asked, my voice notes higher. "Why do you have to bring my dick into this?"

"Oh, believe me, I'm sure your dick has been having a good ol' time the last few days with *our* sister. He already has a dog…or a *bone*…in this fight."

"What?" I exclaimed, covering my junk as Trevor moved closer. "My dick is off limits. There will be no hitting of my dick. I mean, that's going too far…even for y'all."

"Damn," Tripp said as he shook his head. "He's right. That means we get an extra hit if you choose stomach." He looked around. "Fair enough, y'all?"

They nodded.

"Christ Almighty," I said, rolling my eyes. "You're all crazy."

Trevor walked over to me. "Where do you want it?"

"You might as well make the other eye black and blue."

"Sounds good to me."

Trevor reached back, about to throw the punch, when the front door banged opened.

"What in the living fuck are the five of you doing?"

Waylynn's voice caused us all to freeze.

I unfroze first. "Hey, what are you doing here? I thought you were staying home." Walking over to her, I leaned down and kissed her on the lips. It was ballsy with her five brothers in the room, each waiting to knock the shit out of me.

"I figured out their little plan. It didn't take long when Paxton and Corina both said Steed and Mitchell were heading over to Cord's for *poker night,"* she said, using air quotes. "Then when Amelia said Wade was going too, I knew you little bastards were up to something."

Cord stood. "You should probably head on back home, Waylynn."

Her hands came to her hips, her head tilted.

"Oh hell," Wade said. "Y'all done pissed her off."

"Head *back home*? You honestly think I'm going to let you beat my boyfriend up?"

All eyes were on me now.

"Boyfriend, huh?" Tripp growled.

I cleared my throat. "Tripp, listen…"

"No," Waylynn shouted, pointing to me. "You don't say another word, Jonathon Turner. Not one…more…word."

I nodded. "Yes, ma'am."

Waylynn slowly shook her head as she peered at each of her brothers. God, it was hot as fuck the way she commanded a room. "Have you five forgotten who is the oldest out of this bunch? You think because I'm a woman I can't take care of myself?"

"No," five voices said at once.

"Then you all need to start acting like it. This isn't a duel over my virginity, boys. Trust me when I say that went out the door when I was seventeen years old."

I was positive Tripp was about to lose his shit over that bit of information.

"What in the hell gives you the right to do what you were about to do? Did any of you think of my feelings? Or the feelings I have for Jonathon?"

My heart soared to hear her profess her feelings for me in public. Especially to her brothers.

"Waylynn, we just—"

She held up her hand to silence Trevor. "I love each and every one of you so much. But I'm almost thirty-three, y'all. I've been on my own for a while now, married, divorced, and interrupted having sex by an eighty-year-old woman. That was Jonathon, by the way."

All eyes were back on me. Swallowing hard, I glanced at the balcony. "Um, babe, maybe you should keep to your original point," I said, rubbing the tension out of my neck.

"The point is that you can't beat him up or threaten him or even try to keep us apart. I care about Jonathon and the way I feel when I'm with him…"

Waylynn's eyes met mine across the room. We both smiled, and my stomach did that crazy ass drop thing like I was on a damn thrill ride.

"The way I feel when I'm with him is unlike anything I've felt before." She focused back on her brothers. "I'm scared, I won't lie, and it's not because I think Jonathon would hurt me. I truly don't. Opening my heart up again is hard, and the well-known fact that I am older has me anxious."

"Age doesn't mean shit," Cord said, giving me a half smile. "Don't let that bother you, sis."

A sweet smile spread over Waylynn's beautiful face. "I won't, Cord. Okay, listen, I have Dad's blessings, and to be frank, his and Mom's are all I need. But I actually want the blessing of each of y'all too. If you love me and you want me to be happy, you need to let this protective brother mentality go. And if you so much as lay a hand on my boyfriend, I will make sure none of you can use your dicks for a month. Do you remember my sixteenth birthday party and what happened when you threatened Bobby Harding?"

"Shit, I was only eight and I remember it…and nothing even happened to me," Trevor said. The other four covered their junk. Steed groaned while his body trembled.

Tripp narrowed his eyes at his sister. "That was a low move with the Bengay."

Waylynn flashed an evil little grin. "Are we clear, gentlemen?"

Each of them mumbled something under their breath.

"I'm sorry, what was that?" Waylynn asked.

"We're clear," Tripp snapped. "We won't touch him, but let me make something clear."

Walking closer to me, Tripp stood inches from my face. "You so much as make a tear slip from her eyes, and I'll rip your goddamn heart out and serve it to my brothers."

I didn't think I'd ever felt my heart beat so fast. "I promise you, I won't."

How in the hell my voice sounded so calm was a fucking miracle.

Clapping her hands, Waylynn kissed each of her brothers. Wade walked over to stand next to me.

"They would've gone easy on you. I hardly felt their punches."

"Oh, my God. Each of them would have actually hit me?"

Wade chuckled. "Fuck yeah, they would have. Waylynn totally saved your ass."

"Well, shit, I figured they drew straws to see who would throw the punch."

Giving my shoulder a squeeze, Wade flashed a bright smile. "Welcome to the family, dude."

I glanced over to Tripp. He made a motion with two fingers showing he'd be watching me. Forcing a smile, I replied to Wade quietly, "It's a damn good thing she's worth the hazards of dating her."

He laughed loudly. "The Parker women are for certain worth it."

As I watched Waylynn make her way to each brother, I knew in my heart she was more than worth it. I let out a sigh when she walked over to me. "My savior," I whispered, kissing her gently on the lips.

Her eyes watered some before she glanced down and then back up at me. "You know what I'm in the mood for?"

I wiggled my eyebrows, making her giggle. "Yes, *that*. But seriously, I need a big bowl of ice cream."

I wrapped my arm around her waist and headed toward Cord's door. "Then ice cream you shall have."

Glancing over her shoulder, Waylynn called, "Evening, boys. Behave yourselves and make sure you check those boxers before you put them on."

I couldn't help but laugh as we made our way down the stairs.

Life with Waylynn Parker was going to be anything but boring.

CHAPTER 120

Waylynn

My cell phone dinged, and a smile came automatically when I saw his name.

Jon: *Thinking about you.*

Picking up my phone, I replied.

Me: *Same here.*

Jon: *Tell me what you're doing right this second.*

Me: *Staring at fabric samples for the benches and chairs for the lobby and reception area.*

Jon: *Fun times. They should be getting there soon to install the floors.*

As if on cue, the front door of the dance studio opened.

Me: *They just walked in.*

Jon: *I'll be there as soon as I finish up getting these windows in at this house.*

Me: *No rush. See you soon!*

Jon: *Kisses!*

Me: *Hugs!*

Smiling, I ran my fingers along my lips. How I loved Jonathon Turner's kisses. After nearly two weeks of officially being boyfriend and girlfriend, I'd gotten a lot of those kisses. And in places that made my body tremble just to think about it.

"Ms. Parker? I'm Randy Leman, owner of Premiere Flooring. Jonathon said you were expecting us."

I made my way out of the small office in the lobby. "Yes, it's a pleasure to meet you."

"I've gotten the instructions from Jonathon, but do you want to walk through each dance room as well, so we're all on the same page?"

"Sure," I replied with a smile.

Randy smiled bigger, and it wasn't lost on me how he quickly gave me a once over.

"There are four dance rooms," I started, making my way through each area. Each room was connected to the others by a single hallway with my office, the kitchen, and another office on the opposite side. Each room was glass almost all the way around, except on the ends.

"One is the ballet room, one for tappers, and two ballrooms."

"Right."

"From what Jonathon has told me, the subfloor frame will be built, then a high-density foam over the plywood and then the floors."

"That's correct, Ms. Parker."

Turning to look at him, I stated, "Waylynn is fine."

He nodded. "Waylynn, it is."

We stood there for a few brief seconds as he smiled at me. "The performance surface?"

"Yes, I've got the northern hard maple floor ordered for all four rooms," he replied. "It was birch, at first, and Jonathon said y'all changed it after looking at the hardwoods."

"That's right. We decided on maple. How long do you think it will take to install the floors?"

"I've got a full crew here, so I'll say two days at the most, for each room."

I glanced around as we stood in the ballet room. "Wow, okay that's pretty fast."

"It could be faster. We'll see how everything goes."

I took a good look at Randy. He was probably a few years older than me, good looking, and the fact that he couldn't keep his eyes off me should have been flattering. But it gave me the opposite feeling.

"So, Randy, how long have you been installing floors?" I asked as I walked into the next dance room.

He chuckled. "Since as long as I can remember. My father started the business and I guess he figured his sons would follow in his footsteps."

I lifted a brow. "And did they? I mean, clearly you have."

Laughing, he shook his head. "I worked as an engineer at NASA, my younger brother took over the family business."

"You're just filling in?" My curiosity was piqued.

"No, I'm ready to settle my life down, start a family, work less. NASA was amazing, but I worked seventy hours a week and got tired of the grind."

"Wow, I can see how that would get old. Are you married?"

His smile grew wider, if possible. "Not even close. Finding a woman my age who isn't already married or who isn't career driven has proven to be a problem."

I chuckled. "I totally understand. I'm at the same place you are. Ready to have a family and settle into a routine."

A man appeared at the door and cleared his throat to get our attention. "Randy? Are we ready to start bringing in the materials?"

"Yeah, let's get moving so we stay on schedule."

The next hour or so was filled with guys bringing in wood and tools. I stood in the very last room, one of the ballrooms, and watched as they built the frame.

Randy was right in there with his crew, working alongside them. I admired men like him and Jonathon who worked with their employees. My father had always been like that. Never standing back to order people around, always in the thick of things.

My cell phone started ringing. I pulled it out of my back pocket.

"Hey, Momma, what's up?"

"Hello, sweetie. I wanted to make sure you were coming for dinner tonight."

"Yep, I'll be there."

"And will you be bringing Jonathon?"

My stomach fluttered at the mention of his name. "Do you promise not to scare him away?"

She laughed. "Of course!"

"Then, he'll be there with me this evening for dinner. And, Momma, please don't start pryin' into his business."

"What are you talking about, Waylynn Parker? I've known Jonathon Turner since the boy was in diapers. I already know all of his business. Heck, I've seen all of his business."

I rolled my eyes. "Oh Lord, please don't remind him of that tonight. I forgot what town I was living in and how much of a busybody my mother can be."

"Mind your tongue, young lady. Bring me some of Lilly's homemade bread, will you? I've made a lasagna that will go perfectly with it."

"Yes, ma'am."

"Better make it two loaves. Your brothers like it as well."

Chuckling, I replied, "I'll buy three...just in case."

"Perfect. Seven sharp! Not a minute later."

"Wait! Is Aunt Vi gonna be there?"

"Yes, of course, it's family dinner night."

Perfect. I needed to talk to my aunt in private. I was positive she would know what it was like to date a younger man and would be able to give me advice. I'd already had one person make a comment to me at Lilly's when I ran by earlier for breakfast.

"Great. I'll see ya tonight," I said.

"Love you, sweetheart."

"Love you back."

Hitting End, I glanced up to see Randy watching me.

"You heading out?" he asked.

"I've got a few things to take care of. I'm sure Jonathon will be stopping by in a bit to check up on things."

He looked down at the tool in his hand and then back up at me. "This may be forward, but I was wondering if you'd like to have dinner sometime."

"Dinner?" I asked, completely taken aback.

"I know I shouldn't be asking, but it sounds like we have a lot in common."

Giving him a friendly grin, I replied, "Thank you for the invitation, but I'm actually seeing someone. Jonathon, to be exact."

His eyes widened. "Really?" Then he laughed. "Isn't he a little young for you?"

I swallowed hard. "Last time I checked he was out of college and a grown man who owned his own company. Do you have a problem with a woman dating a man a few years younger?"

"A few years? Don't get me wrong, Waylynn, you would pass for twenty-five, but I'm pretty sure you're around my age."

Folding my arms across my chest, I asked, "And how old are you, Mr. Leman?"

"Thirty-four."

"If you want to continue putting in the wood floors of this dance studio, I highly suggest you take a few steps back and think about your choice of words the next time you speak to me, or any other woman, for that matter. This isn't 1950, Mr. Leman, and a six-year difference isn't mind-blowing."

He held up his hands. "I'm sorry if I overstepped."

"Overstepped? You took a fucking leap off the building."

"What's going on?"

Jonathon's voice caused my rapid breath to settle a bit.

"Mr. Leman here thinks I'm too old to be dating you...darling."

"Now, wait a minute. I didn't say that."

Tapping my finger on my lips, I repeated his words. "Let me think, what was it you said again? Oh, that's right, 'isn't he a little young for you' were your *exact* words."

"Randy, what in the hell?"

"Listen, it was a mistake to ask you out."

"You asked her out?" Jonathon asked in a raised voice. "Are you out of your goddamn mind? Do you do this on all your jobs?"

"No! I thought she was giving me the signal."

My mouth fell open. "The signal? Being polite and talking to you is your *signal*? Holy shit, dude, maybe you should—"

Jonathon stepped in front of me. His hands cupped my face, lifting my eyes to his.

"Why don't we go to your office?"

I closed my eyes and let out a breath before agreeing to go. Jonathon guided me through the room and into the back hallway that led to my office.

The moment the door shut, I spun around. "I was not leading him on!"

"I know you weren't."

"He actually told me I was too old for you!"

"Fuck him."

I rolled my eyes. "Asshat."

"He is. Don't worry about what he says or thinks."

Leaning against the desk, I let out a sigh. "That's twice today someone has brought up our age difference."

"Waylynn, if it was reversed and I was older, no one would bat an eyelash. I don't care what people say or think...and neither should you."

My head dropped back as I let out groan. "I'm trying not to, Jonathon. I am! It's just so hard."

His lips touched my neck and the stress left my body. I swore the man had magical lips and fingers. As well as another very magical tool of his.

"Is that better?" he whispered, hot breath spilling onto my neck.

"Almost," I panted, every single sense seduced by his touch.

"What will make it better, babe?"

My body flooded with warmth, and my brain fogged. "Um...ah ...oh, God."

His fingers pulled and teased at my nipple through my shirt. "Lie down on the desk, baby. Let me fix this."

I laid back on the desk as he pulled my ass to the very end and lifted my skirt up.

Note to self: wear skirts always. Easy access.

Jonathon's fingers quickly moved my panties to the side. A low growl from the back of his throat caused my heart to quicken. One movement of his tongue had me letting out a soft moan as my orgasm built.

Lacing my fingers in his hair, I pulled him close. I couldn't get enough of this man and his ability to make me forget everything but us.

The knock on my office door made me jerk, but Jonathon kept on. Moving his fingers in and out of me while his mouth and tongue did a number on my sensitive clit.

"Wait!" The word was low and breathy.

Jonathon didn't hear me and continued, even as the person knocked again. The idea that someone was on the other side of the door fueled the fires. Covering my mouth, my body shook with an all-encompassing orgasm. Every single nerve ending in my body sparked.

Lifting his head, Jonathon smiled as I stared at him, my chest rising and falling with deep breaths.

A piece of paper slipped under the door. Jonathon and I looked at it and then lost it in a giggling fit.

Adjusting my panties, Jonathon pulled my skirt down, then stood. He reached for my hand and pulled me to an upright, seated position.

"Good job keeping it quiet there, Ms. Parker."

I scoffed. "It was harder than it looked, Mr. Turner. That tongue of yours should be a patented sex tool."

He winked. "Feel better?"

"Yes."

His placed his hand on the side of my face. Leaning in, I closed my eyes. "I promise it won't bother me the longer we're together. It's just hard right now. I hope you're not angry with me for lashing out at Randy like that."

"Waylynn, nothing on the face of this Earth would have me thinking an ill thing toward you. I'm here, by your side, through everything. Don't forget that."

"Everything, huh?"

He kissed the tip of my nose. "Everything."

"Okay, let's test that, shall we?"

Pulling back, he stared. "Give it to me."

"Dinner at my parents' tonight."

"That's easy. I've been there a hundred times or more."

"It's family dinner night."

The grin vanished.

"Family dinner night? So, Cord will be there…and Tripp?"

Laughing, I wrapped my legs around him and pulled him close. "You still by my side?"

"Yes...and inside you after dinner."

I sank my teeth into my lip at the delicious thought.

"I think today just became my favorite day."

Jonathon laughed. "You said that yesterday."

Tracing my finger along his stubble-covered jaw line, I gazed into his eyes. "I have a feeling I'm going to be saying that every day for a long time."

"I do too."

CHAPTER 13

Jonathon

I stopped at the gate and looked at the sign above the massive rock entrance.

Frio River Ranch.

Growing up in Oak Springs, it was no secret that the Parker family was the wealthiest in the county. Hell, all the surrounding counties. The thing I admired was that none of them acted like it. Cord and his brothers were always either working their father's ranch or one of the local ranches hauling hay, plowing fields, or some form of manual labor. Nothing was ever handed to those kids. They worked alongside me on my own father's ranch from time to time.

Glancing down, I stared at my father's college ring. I put it on the day he died and hadn't taken it off since. I couldn't help but smile. He'd have loved Waylynn. Just like I knew my mother and Rip were going to love her.

With my window down, I punched in the code I'd known since I was little and watched the gate swing open.

I'd driven this driveway a million times, but this time felt different. Everything felt different since Waylynn and I had started dating.

A horn honked behind me and I glanced in the mirror to see
Cord. I lifted my hand and hit the gas to go a little faster. I pulled up
and parked next to the row of trucks.

After a few deep breaths, I climbed out of my truck and started
toward Cord, who was waiting for me.

"What's wrong, Turner? You nervous?"

With a half-hearted laugh, I replied, "Slightly."

"Why? It's not like you've never been over to dinner on family
night."

After placing my hat on my head, I shook his hand. "Yeah, well,
I didn't have all your brothers wanting to hit my face then. And I
certainly wasn't dating one of your sisters."

Cord let out a roar of laughter. The bastard was enjoying this.
"You know we weren't really going to kick your ass."

"I know you're a damn liar."

"True, we were going to kick your ass. My sister saved you
from another black eye and possibly a broken nose. Trevor likes going for the nose."

Reaching up, I rubbed my nose. "I like my nose. It's one of my
favorite features."

Cord slapped my back. "Pussy. Come on, let's get on inside. I'm
sure my parents are chomping at the bit to get to you."

"Aw hell," I mumbled, following Cord up the front porch steps.
The door opened and there she was. My beautiful girl dressed in a
long black flowing skirt, black cowboy boots, and a white, off-the-
shoulder shirt. I loved it when she wore shirts that exposed her neck.
I also loved it when she wore skirts and she was wearing them more
and more often, for a good reason. My dick jumped in my pants
thinking back to earlier in her office, wondering if she was going
commando under all that black fabric.

"Hey there, beautiful!"

Waylynn's eyes lit up as they swept over my body. I knew the Parkers tended to keep things casual, but not *too* casual on family dinner night. I was dressed in new jeans, boots, and a shirt that showed off how damn hard I worked out in the gym.

"Hello there, handsome."

Before I got to the top step, she wrapped her arms around my neck, pulling me in for a kiss.

"Gross," Cord said. "Do you not even care how this freaks me out? Hello? Um…does anyone remember Cord is standing here?"

When our lips parted, Waylynn looked at her brother. "Oh, hey Cord. Good seeing ya."

Taking my hand in hers, Waylynn guided me to the front door.

"Asshole. Stealing my sister from me."

"I didn't steal your sister from you."

Cord shot me a dirty look. "Yeah, ya did."

"No, I didn't."

"Did too."

"Did not."

"Oh, for the love of Christ, are you two five or something?"

We both turned and faced Waylynn, unsure what she was talking about. "Do you hear yourselves? Cord, stop being a dick."

"Hey! I'm not being a dick. You just sucked face with my best friend in front of me, Waylynn. Can you at least let me get used to the idea that you're together without advertising it."

Waylynn folded her arms across her chest and stared at Cord. "So, I shouldn't tell you we had hot sex this morning in the shower?"

Scrubbing my hands down my face, I groaned. "You're trying to get my balls cut off, aren't you?"

"Seriously, Waylynn? I need to wash out my damn ears," Cord said.

"Then I really won't tell you what happened in my office this afternoon…" Waylynn teased.

"Waylynn!" I said, covering her mouth with my hand. "I would like a chance to live, so please stop talking."

Cord poked his head over my shoulder. "Yes! Please shut the fuck up."

I was pretty sure Waylynn was saying, "Fuck you too," but my hand was still covering her mouth.

"I'm going to get a drink. Get all the damn touching and feeling over with before you walk any farther into the house so I don't puke."

When he turned the corner, I dropped my hand from her mouth. "Please tell me you know what you're doing. I'm pretty sure if you keep this up I'm going to end up in a dark alley and my ass is going to be kicked by people who know people who know the Parker brothers."

She winked. "I just like getting them all riled up. It's fun!"

"For you! My face isn't going to be having any fun when it gets broken."

Her fingers traced the outline of the barely visible black eye. "Sure did take a long time to go away."

"Cord's strong."

Waylynn grinned. "I don't want this handsome face to get a scratch on it, so I'll be good."

My hands landed on her hips, pulling her close. "Waylynn Parker, you don't know how to be good when it comes to teasing those brothers of yours."

"That is the God's honest truth right there. Trust me, one day you'll appreciate it, and it will be funny."

"I hope that day comes soon."

"The last two weeks have been…amazing," she said. "Please tell me this isn't the new relationship high, and in four months were gonna be on the sofa with bowls of popcorn watching stupid reality TV shows."

I laughed. "I have a feeling I'm always going to feel this way about you. You've ignited my heart, Waylynn."

Our eyes met and it felt like we were totally alone. Completely lost within each other.

"Promise me you won't be reckless with my heart."

My chest tightened to hear her voice shake. "I swear to you on this day, I will hold your heart in mine and never let it go."

Her eyes filled with tears, speaking volumes more than words would ever be able to. "Kiss me."

Smiling, I did as she asked. The tenderness of that kiss would forever be ingrained in my heart. It was in that moment I knew...

I was in love with Waylynn Parker.

CHAPTER 14

jonathon

The large table in the dining room looked the same as usual. The color on the walls was the same. The people sitting around the table were the same, expect for a few additions.

"So, when can I call you Uncle Jonathon?"

I looked down at Chloe. She was a sweetheart and adorable to boot. Those Parker blue eyes stared back up at me. The way she batted those eyelashes told me she knew exactly what she was doing. Oh, yeah, she had her family's blood flowing through her.

Little stinker.

"Well, I guess you could call me that whenever you want. I feel like your Uncle Cord is my own brother, and I've always loved your family like it was my own."

Her eyes lit up. "Does that mean you're gonna marry Aunt Waylynn?" Chloe leaned in closer and shielded her mouth in an attempt to whisper. "Aunt Meli told me what to ask and say, so that's what I'm doing."

I nodded. "I see. What else are you supposed to ask me?"

Chloe glanced around the table to see if it was safe to keep going. I did the same. Everyone was lost in conversation except for Melanie. She was grinning from ear to ear watching Chloe and me.

"Okay well, you have to promise not to tell cuz I'm a good secret keeper."

"I see that," I said, crossing my heart in a promise.

"I'm supposed to find out if you like kids. Do you?"

Leaning in closer, I replied in a hushed voice. "Very much so. I have five younger siblings. The youngest is almost seven."

She pulled back. "Really? I'm six."

"I know. He's in your class. His name is Rip."

Her mouth opened in shock. "Rip is your brother?"

With a nod, I added, "He sure is."

Leaning back in her chair, she frowned as if she was in deep thought. When she started to tap her chin, I had to hold back a laugh. "What are you in such deep thought about, young Chloe?"

"If Rip is your brother, and he's already cute, *and* he grows up to look like you, he's gonna be even more cute. I need to add him to my list of possible husbands."

I nearly choked. I made a mental note to talk to young Rip in a few years about Chloe Parker. Clearly, she had a lot of her aunt's blood flowing in there. Poor Steed was in for the ride of his life with this one.

"I'm sure he'd be honored to know he made your list."

She smiled. "You're on Aunt Waylynn's list. I heard her telling Grammy that y'all had only just started dating, but that she felt something deep down in here..." She pressed her hand to her chest. "She said it was unlike anything she'd ever felt. I don't know what that means, but I think it's good and probably means you're on her list."

My gaze drifted over to Waylynn. She was deep in conversation with her Aunt Vi. "That's a very good thing, Chloe, and I hope you're right."

"So, back to kids. You like them, so we can check that off the list."

"We have a list going?" I asked.

Chloe giggled. "There is *always* a list, Uncle Jonathon."

This time I did laugh. If I were blessed with a child half this amazing, I'd consider myself the luckiest damn man on Earth.

"I like you, Chloe Parker. You make me laugh."

Her cheeks blushed. "I like you too, but only as a friend." Her head tilted with a concerned look.

"Oh, same here. I mean, I've given my heart to Waylynn, and only her."

Chloe gasped and covered her mouth. Then she quickly stood on her chair. "Uncle Jonathon just said he loves Aunt Waylynn!"

Nearly everyone at the table, myself included, cried out, "What?"

My eyes snapped over to Waylynn. "I said I had given my heart to you. That's all."

Melanie cleared her throat. "Chloe Lynn Parker, we do not burst out like that at the dinner table. Sit down, please. And we certainly do not spill the beans when someone says they love someone."

"Mother!" Waylynn gasped.

"I didn't say that," I quickly added, taking note of all the death stares I was getting from Waylynn's brothers.

Melanie raised a brow. "Of course you didn't, Jonathon. Anyone for dessert?"

The room started to spin, but quickly righted itself when Chloe pulled on my arm. "Sorry, Uncle Jonathon, for outing you. I got a little excited."

"Chloe, I didn't say I loved Waylynn."

Reaching for her glass of water, she half-shrugged. "Oh, you did. You just don't know it. Momma says boys say things all the time that they don't know they say 'cause they say 'em in a different way, but what they say is really what they mean, but they just don't know they mean it yet."

I stared at her. "I have no clue what you said."

Chloe took a drink and set her glass down. "That's another thing Momma says. Boys don't understand girls. It's okay, Uncle Jonathon... It took Daddy awhile to figure it out too. You'll get there."

When she patted me on the shoulder, I sat back in my seat.

I had just been schooled by a first grader.

Damn, I want to have kids.

I glanced across the table and caught Waylynn's gaze. I smiled, and she returned it with a smile of her own. We must have sat there a good two minutes, staring at each other.

The doorbell rang, and Chloe jumped up. "I'll get it!"

"Sit back down, young lady," Steed ordered.

Trevor stood. "I'll grab it."

"Chloe, are you talking Jonathon's ear off?" Waylynn asked, folding her hands and resting her chin on them.

"No, ma'am. I'm just asking him some questions for Aunt Meli's list."

"Oh crap," Amelia said as Waylynn turned to look at her.

"List? What list, Meli?"

"Huh? A list?"

"Yeah, the list you're having our niece ask Jonathon about." Waylynn stated.

Amelia's eyes bounced back and forth from me, to Waylynn, to Chloe.

"I know of no such list. Chloe? Do you know of a list?"

Chloe looked confused. "The list we made earlier. Remember? I'm supposed to keep it a secret!"

"This is when Amelia will swear, then Chloe will jump up and run around the room cursing as well." Wade chuckled as he raised his drink to me.

"No, she will not!" Paxton said, pointing to Chloe who covered her mouth and giggled.

"I'm so lost," I admitted.

Waylynn shook her head. "Don't worry about it, Jonathon. The less you know, the better."

"Ah, Waylynn, can I speak with you for a second." Trevor asked.

Glancing at Trevor, Waylynn asked, "Why?"

"I need to talk to you in private."

I could tell Trevor was hiding something.

"Seriously, Trev, what is it and why can't you just tell me now?"

He rubbed the back of his neck. "You need to follow me to the library."

"The library?"

"Trevor, who was at the door?" John asked. By now, everyone's attention was on Trevor.

He blew out a deep breath and looked at the floor. "Jack's here. He's waiting for Waylynn in the library."

The air from my lungs whooshed out in one quick breath. What did Jack want with Waylynn? Maybe to tell her he'd changed his mind about starting a family.

Fuck. Fuck. Fuck.

Slowly standing, Waylynn stared at me, a look of complete darkness in her eyes. I had no idea how to read her in that moment. Was she angry? Scared of her feelings for him? The thought that she might still have feelings for him made me sick to my stomach.

"If you all will excuse me."

She forced a smile, but it didn't come anywhere near her eyes. They were void of any emotion at all.

Sitting back in my chair, I blew out a frustrated breath. Cord hit my side, and I looked at him.

"Dude, don't even worry. I know Waylynn has no feelings whatsoever for that asshole."

I nodded.

John tossed his napkin on the table. "That sonofabitch had the nerve to show up at my house? I'll rip him apart piece by piece."

Melanie cleared her throat. "Sit back down, John Parker. This is Waylynn's issue and each of you will let her handle it. Trevor, come sit down and let your sister take care of Jack."

Trevor looked like he wanted to disobey his mother, but he didn't. He walked over and took a seat. "This is bullshit. He shows up one day and asks to talk to her. I almost beat his face in the second I saw him."

"Looks like the heat's off you for a bit," Wade said to me.

I tried to laugh, but I could only muster a fake-sounding version of humor.

Melanie stood and motioned for us all to do the same. "Let's clear the table, y'all, and then cut into some of that pie Corina brought."

"That sounds like an amazing idea. Lord knows I'm craving apple pie!" Corina said, trying to make light of the heaviness that had settled in the room.

Walking over, Tripp hit me on the back. "Don't worry, Jonathon. Waylynn would never let him back in. Ever."

With a nod, I attempted to keep my voice even and calm. "I know she wouldn't. It was just a surprise, as I'm sure it was to her, as well."

I wasn't so sure I believed that. Waylynn hadn't seemed all that surprised that her ex-husband was waiting for her in another room. In fact, Amelia and Melanie didn't seem surprised either.

Amelia walked by, and I reached for her arm. "Amelia, can I ask you something?"

She looked around everywhere but at me.

"Did Waylynn know Jack was coming over tonight?"

Her eyes snapped to meet mine. "What? No, of course not."

"Then why did she not seem surprised? And neither did you, and your mother."

"The only thing I can say is that none of us knew he would be showing up, but Waylynn mentioned he has been calling her cell phone. She's been denying the calls, so I guess that's why we don't seem surprised he's here."

I sighed, my hand pushing through my hair. "She didn't tell me he'd been calling her."

"I'm sure it was only because she didn't care."

Glancing back over my shoulder, I looked at that hallway that led to the library.

"I know you want to go bursting in there, but you have to let her handle this."

My stomach rolled and I felt sick. I needed air, a distraction, an escape. "I'm going to head outside for some fresh air."

Amelia nodded. "Okay, I'll let Waylynn know where you are."

As I headed toward the living room, a sinking feeling hit me. Everything had been going too well. Too well. Waylynn had moved past her fears and was giving us a shot.

And now? Now one of her biggest fears was in the room with her, and everything felt wrong and out of place...and I was helpless to stop it.

CHAPTER 15

Waylynn

I stared at the fireplace for the longest time before I finally spoke.

"Why are you here, Jack?"

"You wouldn't take my calls. I was desperate to talk to you, sweetheart."

He touched my arm, and I jerked away. "Don't touch me."

"I'm sorry. I'm sorry, pumpkin."

Spinning around, I looked at him with nothing but pure anger. "Do not call me that. I'm not your sweetheart, your pumpkin, your baby. I'm no longer your wife. I'm nothing to you but the woman who stood by your side for years like a damn fool."

"Don't say that. Waylynn, we had some amazing times together."

I scoffed. "Whatever good times we shared vanished when I saw you with your whore of the month."

He flinched.

"I'm going to ask you again. Why are you here?"

"I want you back."

His words played in slow motion. When they finally sank in, I laughed. "You've got to be kidding me. You paid me a hefty little price tag to disappear from your world—or did you forget? Never mind the fact that your lover is carrying your baby."

"I don't love her. She's not you, Waylynn."

"No, she's about ten years younger than me, Jack. What's wrong? Can't keep up with her?"

"You're the one I want. Now that I've lost you, my eyes are open. I was a fool, wrong for thinking I could ever live without you. Please, come back to me."

"I have a life here. This is my hometown, and I'm starting a new business."

"The dance studio. I know, I know. I'll give you ten dance studios in New York if you'll come back."

Narrowing my eyes, I studied him. "Why are you so desperate for me to come back? Does your new toy not look shiny enough on your arm? Or are your friends turning their back on you, Jack, for what you did to me? Is it not good for your image to have a child out of wedlock?"

He looked away, and I continued. "This is all about *your* image. This has *nothing* to do with your feelings for me."

"That's not true. I miss you and the life we had. Things were...easy with you. We knew each other inside and out."

"Speak for yourself."

With a sigh, he sat on the sofa. "Waylynn, I'll get down on my hands and knees and beg, if that's what it will take. You want a baby? We'll have as many as you want. Hell, I'll fuck you right now without a condom and get you pregnant, if that's what you want!"

Tears threatened to spill over my anger. "How dare you think you can come in here and say these things to me! In my parents' house! You think I'll jump back into your arms and fly off back to New York? Why couldn't you give me a child when I asked for one,

Jack? When I begged you for one? You got your whore pregnant. Why her and not me?"

"It was a mistake. I got drunk one night and apparently we fucked without protection. I mean, I remember it…I just lost control."

"Nice. Way to sit there and explain how you got your lover pregnant while at the same time trying to win me back. You are such an asshole. I don't know what I ever saw in you. Jonathon is ten times the man you ever were."

Jack stood. "Who the fuck is Jonathon?"

My chin lifted as I crossed my arms over my chest. "My boyfriend."

He laughed. "Boyfriend? You're dating someone?"

"Yes, I am."

"Wait, you mean the construction guy who's working on your studio."

My hands dropped to my sides. "How did you know that?"

He gave me an evil grin. "I hired a P.I. to do a little bit of digging around since our divorce. He's been keeping tabs for me."

I covered my mouth. It felt like my dinner was about to come back up.

"Don't be so dramatic, Waylynn. It was harmless."

"Harmless? You're spying on me, you sonofabitch!"

"If my memory is right, isn't that boy younger than you?"

I didn't answer, and he started to laugh again. "What, did you seduce the poor boy and get him to fuck you so you could get pregnant?"

Anger raced through me as I slapped Jack as hard as I could. "Get out of my house. Now."

Jack rubbed his face as he glared at me. He crossed the room and sat back down, crossing his leg over his knee.

"Last I checked, this was Mom and Pop's house." He looked around then back to me. "You never were good enough, Waylynn."

I sucked in a breath of air. "W-what?"

"At dancing. I saved you the embarrassment of making a fool out of yourself. The only reason you danced at the Radio City Music Hall was because of how beautiful you are. Rumor has it, though, you and the director had a thing. Maybe that's how you got up on that stage."

"Shut up, you asshole."

Jack chuckled. "He was older than me, wasn't he? You went from older guys to younger, huh? All in the hopes of getting knocked up."

Walking over to him, I kicked his leg, causing the other to fall to the floor.

"I have never hated you more than I hate you right now. I would rather die than be back in your bed or carry your last name. And as far as your little private investigator goes, when I find out who he is, I'll have him arrested for harassment. I'll slap a restraining order on you that I guarantee will be plastered all over the *New York Times, The Post, The Journal*. You name it, Jacky boy, and it will be there. I'll spend the rest of my life being the thorn in your side that you can't pay off with money or sex. I left quietly once. Don't test me a second time."

"You always did like to play hardball."

"I've grown up a lot, Jack. I don't play games anymore. Now get the fuck out of this house and off this property. I swear to God if you ever reach out to me again you will be sorry."

He stood, straightened his tie and looked me up and down.

"You look like a goddamn hillbilly. Let the little peckerhead have you. You sucked in bed anyway."

Before I knew what was happening, I saw Jack spin around and Trevor was throwing punches.

"Trevor!" I screamed out.

Jack stumbled back, gripping his jaw and groaning.

"He can't talk to you that way and get away with it, Waylynn."

Steed grabbed Jack by the back of the shirt and pushed him toward the door. "Time to go, asshole."

"I'll sue your ass for this, Trevor Parker."

Steed gave Jack a good push. "I don't think so. If you don't want to be looking around every dark corner for the rest of your life, I suggest you leave our property and never fucking look back."

Jack glared at Steed and then shot me a dirty look. "You're not fucking worth it, and one of these days you'll realize the mistake you made by turning me away."

"Get out!" I shouted.

Jack walked out of the library and hopefully out of my life for good.

Trevor pulled me into his arms. "Are you okay? Did he touch you at all?"

Burying my face in his chest, I fought to hold back tears and lost. "N-no. He d-didn't touch me."

"Fucking dick. We shouldn't have let you come in here alone with him. Don't listen to a word that asshole said, Waylynn."

Drawing back, I wiped my tears away. "I know, Steed. I'm more upset that I let him get to me with harsh words and memories that are best left buried."

Steed hugged me. Kissing me on the forehead, he said, "Let me get Jonathon. He stepped outside."

Jonathon. I couldn't see him right now. Not when I was this upset.

"I need to go back to my place…without Jonathon."

Steed stopped short. "What?"

"I need to be alone and sort all of this out in my head."

"All of what out? Waylynn, whatever Jack said to you, don't listen."

Pinching the bridge of my nose, I exhaled. "Let me go back to my place alone, will you?" My hand dropped and I gave my brothers a silent plea. "I need to be alone."

I walked past them and out of the library.

"Waylynn? Waylynn?"

My sister's voice grew louder.

"Not now, Amelia."

"Waylynn, where are you going?"

"I said, not now!" I screamed, running down the hall to the front door. I could still see Jack's taillights as he drove away. Getting into my car, I left in a rush to my house.

My house. Fucking hell. It was my parents' guest house, for fuck's sake. Even though I paid rent, it still felt like I was living off my parents. Jack's words replayed in my head.

You were never good enough. I saved you the embarrassment of making a fool out of yourself.

Tears streamed down my face as I drove. The full moon lit up the pastures on either side of me. Any normal night, and I'd drive with the lights out to let the moon lead the way. But tonight, tonight I wanted to get out of my own head and away from everyone and everything.

Tonight, I wanted to forget Jack ever existed.

CHAPTER 16

Jonathon

"Another beer?"

Glancing over my shoulder at Cord, I shook my head. "Nah, I've already had a couple and I need to head home." I sat in Waylynn's parent's home surrounded by her family.

"You're not going to Waylynn's place?" Mitchell asked as he gave Corina a look I couldn't decipher.

I shrugged. "No. She told Steed and Trevor she wanted to be alone."

"Then that means you need to go to her," Corina said.

I closed my eyes. "Corina, that makes no sense."

Mitchell let out a chuckle, "Dude, don't question it. Just follow the advice."

"But it doesn't make sense. She talked to her ex, then she decided she needed to be alone to think things through. What kind of things?"

"That's what you need to go ask her!" Paxton said.

"Paxton's right, Jonathon. I think the worst thing you could do is leave without at least stopping by and checking on her. Show her you care enough to at least do that, even if you don't understand why she pushed everyone away."

Amelia sighed lightly. "She's hurting, that's why she pushed everyone away. After what Trevor overheard, Jack got into her head. Jonathon, you need to go get him back out."

My hands went into my pockets, and I looked at the ground. "I don't know how, Amelia."

She stood and walked over to me. Placing her hand on my heart, she smiled. "Yes, you do. Just follow it. You told Chloe today you'd given your heart to Waylynn...now listen to it."

I nodded, knowing they were right. The least I could do was go check on her.

"Alright. I'll drive over there before I leave."

Everyone smiled, and it wasn't lost on me that three of Waylynn's brothers were giving me advice to go to her house. Alone.

"Let me thank your folks."

"They took Vi home. She rode over with us but was feeling too tired and ready to head on home."

"Yeah, she's feeling tired from the party she threw last night," Wade said with a chuckle.

"I've heard Aunt Vi's crowd gets a little crazy."

Amelia and Wade chuckled. "You could say that. We have to keep reminding her that sound travels great distances in the country."

I forced a laugh. All I wanted was go see Waylynn. Make sure she was okay. "Tell them I said thank you for dinner, will you?"

Cord stood and shook my hand, followed by Steed, Mitchell, and Wade.

"Night, y'all."

By the time I had pulled up to Waylynn's, my hands were sweating and my heart rate had doubled. I pulled around the side of the house and parked by her car. I wasn't sure how long I sat there before I finally got out. My fear was so new, and I didn't like it.

I knocked on the door and waited for her to either yell, "Go away," or for her to let me in.

The door opened and the moment she saw me, she smiled.

"Hey, I wanted to make sure you were okay. Mind if I come in?"

Opening the door wider, she stepped to the side, and I walked in. The second the door shut, she threw herself at me, crashing her lips to mine. It was a hungry, desperate kiss. Her hands were pulling my shirt out of my jeans before they worked on getting them unbuttoned.

"Wait, Waylynn," I gasped, holding her at arm's length. "What's going on?"

"I need you, Jonathon. I need to be in your arms, to feel you holding me."

The emptiness in her eyes was still there. She was using sex to cope with what had happened, and there was no way I was going to do that. Get over someone by getting under someone else? Yeah, that wasn't my style.

"I want you too, Waylynn, but I think maybe we should talk first."

Her brows pinched. "Talk? You'd rather talk over fucking?"

"I'd rather talk and then make love to you."

Her eyes softened. "And if I say I don't want to talk?"

She continued trying to unbutton my jeans, pushing them down, letting my dick spring out.

"Commando this evening, huh? I like it."

Her hand moved up and down my shaft as she tried to get me to come all the way up. As she lowered herself, I tried to explain why this was a bad idea.

"Waylynn, baby, I really think we need… Oh, motherfucker."

Her mouth took my entire cock and she started sucking while she worked me with both her mouth and hands. I needed to make her stop; we had to talk first.

"Fuuck," I groaned as she played with my balls and sucked harder.

"Wait. Waylynn…fuck…wait!"

She let my dick go and sat back. "What in the fuck is wrong with you? I'm giving you a damn blowjob and all you want to do is talk?"

"If you'd just let me…"

The doorbell rang, followed by a knock. "Waylynn, darling, it's your mother. I'm coming in."

I was standing in Waylynn's living room with my dick hanging out and Waylynn on her knees in front of me.

"Get in my room! Quick! Last door on the right!"

Pulling my jeans up, I made my way down the hall and into the room. It didn't take long to hear Melanie's voice.

"Sweetheart, I wanted to make sure you were okay."

I leaned against the wall next to her open bedroom door.

"I'm fine, Momma. Honestly, I just need to be alone for a bit."

"The boys told me what that asshole said to you. Please, don't let what he said get into that head of yours. I know you, Waylynn. You'll think and think and think until you drive yourself crazy."

I heard Waylynn sigh in frustration. "Mom, I'm fine. Can we talk more in the morning? I'm really exhausted."

"Darling, I'll let you get some rest but there is one more thing I want to talk to you about. Your father told me a little bit ago that you went to a clinic to look into a sperm donation."

My heart slammed against my chest and my legs about gave out.

"Oh, Christ Almighty. Not now, Momma." Waylynn's voice had lowered.

"Waylynn, I just wanted to know if you were still leaving that option on the table now that Jonathon was in the picture."

"It was just a visit to see how it all worked. That was all. Honestly, my head is killing me, and I really want to get to sleep."

"Okay, well, we can talk about it tomorrow."

Waylynn let out a moan of defeat. "Mom, Jonathon is here. He's in my room. I'm sure you saw his truck outside?"

A few seconds of silence filled the house. "Oh, Waylynn, I wouldn't have brought that up had I known he was here. He must be parked on the other side of the house!"

"He's in my room. It's okay."

"Well, enjoy the rest of your evening."

"Be careful driving home. Thank you for dinner, and I'm sorry Jack spoiled things."

"Nonsense. Tell Jonathon goodnight for us."

"Will do."

When I heard the door shut, I walked into the living room. Waylynn was pouring herself a glass of whiskey.

"How much have you had to drink, Waylynn?"

She held it up and laughed. "Clearly not enough."

"A fertility clinic? When were you going to tell me that little plan of yours?"

"It's not the plan for right now. I mean, it never was. It was more like an option—a Plan B—just in case. I wanted to see how it would work."

"When did you go?"

"Before we got together, so cool your tits. My God, why is everyone getting so up in arms about it?"

I pushed my hand through my hair. "Waylynn, maybe you should put the drink down. Let's talk."

She turned and leaned against the bar. "Jack told me if I came back to him we could have a baby right away."

My heart dropped. "What did you say?"

"What did I say?" She looked at me like I had gone insane.

"Yes, Waylynn, what did you say?"

She downed the whiskey and slammed the glass on the counter. "Well, if you have to fucking ask, maybe you and I shouldn't be dating."

"You brought it up! What was I supposed to do? Say, oh, how nice that your ex showed up out of the blue and asked you to come back. And by the way, he's willing to give you the baby you so desperately want with his magic impregnating dick."

Waylynn looked away.

"So, yeah, forgive me for asking you what you said."

Pushing off the bar, she walked toward me. "I told him no, of course! I told him about us, and he went off and rubbed the age difference in my face. That made three times today. Don't they say, 'three time's the charm'?"

With a fake laugh, she dropped to the sofa. "All I wanted was for you to fuck me so I could forget about this evening."

The sting that left in my chest hurt more than I thought it would. I knew that's what she had been doing, but to hear her say it made it all the more worse.

"Maybe instead of forgetting about it, we should talk."

"I don't want to talk to you about it. Don't you get that, Jonathon?"

"No, I don't. Why don't you explain it to me?"

"Why are you pushing me? Stop pushing me! Fuck, you are smothering me."

Her words felt like a slap in the face. She was drawing a line in the sand, and I didn't know if her words were fueled by hurt feelings or the whiskey she was trying to drown her emotions in.

"Am I now? What do you want me to do, Waylynn?"

Her eyes met mine. "Leave. I want you to leave and go find a nice girl your own age who isn't fucked up in the head. Y'all can do the whole dating thing, get engaged, married, and pop out a few kids."

"You want me to leave? Are you sure about that?"

She stood up. "Yes."

"Look me in the eyes and tell me you want me to leave you alone."

Taking a few steps closer, her hands went to my chest. At first, I thought she was going to reach up and kiss me, but she didn't. "I want you to…leave. I don't want to date you anymore."

"You're drunk."

Shrugging, she took a few steps back. "Don't they say drunks don't lie?"

"Please don't do this, Waylynn."

"Get out!" she screamed. "Just get the fuck out and don't come back!"

Reaching for my keys, I headed toward the door. I wasn't about to sit here and argue with someone who was two sheets to the wind.

"When you sober up, give me a call." I left, the silence so deafening it was like a blow to my stomach.

CHAPTER 17

Waylynn

"Want another cup of coffee?"

Rubbing my temples, I spoke softly. "Amelia, stop talking so loud."

"I'm not talking loud. You've got a hangover, and it serves you right."

I dropped my hands and stared at her. "What?"

"Jonathon told Cord what you said and did to him last night."

A heaviness settled over my body. I had been so mean to Jonathon, and I knew it.

"It was a bad night."

Amelia folded her arms and leaned against my sink. "It was a 'bad night'? Seriously, Waylynn? That's the best you can come up with for telling him to leave you alone and go find a girl his own age?"

I cringed. That part I didn't remember. "I said that?"

"Yes, and to be honest with you, I wouldn't blame him if he did."

Staring into my coffee, I sighed. "Maybe I'm just not cut out for relationships."

A loud bang outside made me jump and place my hands on my head. "What in the hell was that?"

"I don't know, and I don't care. What is the matter with you? I've never seen you as happy as you have been the last week. Why are you pushing him away?"

"Not now, Amelia."

"Yes, now. Why won't you give yourself a chance to be happy?"

I sat there with a deadpan expression.

Throwing up her hands, Amelia paced across the kitchen. "I don't get it. You've got an amazing man who wants to be with you. Who wants the same things you want, but you're so blinded you can't see that."

"I'm not blind, and I do see it."

"Then what in the hell is the problem?"

This time I slammed my fists down. "I'm scared, Amelia! Damn it, I'm scared."

Burying my face in my hands, I exhaled and tried to keep my emotions in check.

I felt my sister's hand on my arm. "What are you scared of?"

My arms fell to my lap as I stared at Amelia. "When I met Jack, I was over the moon for him. I gave up everything to be with him, and at first, it was amazing. I felt like I was walking on clouds I was so in love with him. One day I woke up and everything changed. He didn't greet me each morning with a kiss. He worked longer hours and spent less time with me. When I would mention the change, he would whisk me off to some exotic location and we'd have a romantic weekend, only to have the whole thing repeat itself year after year. Last night when he was here, asking me to come back, all I could think about was—why did I stay all those years? How long would I have stayed if I hadn't caught him cheating?"

"Jonathon is *nothing* like Jack."

"But what if one morning he wakes up and wants someone better? Someone younger and prettier? I know in my heart that Jonathon is not Jack, but it's hard, Amelia. I was ready to do this, but then Jack showed up and turned my world upside down. He put those doubts I have about myself right back into my head and I...I..."

Tears fell from my eyes as I wrestled to speak clearly. "I can't get them out. All I hear is his voice, and then there are the people who keep remarking about the age difference. I thought I was strong enough to ignore it. Maybe I'm not as strong as I thought I was."

"That is bullshit. You're one of the strongest, most confident women I've ever known."

"You have to say that, you're my sister."

Amelia grinned. "Waylynn, you've got to get out of your own damn head. What do you want in life?"

"To be happy."

"What makes you happy?"

I didn't have to think about my answer. "Dancing."

"When was the last time you danced?"

I looked past her and out the window. "Over a year ago."

"Then let's go dancing!"

With a chuckle, I shook my head. "We can't. The floors aren't finished in the dance studio."

Amelia reached for my hand. "I'm pretty sure we can find somewhere. Leave it to me."

I stared out the window, watching everything pass by. Amelia and Corina talked away in the front seat while I tuned them out.

"It's a shame Paxton couldn't come," Corina said, looking back at me. I nodded.

"Did you need anything before we get there?" Amelia asked.

"No, I have everything in my bag."

I placed my hand over my lower stomach. I wasn't sure if I was nervous or if I was feeling cramps. The feeling had been coming more and more over the last few weeks. It had to be nerves. Everything with the dance studio and Jonathon…I was worrying myself sick.

"I can't wait to see you dance, Waylynn!" Corina said as she turned and flashed a perky little smile. I looked back out the window.

I had no idea where Amelia was taking me. Something about a friend of a friend who owned a dance studio in San Antonio.

My phone buzzed in my hand again, an incoming call.

Jonathon.

I needed to apologize, but I wanted to do it when my head was clear. Right now it was anything but clear. I sent the call to voicemail.

"We're here!"

Amelia pulled up to a mansion of a house.

"This is it?" I asked.

"Yep. Wait until you see his dance studio."

"His?" I asked, grabbing my bag and making my way up the steps to the giant wood door. The house looked like it belonged in a historical movie. We didn't even make it all the way before the door opened and a young man stepped outside.

"Amelia!"

"Frank! Oh, my gosh, it's so good to see you. This is my sister-in-law, Corina."

"Nice to meet you, and what a lovely name."

Corina smiled. "The pleasure is mine, and thank you."

He turned his attention on me. "This must be your sister, Waylynn. My God woman, you are a beauty times ten."

I felt a blush rise to my cheeks. "Thank you for the compli-
ment."

He looked me up and down, then sighed. "Dance floor. Stat.
Follow me."

Before I knew it, I was sitting on a pink, fabric-lined bench in
the middle of a dressing room. Opening my bag, I looked down at
my pointe shoes. Pulling them out, I ran my finger along the darn
work and shook my head. I had a love-hate relationship with my
shoes. I knew the pain I was about to experience, especially since I
hadn't danced in so long.

Slipping on my toe pads, I put on the shoes. I laced each one up,
tied them, and tucked the knot under the ribbon.

Taking a deep breath, I stood. The knock on the door caused me
to jump.

"Waylynn, how are you doing?"

"Come in, Frank."

He grinned as he looked at my shoes. "How long has it been
since you've had those on?"

"Long enough to know I'm going to be feeling every step and
flex of my feet."

Laughing, he reached a hand out. "Come on. Let's go get our
dance on."

As we walked down the hall, my heart started to race with that
familiar excitement.

The moment he opened the door, I sighed. It felt like home.

"What's your training in?" Frank asked.

"Classical and contemporary, mostly."

"Shall we?"

The music started, and it was like I had never stopped dancing at
all. Everything came back to me. Each elevation…jetés, entrechat,

cabriole. The way my body glided across the floor and flew through the air. This was what made me happy. This is what filled the void.

And Jonathon…

Frank and I danced for a bit before I finally had to stop. Not only was I in pain, but I was exhausted. At the same time, I felt like a completely new woman.

Glancing up, I saw Amelia and Corina on the other side of the glass window, wearing huge smiles.

"I guess my little sister knows more about me than I do."

Frank looked back at Amelia. "Amelia Parker is one amazing young woman. I have to admit, I was a bit sad to hear she was married. I know her through a mutual friend of ours, Lanny Miller. Lanny and I were in the same dance company."

"I used to babysit Lanny!"

We both laughed.

"Waylynn, you are an incredibly talented dancer. Amelia tells me you were with the New York City ballet."

"I was."

"And a Rockette?"

"I danced with the Rockettes for a bit, as well. That was a lot of fun."

"What made you stop?"

I thought about my answer. "I thought I wanted a different dream with a man I had met. I ended up marrying him, and it turns out he wasn't a dream at all."

Frank grinned. "So you're still in search of your dream man?"

A strange warmth filled my body. Glancing at my feet, everything felt perfectly clear. "No. I believe I've found my real dream, at least the beginning of it."

His brows lifted. "I'm opening a dance studio in Oak Springs, and I've met someone who has sparked something new inside of me. I just needed to take the blinders off. Thank you for letting me use your studio and dancing with me. It felt amazing."

"I'm glad I could be of help."

I smiled. "You wouldn't be interested in a teaching job, would you?"

"In small town America? Hell, no!" We both burst out laughing at his honesty.

"Seriously though, thank you so much. I hadn't realized how long it had been since I strapped on my shoes and let go. I needed it."

"I may not be interested in teaching, but I'd sure love to be a guest dancer—with you—if you're open for that."

"Yes! I'd love that."

Standing, I shook his hand once more. "I should get going. I bet they're starving."

"It was a pleasure, Waylynn. You're welcome any time."

"Thanks, Frank."

I changed out of my shoes and pulled my phone out of my bag. I didn't want to talk to Jonathon over the phone. I needed to talk to him in person.

Me: *I'm in San Antonio with Meli and Corina. Can I call you later?*

He didn't respond right away. As a matter of fact, I didn't hear from him at all. Not even by the time we had gotten back to Oak Springs and Amelia dropped me at home.

Before I got out of her car, she reached for my arm. "Everyone's planning on heading to Cord's Place tonight. You want to go?"

"Everyone?"

"Yeah, Mom and Dad are watching Chloe and Gage. Please come."

"Let me see what Jonathon is doing and I'll let you know."

"I talked to Cord earlier. He said that Jonathon and Dustin were planning on being at the bar later tonight."

My chest squeezed. "Okay. Well, then, I guess I'll see him there."

She nodded. "Have you called him?"

Peering at my phone, I replied, "I sent him a text saying I wanted to talk. He hasn't answered." I shrugged. "I think I'll head to the dance studio and check on the floors."

Amelia gave me a sympathetic smile. It was my own damn fault. I had pushed Jonathon away…again.

"Talk to ya later. Thanks again, Meli! I had a great afternoon."

"Bye. Love you, sis!"

As I walked into my house, I tried to push away the dread that was taking root in my chest.

Sitting on the sofa, I closed my eyes. My voice barely above a whisper, I spoke his name, willing him to call me.

"Jonathon."

The only thing that followed was silence.

CHAPTER 18

Waylynn

Cord's Place was packed. Not surprising for a Friday night. The music was playing and there wasn't an open spot on the dance floor.

"Wow! Why is it so packed in here tonight?" I yelled, following Paxton and Amelia. Corina was pulling up the rear.

"What did you say?" Corina hollered.

Stopping, I faced her. "Why is it so packed tonight?"

She shrugged. "I don't know. Mitchell texted and said they'll be here in a few minutes. I guess they were plowing one of the pastures."

Paxton pulled on my shirt. "Cord saved us a table close to the bar!"

I gave her a thumbs up. Perks of knowing the owner.

When we finally got to our table, Cord appeared. "Evening, ladies. What are we drinking?"

"Water for me!" Corina shouted.

"Coke for me," I added.

"What's wrong, big sis?" Amelia asked. "You still hungover from last night?"

Rolling my eyes, I replied, "Something like that, smartass."

Cord pointed to Paxton and Amelia who ordered beers.

Amelia was bouncing in her seat, itching to get out on the dance floor. "Where are the guys? I'm dying to go dance."

"Want to dance? I'll dance with you," Paxton said.

My sister jumped up, grabbed Paxton, and pushed her way through the crowd.

Corina and I both laughed.

"The girl likes her country dancing."

I agreed. "Yeah, she does."

Cord came back with our drinks and a beer for himself. Some girl was giving him the eye, and I was positive he would be ditching us soon and disappearing with her.

"I'd say business is doing good." I said with a wink toward my brother.

He raised his glass of beer to my Coke. I caught the girl shooting me a dirty look, so I focused in on her and raised my Coke to her, as well.

"Who's that?" Cord asked.

"Some whore giving me the evil eye because she thinks I'm stealing her hot piece of ass."

"Hey! Don't talk about me like that. I have feelings, you know."

Corina laughed. "Please. If you had seen her looking at you before you walked up to us, you'd have bypassed us and went straight to her."

Cord pretended like he had been hit in the chest. "How could you, sweet sister-in-law! Are you saying I'm...cheap?"

Corina half shrugged. "If the boot fits."

"Ha!" Cord dropped his head back and laughed, but then his face turned serious. "But you know what? Tripp told me someone who's not from around here applied for a permit to sell alcohol. Tripp's been hinting to me it's an Irish Pub."

I sat up. "No way! I love Irish pubs."

Cord narrowed his eyes at me. "Seriously?"

"What? I do."

"You didn't think you would be the only bar on the square, did you, Cord? With the way the town is growing, I'm not surprised."

"Well, I don't like it one damn bit. We have a fine establishment here at Cord's Place."

"A little competition can't hurt anyone," I added.

He rolled his eyes and took a drink of beer.

"What else do you know about it?" I asked.

"I know I don't like the owner."

Laughing, I glanced to Corina. "How can you say that? You don't even know the guy!"

"They're opening up on the corner where the old pharmacy was."

"Good location."

Cord pointed to me. "Stop it, Waylynn."

"I'm just saying, stop freaking out until you know more about the place."

"Freaking out? I'm not freaking out!"

Corina attempted to hide her laughter. I—on the other hand—laughed right in my brother's face.

"Oh sweet brother, you are freaking out. Big time!"

I looked up to see Tripp, Mitchell, and Steed all walking up. I couldn't help a smile.

"I'm not sure I'll ever get used to the way women look at them," Corina said.

"You have nothing to worry about, Corina. Look at how my brother can't seem to take his gaze off of you. The man only has eyes for you."

"And I him."

Mitchell leaned down and kissed Corina.

"Gross. You nearly swallowed her whole, Mitchell."

"Hello to you too, Waylynn."

I slid down a seat so that Mitchell could sit between Cord and Corina.

"You not manning the bar?" Tripp asked.

"Just informing the girls here about the new bar coming to town."

Steed leaned over and gave me a quick kiss on the forehead. "Hey, beautiful."

"Hey, Steed."

Tripp sighed. "Jesus, I should have never told you. If I had known you were going to act like a baby I'd have kept my mouth shut."

I grinned and took another drink. "If it's not an Irish pub, what is it?" I asked.

Tripp grinned. "All I know is they applied for a liquor license."

"That's what you're bellyaching about, Cord?"

He looked away and must have caught sight of the floozy making eyes at him. He stood up. "It's been real, but I see fun over there. I need something to take my mind off the competition, if you catch my drift."

He turned and ran right into someone.

"Shit!" Cord yelled as the drink the girl was holding spilled all over him.

"I'm so sorry!"

"Did she say oil was so sorry?" Corina asked.

"I think she said I'm, but it sounded funny." Mitchell replied.

It wasn't hard to notice Cord was instantly taken with her. As he should be. She was drop-dead gorgeous, and I knew she wasn't from Oak Springs.

"Wow. Do you see how green her eyes are?" Corina said, leaning in closer to say it in my ear.

I nodded.

"I didn't mean to run into you," she said.

Cord flashed her that famous Parker grin. "No worries, sweetheart." He stepped around her and headed over to the bitch who'd been giving me dirty looks.

The green-eyed beauty watched Cord walk over to the girl and start putting the moves on her. Glancing back at us, she smiled.

"Have a nice one."

I couldn't help but smile. This girl wasn't from Oak Springs, or even America. She was from Ireland.

"You too!" everyone said.

Once she walked off, I looked around the table. "She's Irish!"

"What?" Mitchell and Tripp said as Steed busted out laughing.

"Oh, goodness. Cord just met his competition, and he didn't even know it!" Corina said.

Steed glanced over to Cord. "Do we tell him?"

I laughed. "Hell, no. I say we keep letting him believe his new competition is a man."

"How did he not catch the accent?" Tripp asked.

"Because he had one thing on his mind."

"I agree with Waylynn, but did anyone happen to notice how he looked at her and how he is currently watching her at the bar?" Corina stated. "Good thing Trevor is off tonight, because I can promise you he'd be all over that girl."

Watching Cord, I noticed how he was still eyeing the Irish girl, his "competition."

"Oh, this is going to be so much fun," I said as I leaned back in my chair and watched Cord's eyes follow her out the front door.

Corina and I looked at each other and grinned.

I'd never seen Cord watch a woman with as much intensity as he just did. Cord Parker had just met the game changer and the poor bastard didn't even know it!

"Hey, isn't that Jonathon on the dance floor?"

My heart dropped, and I spun in my chair. I swallowed hard as my eyes searched the crowd. When I found him, I quickly looked to see who he was dancing with.

"That's Evie, Jonathon's sister."

"I didn't realize he had a sister," Corina stated.

"He has three sisters and two brothers."

"She's pretty."

"Oh, hell. Once Trevor lays eyes on Evie, shit is going to hit the fan," Steed said.

"What do you mean?" I asked.

Looking at me, Steed continued, "Once Trevor finds out who Evie's brother is, he's going to go after her. Tit for tat sort of thing."

Mitchell and Tripp laughed while I glared at them.

"Um, no. Evie is off limits to Trevor and to you, Tripp."

"Me? What makes you think I would go after her?"

"You have a dick, that's what."

Tripp nodded. "Reason enough."

When Evie looked our way, she waved, pulling her brother with her as she ran over to the table.

"Hi, Waylynn! Here she is, Jon. It's Waylynn."

Giving me a warm smile, he replied, "I can see that, Evie. Thanks."

"He's been waiting for you to show up. Have you been here long?"

"Not very long."

I couldn't pull my eyes from Jonathon. He looked around the table and shook my brothers' hands, then he gave Corina a hug.

"Mitchell, I'm in the mood for a dance!" Corina said. My brother took her hand and led her to the dance floor. Paxton was making her way back to the table.

"Well, Wade showed up and Amelia dropped me like a hot plate!"

Everyone chuckled. Kissing Steed, Paxton sat down next to him. "Hi Jonathon! I thought that was you on the dance floor."

He tipped his hat toward Paxton. "Evening, Paxton."

"Jonathon?"

Looking over, I found Bethany Lenard, Jonathon's ex and the bitch who wrote that trash article. One quick sweep of her body, and I wanted to gag. She was dressed in a tight, short skirt with a shirt that showed her stomach and cleavage. This girl left nothing to the imagination.

"Hey, Beth. How's it going?"

"Okay, I heard you were looking for me last night."

My heart dropped. Did Jonathon get so upset with me he went in search of another woman?

I looked away, trying to keep the bile down my throat. *How could he?*

"No, I wasn't looking for you. Sorry."

"Are you sure? Cause my roommate said you stopped by last night. I was on a date."

My eyes lifted to Tripp's, and he shook his head. When I looked at Steed, he didn't seem too bothered by the fact that Jonathon had left my house and went to this whore's.

"Bethany, I didn't stop by your place last night."

Bethany's gaze was bouncing from me to Jonathon. "That's not what my roommate said."

Jonathon laughed and shook his head, all the while my head pounding again. I went to look away when his words froze me in place. "I was at Waylynn's all night, so I couldn't possibly have been at your place."

My eyes nearly popped out of my head. He was lying. Oh my God, did he think I was so drunk I wouldn't remember him leaving? I stood up to call his ass out when Tripp grabbed my hand.

"Don't."

Looking at my brother with a confused expression, I asked, "What?"

Tripp moved into Corina's seat and placed his mouth next to my ear. "Jonathon slept in his truck at your place all night so that he could check on you. He sent a text to let Steed know. We all ate breakfast together this morning at Mom and Dad's."

Relief washed over me. Then confusion. "How did she know we were fighting?" I asked in a hushed voice.

"That, I don't know."

When I turned around, Bethany was staring at Jonathon. "One of these days you're going to get tired of her and come crawling back to me."

Jonathon shook his head. "I highly doubt that. Enjoy your evening, Bethany."

Bethany stomped off like a child who had just gotten her toy taken away. I stood up as Jonathon faced me.

"I guess I'll be calling it a night. Night, y'all." He tipped his hat at me and added, "Waylynn."

Then he walked away. Leaving me standing there like a complete idiot.

I closed my eyes and shook my head. Turning, I looked between my two brothers and Paxton.

"What just happened? Why did he treat me like an old friend he was saying hi to?"

Paxton shrugged. "I don't know, but I think you best go after him and find out."

Grabbing my purse, I felt my anger starting to boil. How dare he walk away? "Oh, that is exactly what I intend on doing. Excuse me, y'all."

CHAPTER 19

jonathon

My truck was parked on Main Street, so I got to it pretty quickly. Right as I opened my door, I heard her call out my name. And I knew it was time to give Waylynn Parker a taste of her own medicine. I got in my truck, started it up, and pulled onto the road. I looked in the rearview and watched her stand on the sidewalk, her hands at her sides.

Shit. What if she didn't drive to the bar. I swung a U-turn and started back down Main. Waylynn stepped into the street to flag me down. Yep, no car.

I came to a slow stop and rolled my window down. "Waylynn? What's the matter?"

"Don't you 'what's the matter' me, Jonathon Turner."

She marched around the front of my truck, and it was all I could do not to start laughing. Once she was in, she hit me on the shoulder.

"Ouch! What in the hell was that for?"

"For making me think you were gonna drive off and leave me here."

"I was driving off, until you ran into the road."

Her mouth fell. "You were honestly going to leave without me? I've been calling you."

"I don't have my phone."

She snarled her lip. "Really? Where is it?"

"Probably somewhere in your folks' house."

Her mouth snapped shut. "Your phone is at my parents' house?"

"I sure hope so, or I've lost it. I'm pretty sure I left it on the counter there." I glanced out the window.

"That's why you didn't return my calls or text today."

"That would be why."

Waylynn remained silent for a few seconds before she cleared her throat. "I'm sorry for the way I acted last night. I didn't mean anything, and I hope you know that."

"I do."

The weight of her stare made me peek at her. "I know you didn't mean anything, and I know you were upset, Waylynn. I only wish you would have let me talk to you instead of pushing me away and getting drunk. If we want this to work, we need to talk to each other."

"I was confused last night, but today my mind has been cleared, and I realize how stupid I've been acting. I've been so caught up in what everyone else thinks about me or *will* think about me, that I let it cloud what my heart truly wants."

"I asked you this before, Waylynn, and I'm asking you again...what do you want?"

"Happiness. Love. My dreams. You."

I reached for her hand. "That's all I want for both of us, Waylynn. Together."

"I also need you to know that when I went to the fertility clinic, it was just to ask questions and it was right after I found out about Mitchell and Corina. I was feeling sorry for myself and acting foolish. I want a baby still, though. If things work out with us…I mean…I want a baby soon."

I pulled over and put the truck in park. I needed to look into her eyes as I spoke to her. When I kissed the back of her hand, her eyes finally seemed to shine again.

"I want to start a family too, Waylynn. I wasn't feeding you lines of bullshit to get into your pants. You were acting with your heart and that can never be a foolish thing."

She let out a gruff laugh. "Oh, trust me, your heart can lead you astray. At least it can until you learn how to listen to it. I was able to do that today. I went dancing."

My brows lifted. "Dancing? Where? I was at the studio most of today."

I chuckled. "Amelia, Corina, and I went into San Antonio to use a dance studio that a friend of Amelia's owns. It was the first time I'd danced since I've been here and there was something very therapeutic about it. When I was finished the fog had lifted."

"So, no more worrying about what people say about us?"

"No more."

"Jack?"

"Nothing he said to me or anything about him matters at all."

"Good. Now let's go to my place and fuck like rabbits because seeing you in that dress is making my dick hard as a rock."

Waylynn fanned herself with her hand. "Oh my! You do know how to sweet talk me, Jonathon Turner."

I opened my eyes to the most beautiful sight I'd ever seen. Waylynn Parker in my arms.

"Good morning, beautiful. What's the plan for today?"

She peeked up at me. "Christmas."

"It's only a few weeks away."

Sitting up, she grinned. "Today is decoration day at my parents' house. They've always done it on their wedding anniversary. When does your family decorate?"

"Thanksgiving. It looks like someone threw up Christmas at my folks' place."

Then it hit me. Waylynn hadn't met them yet.

"What do you say we get up, eat breakfast, and swing by my folks' before we head to yours."

Chewing on her lip, her eyes filled with worry.

"Stop doing that. You'll make it swell up, and then I am going to have to kiss you all morning to make it better."

She bit down harder, then laughed. "I'm nervous about meeting them. I mean, I'm sure I've seen your mom and probably even met her when I was younger."

I kissed the tip of her nose. "She's going to love you. Now, roll over."

"Why?" she asked with a giggle.

"Because I'm going to make love to you to start the day."

Doing as I asked, Waylynn rolled over. I kissed her stomach tenderly and moved my lips over her body, stopping at each nipple for a few seconds to give them attention. Waylynn's hands laced through my hair and pulled slightly as I sucked. My hand rubbed against her pussy, causing her to squirm.

My lips moved to her neck while her legs wrapped around me, pressing my hard dick against her.

"I've got something to tell you, sweetie. I'm on the pill," she blurted out.

My head popped up. "What?"

Her chest was heaving with each excited breath. "I'm on the pill. If you're comfortable with it, you don't have to wear a condom."

We'd already had the talk, each of us sharing our sexual past. Neither of us had much of one to speak of. Waylynn had lost her virginity to a high school sweetheart and then married Jack. Once she found out he had been cheating, she'd gotten tested and everything came back clean. I had lost mine in high school and then only been with two other women. I wasn't as adventurous as Cord when it came to women. I'd always worn a condom, but I'd still gotten tested after my last breakup.

"Are you...are you sure?" I asked, my heart pounding so loud it almost made it hard to hear her answer.

"I'm very sure."

"Fucking hell. I'm going to come before I get all the way in."

Her smile nearly lit up the whole damn room.

"I want to feel you. Please, go slow."

Burying my face into her neck, I fought to keep my emotions in check. I'd never had a woman make me tear up...until Waylynn. The emotions she brought out in me were crazy.

Slipping my fingers inside her, I worked them in and out. She was so fucking wet and ready. My dick was painfully hard, but I didn't want to rush this. I wanted to feel every single thing as I slid inside of the woman I was falling in love with. I didn't care that things were moving fast, there was no denying what my heart was feeling.

I positioned myself and slowly pushed in. Both of us moaned. My eyes nearly rolled to the back of my head as I took in the way she felt. Without a condom, I felt like I was losing my virginity all over again...and based on how intoxicating Waylynn felt, I wasn't sure I'd last much longer than I did the first time I lost my virginity.

"Christ Almighty, you feel so good, baby," I panted.

Her legs pulled me closer, her need for me to hurry evident.

"Sweetheart, you just told me to go slow."

"You're going *too* slow!"

Smiling, I pressed my lips to hers as I pushed all the way in and froze. Her arms were wrapped around me with her fingers gliding over my back. Pulling her mouth from mine, our eyes met. "Jonathon, it feels so...amazing."

I slowly pulled out and pushed back in. Her mouth opened in the perfect shape of an O. When I did it again, her eyes closed and she whispered, "Yes."

"It feels so good, baby. God, Waylynn, you feel so good."

Going this slow, I wasn't going to last much longer. When our mouths crushed together again, things turned more passionate. Our tongues danced, and her nails dug into my back. Picking up the speed, I broke the kiss and pulled her legs up.

"Yes. Harder. Oh God, yes!" Waylynn hissed as our sweet lovemaking turned faster. The sounds of our bodies hitting and the way her tits bounced with each thrust drove me harder.

"I'm going to come," she said, her eyes locked with mine.

Her sweet moans of pleasure were all it took for me to come along with her. The moment I came, I knew she was the only woman I'd ever make love to again. There could never be another. She was the one I wanted to see pregnant with our child. To whisper I love you to each night and every morning.

The feel of her pussy holding my cock so deeply was like magic. When I finally stopped, I dropped over her, my arms catching my weight.

Waylynn's hand brushed my face as she gently ran her thumb over my cheek. "I've never felt anything like that before in my life."

Leaning into her hand, I replied, "Neither have I. I'm falling in love with you, Waylynn Parker, and there is no turning back. You're mine. Forever."

Her eyes filled with tears as she bit on that damn lip again before whispering her reply.

"I've already fallen."

CHAPTER 20

Waylynn

"There's nothing to be nervous about."

I looked at Jonathon as we walked up the sidewalk to his parents' house. It was a large ranch house, not as big as my parents', but still big. It was covered with Christmas lights and decorations. Even the front walkway had decorations lining it. The windows had the snow sprayed into the corners. I smiled. I'd begged my mother for years to do that, and she refused. Said it was too hard to wash off.

"I've always wanted the snow in the corners of the window."

Jonathon laughed. "I bet you got the real thing in New York."

"Yes! And then some."

Before we hit the first step, the front door flew open and the cutest little girl came running out. Her blonde hair was full of curls, and she had the most beautiful blue eyes.

"Blonde," I said, surprised. I looked at his tussled brown locks. All he did was run his fingers through his hair this morning and it was simply perfect.

"The blonde hair is from Rip," Jonathon explained. A pull in my lower stomach had me wanting him…again. After this morning, I was positive I could never have another man make love to me like Jonathon did. It was beyond beautiful. It was a…dream.

"There is my beautiful girl!" Jonathon gushed, picking up the young girl and giving her a hug. She laughed in delight.

"I've missed you so much, Jon! Where have you been?"

I watched the interchange and wondered how many times Jonathon would come over to his folks' place and visit. Did they do weekly dinners like my parents did? I would think with four younger siblings, it'd almost be a requirement.

"I just saw you a couple days ago, squirt!"

"That's not the same. You used to come over more!"

My lips pressed together. I hoped I wasn't the reason he hadn't been coming over as often.

"Well, remember last time, I told you there was another girl in my life."

She nodded and turned her attention on me. Her eyes grew big. "You're the new girl in my brother's life, huh? You are very pretty."

Feeling the heat on my cheeks, I pressed my hand to my chest. "Why, aren't you the sweetest for saying something so nice."

"It's the truth. I don't ever lie. If I do my momma will have no problem swatting my bottom."

Trying not to laugh, I nodded. "I don't blame you. Neither would I."

"Hope, this is Waylynn Parker."

The young girl gasped. "Cord's sister?" I nodded. "No wonder you're so pretty. He's so handsome. I'm going to marry him someday."

"Oh, does Cord know?"

Hope nodded. "Yep. He laughs when I tell him, though. He doesn't believe me."

My eyes snapped over to Jonathon. He winked. "Come on, there are plenty more where this one came from."

Hope reached for my hand and pulled me in. "Come on, Waylynn, momma is so excited to see you. She said she was gonna pee her pants."

This time I did laugh.

"Don't pull her arm out of the socket, Hope!"

After walking through the front door, I felt like I had stepped into a winter wonderland. The large foyer held a small tree on a round table. Around the base sat fake snow and little trinkets.

"Oh, my gawd! She's here!"

Another girl, this one much older and gorgeous to boot, came rushing over to me.

"Waylynn! It's so amazing to meet you!"

Hope refused to let go of my hand as the older girl crushed her body against mine in a bear hug. When she pulled back, she looked me up and down and shook her head.

"You Parkers. I swear to God, your parents know how to breed 'em."

I laughed. "You must be Hollie."

She smiled big. "I am!"

"You're a senior this year?" I asked as Hope continued to pull me farther into the house. We were now in a living room that had a giant tree in the corner. I glanced around the room, taking in all the decorations. The tree had to be ten feet tall. The fireplace was done up in lighted garlands, with seven stockings held up by snowmen. It was adorable. They even had a train running around the circumference of the tree.

"Sure am. Heading to Texas Tech next fall."

Glancing at Hollie, I grinned. "How exciting. Do you know what your major is?"

"Nursing."

"That's wonderful!"

Jonathon placed his hand on my lower back, and my entire body trembled. He must have felt it because he pulled me closer, pressing his lips to my ear. "You nervous?"

I shook my head. "That's just what you do to me."

I loved how his eyes lit up and that crooked grin appeared. I was falling in love with him faster as the seconds ticked by. And this family made falling in love with him even easier.

"This isn't even the living room where we open presents," Jonathon chuckled.

"No way! That tree is amazing!"

"Oh, our mother is a nut when it comes to decorating for fall, Halloween, and Christmas. She starts in August," Hollie said.

"August?"

Hollie rolled her eyes. "Don't even get me started with it. Come on, my folks are in the kitchen, and I'm sure my mom is chomping at the bit to see you."

Hope pulled me along as Jonathon kept his hand on my lower back. We walked through a large dining room with a huge farm table completely decked out. My mother would have decoration envy if she saw this house. There were even name holders for the table seating.

To my right, I could see into the large kitchen. A beautiful older woman, maybe in her late forties, was standing at the island making a pie crust. Her dark hair looked exactly like Jonathon's. She smiled the biggest smile I'd ever seen. I could see where Jonathon got his good looks from. His mother was breathtaking.

"Waylynn Parker! My goodness, look how beautiful you've become."

I didn't really remember Jonathon's mom. Maybe we'd met a few times when she had dropped Jonathon off at the house, but I never paid close attention to my brother's friends.

Wiping her hands on her apron, she took it off and tossed it onto the island. Her arms were extended, and Jonathon gave me a small push toward her. I was quickly engulfed in a hug.

"Thank you," she whispered into my ear before pulling back and giving me a once over. "My goodness. You are a pretty thing."

"Alright, Mom. Don't scare her off. Waylynn, this is my mother, Kristin Myers. Mom, Waylynn Parker."

"It's a pleasure meeting you officially, Mrs. Myers."

"Please, call me Kristin. It's my pleasure meeting you. Jonathon has told us so much about you. Your life in New York! The dance studio. I can't wait to see it. Hope has been begging to take dance lessons, but I didn't have the time to drive to Uvalde. To have a place right here in Oak Springs, it's so exciting!"

My heart leapt with joy. "I'm not sure what to expect, but I'm certainly excited. We're going to have an open house next week and do tours for those who are interested in signing up."

Kristin's eyes lit up. "Oh, I'm going to tell my reading group! They have been asking."

I grinned. "Thank you so much. I truly appreciate it."

"Mom, we can't stay long. Waylynn's family is decorating their house today for Christmas."

"Wait. What? You mean she comes from a normal family that doesn't go from cutting the turkey to putting up the tree all within an hour?" Hollie chipped in.

"Stop that, Hollie. I have to get it done so I can go shopping!"

Kristin turned to face me. "Black Friday and all that."

I shrugged. "I've never gone shopping on Black Friday."

"Oh hell," Jonathon whispered as Hollie slowly shook her head.

"You've gone and done yourself in, Waylynn." She looked at her brother. "You better marry her before next Thanksgiving or Mom will scare her off for sure if she takes her shopping."

With a chuckle, I said, "I love to shop…"

Jonathon put his hand over my mouth. "If you know what's good for you, don't say another word."

My eyes widened as Hollie and Hope laughed. Kristin grabbed a handful of flour and threw it at both girls, then tossed her napkin at Jonathon.

"Don't listen to them, Waylynn. I'm not *that* over the top."

"Oh, sure Mom," Hollie said. "You only leave the house on Thanksgiving night at midnight, and we don't see you until Sunday morning at church."

Hope covered her mouth and laughed. "Last year, Momma fell asleep in church and Dad had to keep waking her up."

"We talkin' about Black Friday shopping?"

A tall man with light blonde hair walked into the kitchen. He was handsome as hell and looked exactly like Hope. She ran over and jumped into her daddy's arms. The way he kissed her and then Hollie made my heart skip. I already knew that Hollie's birth father was Ned Turner, Jonathon's dad. But the way Rip loved both of them was absolutely equal.

He made his way over to Kristin and planted a long kiss on her lips. I peeked over to Jonathon who gave me a wink.

"Rip, this is Waylynn Parker. Waylynn, this is my dad, Rip Myers."

I wasn't the least bit surprised Jonathon called him *dad*. From what Jonathon had told me, Rip had adopted the older kids and had told them they could take on his last name or keep their father's. They all decided to keep Turner, but also add Myers. Jonathon's legal name was Jonathon Turner Myers.

Reaching my hand out, Rip shook it. "It's a real honor to meet you, Waylynn. Jon's told me a lot about you."

"Has he?" I asked, peering back to Jonathon. "All good, I hope."

"Of course. I can't wait to see his handiwork at the dance studio."

"Next week!" Kristin exclaimed. "Waylynn's having an open house."

Rip nodded. "Well, I've gotten to see a lot of it already. I do a lot of the electrical work for Jon. It was my trade before I met Kristin."

"I didn't know that," I said.

Rip grinned. "I like to do a little here and there just to keep up with things. Plus I love the work."

"He's damn good as well. Best electrician I've ever had," Jonathon replied with a proud smile.

I loved watching this family interact with each other. It reminded me of mine.

Jonathon let out a sigh. "As fun as this is, we've got to run, y'all."

Jonathon kissed his mother on the cheek, then did the same to Hollie. He pointed to her and softly said, "Behave, you hear me?"

He cheeks blushed and she nodded. Turning, he picked up Hope and gave her a kiss on the cheek. "I love you, sweet girl. I'll be back for dinner."

"Waylynn, I know it's your family night, but if you can stop by for dinner later, we'd love to have you. I'm sure the boys would love to meet you."

"I'd like that very much. Thank you for the invite."

Placing his hand on my back, Jonathon led me out of the kitchen and through the house. I tried to take everything in again as we meandered through the rooms and back onto the porch.

"Well, that wasn't so bad," Jonathon said.

My fingers laced with his as we made our way down the steps and sidewalk. "It was lovely! Your mother is sweet and so beautiful. I see where you get those good looks."

Jonathon's face blushed, and boy did that turn me on.

"You should have seen my father. Evie is the spitting image of him."

"Do you have a picture of him?" I asked.

Dropping my hand, he took out his wallet and pulled out an old photo that was folded in half.

"It's the last picture we took together. I was at a 4-H show and I'd won first prize with my pig, Wilbur."

I laughed. "Not very creative with the name there, Turner."

"No, I wasn't."

Running my fingers along the man's face, I saw Jonathon. He had short, dark hair, and even though the photo was old, you could see his blue-grey eyes.

"You look like him." Our eyes met. His sadness made my chest ache.

"I miss him. There isn't a day that doesn't go by where I don't think about him. Rip has been a great stepdad. He's never once pushed us, left it up to us on when and if we wanted to call him dad, as well as taking on his name. He's been so good to my mother, but he also knows that my dad was the love of her life."

"She told him that?"

He nodded. "Yes. When he asked her to marry him, she told him he'd have to share her heart."

"Wow," I whispered. A chill swept over my body.

"I truly believe a love like my folks had is a once-in-a-lifetime thing. I feel like Rip has that with my mother and she does love him, but not like how she loved my father. Does that make sense?"

I smiled slightly. "Yes."

Glancing at the photo, I pressed my lips together. I wanted desperately to tell Jonathon how deep my feelings were for him, but we'd have that conversation at a later date. Today was not the time. Handing back the photo, I watched as he carefully folded it and put it into his wallet.

With a deep breath, I took his hands in mine. "Now, are you ready to go see *my* crazy family?"

"Always! I can't wait to see what type of new questions Chloe
has from her *list* today."

CHAPTER 21

jonathon

"Stop the truck!"

I slammed on the brakes and pulled onto the shoulder. Waylynn jumped out of the truck and started running down the road.

"What in the fuck?"

I followed her, stopping when I saw her lean down and pick up a giant turtle.

"I've got you, buddy. You shouldn't be crossing the road. It's dangerous! I'll get you over there."

My chest fluttered at the sight of Waylynn rescuing a turtle. She walked it all the way across the street and put it on the other side of the fence.

"Go on! And stay away from the road!"

When she turned back, she saw me staring.

"He would have died if we didn't help him. Didn't you see him?"

"I saw him, but I would've drove over him."

Her mouth fell. "Jonathon Turner, you could have run him over."

"No, I straddled him."

"Okay, but what about the next car or the next? The poor thing was terrified."

I laughed. "How do you know he was terrified?"

"Wouldn't you be if a giant truck *straddled* you?"

Trying not to laugh, I said, "I guess I would be."

We headed back to the truck and I walked over to the passenger side. After opening the door and helping her up, I leaned in. "Do you always pull over and save them?"

She looked at me like I had asked her the stupidest question ever. "Um…yeah. Don't you?"

I do now.

"I love your kind heart."

She grinned. "You avoided the question."

"Well," I said, reaching for her seat belt and pulling it across her. "I certainly do now. Especially knowing how important it is to you."

"Thank you. It goes for all animals, you know. If you see them loose or in trouble, you have to stop."

"I do?"

"Yep. I once chased about six donkeys down the street until we got them back through their owner's ranch gate. Then there were the goats I made my father round up. The best one was the longhorn who kept trying to attack Tripp." She laughed as the memory came back. "Yeah, that one was funny as hell."

I shook my head and chuckled as I shut the door.

Talking to myself as I rounded the truck, I mumbled, "Life with this woman is going to be interesting."

I pulled onto the road and found myself frantically watching for damn turtles.

For the love of Pete! What does this woman do to me?

"Do you like Christmas?" Waylynn asked out of the blue.

"I love Christmas. Do you?"

She smiled. "It's always been one of my favorite holidays. Your sister wasn't kidding about your mom liking to decorate. How many trees does she have total?"

"Hmm, let me think. I know of at least five."

"Five!"

Laughing, I added, "Maybe six if she puts the one up outside."

"Holy shit. Why so many trees?"

I shrugged. "Beats me. Hope has one in her room and each year the theme changes. Last year, I think it was fish."

"Fish?"

"It was a phase she went through."

Waylynn giggled. "Well, I want to do a themed tree."

"Oh yeah? What would it be?"

"I'm thinking red and white. That would be fun. Or red and silver. Or silver and blue. Oh! A moose-themed tree!"

Glancing her way, I asked, "A moose-themed tree?"

"I like moose."

"I'd say, if you want to do a whole damn tree of them."

"No themed tree for you?"

I thought about it for a few seconds as I turned down ranch road 47 that led to the Frio River Ranch.

"Let me think, if I did a themed Christmas tree, what would it be? Probably hunting."

"No. Pick something else."

I glanced at her before looking back at the road. "What's wrong with a hunting theme?"

She shook her head. "Maybe in the garage."

"The garage? You'd put a Christmas tree in the garage."

Facing me, she winked. "If it was a hunting-themed one, yes. Pick something else."

I chuckled. "Okay. Tools."

This time she laughed harder. "Oh my gosh, how cute would that be?"

"What if we did tools on one side and dancing stuff on the other?"

Feeling her stare, I looked at her. "What's wrong?"

Her eyes softened and seemed to shine a little more. "Nothing."

"You don't like my idea?"

Her fingers laced in mine. "I love that idea."

We pulled up to the gate of the ranch and I punched in the code. "Remind me to give you a remote to open the gate."

"You planning on me visiting a lot?"

She grinned. "I know you live closer to town, so I'm guessing I'll be staying with you more than you'll be staying here."

"Makes sense. I hope you like classic rock. I fall asleep to music playing each night."

"Really? You haven't so far."

"That's because you exhaust me with all the sex, and I pass the hell out."

"I can back off if you want."

"Fuck, no! I don't want that. Especially now that I get to have you bareback."

She squeezed my hand. "I thought that might be your answer."

We drove down the long driveway and planned out which days I would stay with her and which she would stay with me. We settled on her coming and staying with me for the next few days since so much would be happening at the dance studio, in order to get things ready for the open house.

"Looks like everyone is here, except for Tripp. I don't see his truck."

I pulled in next to Mitchell's truck. "Maybe he's working late."

"*Pssssh.* No, he always comes late because he hates doing this. He used to love it when he was dating Harley. She was always big into decorating."

"Whatever happened with her dating that guy she met in college?"

"Don't know. Tripp never did find out. I guess he doesn't bring it up to her folks whenever he sees them, and they don't either. They loved Tripp like a son, and I think they were caught just as off guard as Tripp was."

"That's a damn shame. They were good together."

We walked up the porch steps hand-in-hand. "Did you know she's moving back to town to be the new vet?"

"I heard. That can't be easy for Tripp."

"He's acting like it's not bothering him, but I know it is."

Waylynn walked into the house with me following. She busted out laughing when she saw the tall skinny tree in the foyer. It was a flocked tree with white lights.

"Tree number one. Let's see if my mom goes as crazy as yours."

I rolled my eyes. "Let's think for a second. Foyer, formal living, family room, my folks' bedroom, and a small one in the guest bathroom. You mom will have to beat that."

"Holy crap. Don't tell my mother. She'll want more."

I motioned like I was sealing my lips and tossing the key.

"Waylynn! Sexy Jonathon! Come in and join the party!"

With a moan, Waylynn turned to me. "Looks like Aunt Vi's got herself some booze!"

I laughed and smacked Waylynn on the ass when she turned around, causing her to let out a small scream. Vi motioned to us as she held up her glass and called out, "Awww! Here's to love!"

As Waylynn walked up to her aunt, she replied, "Amen to that!"

The two women set off toward the family room where everyone was gathering while I paused for a moment.

Here's to love.

Waylynn didn't take pause at all to that comment. It was as if it had been the most natural thing in the world. For me, it had been. I knew I was falling in love with her. She said she was falling, as well.

In my mind I thought it was way to soon...but my heart wasn't going to hear any of that. I wanted to tell her out loud that I loved her. Soon.

"Is everything okay?"

I glanced up to see Waylynn. "Yeah. Sorry, I got lost in thought for a moment."

She grinned. "Does it involve you naked and me on top?"

"It certainly does now."

Following her through the house, we made it to the family room. A giant tree stood in the corner. It had to be at least ten feet tall. John stood on a giant ladder, stringing lights.

Chloe was sitting on the floor organizing decorations with Paxton and Amelia.

"Hey, how's it going?"

I turned and smiled at Cord, his hand out for a handshake.

"It's going. How about you?"

He grinned. "Doing great. So, is this how things are going to be? I only get to see my best friend at family events with my sister?"

I chuckled. "No, not at all. I was going to call and see if you wanted to head to Llano next week for a quick hunting trip after the open house."

Appearing to think about that for a few seconds, Cord asked, "What days?"

"Tuesday, Wednesday, and coming back Thursday. The lease is quieter during the week. Roy said he saw a huge twelve point."

His eyes lit up. "Really? Damn, let me see how Tammy feels about holding down the fort for a couple of days."

"Tammy? Who's that?"

Wiggling his brows, Cord leaned close. "My fucking hot new manager who has a body to die for."

"Tell me you haven't."

He laughed. "No, I'm not that much of a douche, but she's pretty and knows how to flirt."

I put my hand on his shoulder. "Just be careful, dude. That's an area you don't want to mess around in when you're the boss."

"Believe me, I know. If she wasn't so good at her job, I'd fire her just so I could screw her."

"You'll never change, Cord Parker."

He winked. "I hope not. I'm having too much fun."

A slap on my back had me turning to see Mitchell. "How's it going there, Jon?"

We shook hands, and I replied, "Never better."

"My sister is good for you. I don't think I've ever seen you looking so…happy."

With a huge smile, I agreed. "I haven't ever been this happy. Feels like I'm living in a dream, to be honest."

Mitchell nodded while Cord let out a groan.

"For fuck's sake. Now *you've* got the damn Smurf smile."

Drawing my head back, I asked, "What?"

"Ignore him. He's just jealous he hasn't found anyone to bring out his inner Smurf."

"Fuck you, Mitchell."

"Cord Parker!" Melanie shouted from across the room.

"It's bad enough little ears are around, but to curse when we're putting up the Christmas tree?"

John laughed as he made his way down the ladder. "It's not like the tree will get its feelings hurt, Melanie."

"You hush up, John Parker, or no banana bread for you!"

John walked over to us, extending his hand out to mine and whispered, "You'd think by now she'd know I can't stand her banana bread."

Each of us let out a chuckle.

"How's it going, Jonathon?"

"Very well, sir. Yourself?"

"Good and even better if someone hides the banana bread. Waylynn tells me the place is nearly done. Just a few touch-ups here and there, and you're ready for the open house on Monday."

"We are, indeed. The interior decorator had some problems getting all the chairs ready, but that won't affect the open house."

"I've been meaning to head down there and take a look. Are the floors still going in?"

"They should be completely finished by tomorrow."

He nodded. "Good. Waylynn seems to be over the moon about it all."

Glancing her way, she was holding Gage as she helped Chloe put decorations on the tree. I couldn't help imagining having a baby together someday.

"I believe she is pretty excited about it."

John hit the side of my arm. "I don't think the dance studio is the only thing making her happy, son."

"I reckon not, sir. She makes me just as happy."

John flashed me the same smile all of his sons had. "Just remember, she looks all sweet on the outside, but that girl is just like her momma. There is a reason I don't tell my wife I don't like her banana nut bread. You'd do good to remember that."

I chuckled. "Yes, sir. I will."

Trevor walked into the room dressed in a cooking apron that read, "Real men aren't afraid to bake."

"I've got butter pecan cookies!"

Amelia and Steed nearly knocked each other over trying to get them.

"Holy crap, are they that good?" I asked as Cord made a beeline toward Trevor.

John laughed. "Trevor is the baker in the family, and he only makes these cookies on December 9, decoration day."

"Huh, I'll have to try one."

"Jonathon, hold Gage!"

Waylynn placed the four-month-old baby in my arms and took off with the rest of the Parker siblings. The only one not heading for the tray was Mitchell.

"Man, Turner. You're a natural at this whole baby thing."

I stared at the baby in my arms. Gage's eyes were everywhere, taking in all the colors and lights.

"I like kids. Seems like yesterday Rip Jr. was this age." Glancing up, I smiled at Mitchell. "Are you excited about becoming a father?"

His face lit up brighter than the Christmas tree, and I couldn't help but notice how he looked lovingly at Corina.

"I am excited. Seven months to go. She's got the tiniest little belly bump. I can't wait to watch the baby grow."

"Are y'all going to find out if it's a boy or a girl?"

"I think we will find out."

Waylynn walked back over and reached for Gage. I turned away and her mouth dropped open. "Don't be a baby hog, Jonathon!"

"Me? You've had him since we first walked in."

She reached for the baby again, and I pulled away.

"Jonathon Turner, give me my nephew."

Gage laughed, and I looked down at him. "That's it, buddy. We guys need to stick together."

Steed laughed as he walked up and kissed his son on the forehead. "Waylynn, you get to see Gage all the time. Let Jonathon hold him."

When her hands went to her hips, I knew I had two options. One? Give her the baby and enjoy my evening. Two? Keep the baby and incur the wrath of Waylynn Parker.

Option one it was.

"Fine, you can take him back."

I handed Gage back to Waylynn. She flashed me that gorgeous smile and leaned in to kiss me. "Thank you, babe."

Heading back to the tree, she ate her cookie and held onto the baby like her life depended on it.

"How do you feel about kids, Jonathon?"

Not taking my eyes off of Waylynn, I answered Steed. "I love them."

"Probably has something to do with having younger siblings, I would think," Steed added.

"Yeah, you're probably right."

He bumped my shoulder, causing me to look at him.

"There isn't anything more amazing than becoming a father. I know Waylynn's ready to settle down. What about you?"

"Yes, I'd like to get settled and have a family."

"Take it slow, get to know each other. I know y'all have known each other for a few months, but I know the path my sister wants to take and I don't want to see her hurt."

Placing my hand on his shoulder, I gave it a squeeze. "I hope I'm half as good of a brother to my sisters as y'all are to Waylynn and Amelia. It's clear how much y'all love your sisters."

He nodded, as did Mitchell. "Take care of her, Jonathon. That's all we ask for."

Facing the two brothers, I nodded. "I promise you I will. I have no intentions of ever hurting her or leaving her."

A strong slap on my back caused me to stumble forward. I turned to see it was find Tripp.

"Good answer, Turner. Good answer."

Cord walked up and handed me a beer. We sat on the sofa and watched the girls decorate the tree. Waylynn and Chloe were stringing popcorn, only they were eating more of it than they were stringing.

A strange feeling moved over me that caused goosebumps. Something about this moment felt too perfect. Too right. I pushed it aside, but something deep down inside had my stomach in knots.

"It's a surprise for your father," my mother said with a wide grin.

"Dad is going to flip out when he sees you bought him a new .22 for his birthday, Momma!" I said, helping her hide the gun in the attic.

"Someday when y'all go on that hunting trip to Montana he always talks about, he can use it for that."

A Montana hunting trip was all my father and I ever talked about. It was our dream.

Too bad we never saw it come true.

CHAPTER 22

Waylynn

"Okay, everyone ready?" my mother called out.

"Ready!" we all shouted, Chloe being the loudest.

My father hit the switch and the giant tree came to life. An internal warmth spread through my body as the sounds of Nat King Cole's "The Christmas Song" filled the air.

The sight was beautiful, and not just the Christmas tree. It was everything. The one thing that stood out the most was my parents. They looked up at the tree, around the room to their family, and then at each other. It wasn't just a passing look. No, this was a look of utter love. The way they gazed into each other's eyes left me breathless. Their love was like a fairy tale, only more amazing.

"It looks beautiful, John," my mother softly said. "Every year I'm in awe in this moment."

Lifting his hand, he brushed a piece of her dark blonde hair to the side. "Not nearly as beautiful as you, darling."

And there it was. The most intimate of exchanges. I'd witnessed them my whole life, but never really paid attention. When I glanced around the room, I saw it again and again. Steed and Paxton. Amelia and Wade. Mitchell and Corina. The love that filled this room brought tears to my eyes.

Then I felt his arms around me, and I knew. It wasn't because my heart had never felt this way before. It wasn't because every time I was around the man I wanted to strip him naked and ride him for hours.

It wasn't any of that.

It was the way he looked at me. The way his eyes seemed to take on a completely new look when he gazed at me. It was the way he held my hand. The way he kissed me passionately, yet somehow soft and sweet.

"You're lost in thought, my sweet Waylynn."

His voice was like a blanket wrapped around my body on a cold winter night.

I had no idea what made me utter the words, but I knew they were right. I felt them deep within my soul as the song "Unforgettable" started playing.

My voice was low and soft as I wrapped my arms around his neck. I lifted on tippy toes and whispered, "I love you."

For as long as I live, I'd never forget the smile on his face. His fingers dug into my hips as he pulled me closer.

"You've just made me the happiest man on Earth, Waylynn Parker." He pressed his lips to mine. We kept it sweet and innocent, remembering my father and brothers surrounding us. He drew back and leaned his forehead against mine.

"I love you too."

Someone pulled on my sweater, causing me to look down. Chloe stared up at us with those big blue eyes.

"Aunt Meli told me to come over here and ask what y'all are whispering about." Her hand came up while she talked. "Well, really she told me to sneak over and listen to what you were saying, and I'm supposed to see if you used the..." She hid her mouth with her hand. "Love word."

Jonathon bent down and looked Chloe in the eyes. "You go back and tell your Aunt Meli that she needs to work on her little spy not spilling her secrets."

Laughing, I bent over and kissed Chloe on the cheek. "I love you, Chloe Cat."

Chloe's cheeks turned pink. "I love you too, Aunt Waylynn!" And like that, she took off to Amelia.

Jonathon stood. "She obviously didn't hear us, or she'd be running around the house ratting us out."

I folded my arms and stared at my sister, who raised her wine glass. "Remind me to never let Chloe Parker in on a secret!"

Wrapping his arm around my waist, Jonathon agreed.

"All right, y'all, it's time for dinner!"

"When in the world did your mom have time to prepare dinner?" Jonathon asked.

"She didn't cook. This is the one time of year she has someone come in and cook up a dinner so that she can spend time with us. It's usually on decoration night and Christmas Eve. Momma likes to spend time with the family and the idea of being in the kitchen the whole time doesn't thrill her."

"Makes sense to me."

As we started toward the kitchen, the front doorbell rang.

"I'll get it," Tripp said. He stopped abruptly as he walked by us. "Holy fuck."

"What's wrong?" I asked, turning to look out the window. You could see the front drive perfectly from the family room. The old truck parked behind Tripp's was easily recognizable. So was the woman getting out of it.

Covering my mouth slightly, I whispered, "What is she doing here?"

"Who?" Jonathon asked, looking at a stunned Tripp and then back out the window. "Who is she? I don't see anyone."

Looking at Jonathon, I softly said, "Harley."

"Oh. Shit."

I turned to Tripp to say something, but our mother called out. "Are you getting the door, Tripp? Waylynn, Jonathon, come eat dinner."

All three of us spun around to face my mother.

"Yes, I'm getting the um…the…"

"Door?" I finished for him.

"Waylynn needs something out of the truck. Come on, sis."

Tripp pulled my arm as he dragged me toward the front door. I reached out for Jonathon's help, and he shook his head.

"You're on your own."

My mouth dropped. "You just said you loved me, Turner! Now you're leaving me?"

He winked before turning and heading to the kitchen.

"Tripp Parker, why are you dragging me into this?"

He looked scared to death. "I can't talk to her alone, Waylynn, and Mom can't find out she's here. If she does you know she'll invite her in."

"Just see what the girl wants and send her on her way."

"What? The last time she talked to me she told me she'd met another guy. I'm pretty sure this conversation ain't gonna be that easy."

I chewed on my lip. "That's true."

The doorbell rang again. Tripp and I headed to the door as I yelled, "We got it!"

"Jesus, Waylynn. A little louder next time. I'm not sure the entire city of Austin heard you."

"Hey, if we don't answer this door soon, Mom will be answering it."

Tripp took a deep breath with his hand on the knob.

"Just do it. It's like pulling a Band-Aid off."

Jerking the door open, Tripp and I stood there like statues to face Harley Carbajal. She was just as beautiful as I remembered her. Her long black hair was pulled up into a ponytail and she wore jeans, cowboy boots, and a T-shirt that said I love dogs. I couldn't help but smile.

I could feel Tripp tense next to me.

Clearing my throat, I figured someone needed to speak. "Harley, fancy seeing you here. What brings you by?"

She smiled and stepped closer to me to give me a hug. "Way-lynn, it's wonderful seeing you! I heard you're opening a dance studio. That's amazing. The town will surely love that."

"How would you know?" Tripp asked. "You don't live here. Don't you remember? You didn't want to settle for a small town like Oak Springs?"

Oh, hell. Tripp had just word-vomited and I was incapable of stopping it.

Then he went in for the kill. "Or was that just because you were cheating on me and fucking a city slicker?"

I took a step back. "Okay, well, I'll be going…"

Grabbing my hand, Tripp kept me rooted to the spot.

"I guess I deserve some of that," Harley bit back. "I had no choice but to come to your folks' place. I knew you'd be here tonight."

"Wait, you came here knowing we would all be here? To do what?" I asked. Now I was mad. Why would she see Tripp for the first time in front of the entire family?

"I wanted to talk to Tripp."

"You come here when you know I'm with family? So I don't make a scene, Harley? If I wanted to talk to you I would have returned the messages you left at my office all week."

"You won't let me explain. The least you could do is—"

I held up my hands. "Whoa! The least *he* could do? I'm sorry, are you forgetting who broke up with whom? You met another person at college and dumped my brother with the stupid-ass excuse that you didn't want to settle in Oak Springs. And you think he needs to do anything for you? You've got some nerve, Harley."

Glancing down, she nodded. "I guess you're right on that point, Waylynn."

When she looked back up, her eyes were filled with tears. I turned to Tripp and willed him to be strong.

Do not break for her! Make her earn back your trust, Tripp Parker! Right now her trust level is zero, so do not fall for this nonsense.

"I figured with me moving back to Oak Springs after the holidays, it was probably a good idea that we talked and maybe we could be friends?"

I huffed. *Please. You want back in my brother's pants.*

"I'm sorry, Harley, but I don't think we have anything to discuss right now. I'm with my family, and they're waiting on us for dinner."

She nodded. "I understand. Can we at least have coffee once I get back in town and settled? I'd like to explain things a bit more to you."

Tripp looked at me and I rubbed the back of my neck, silently telling him no. It had been our silent communication since we were little. A way to "talk" to each other when we got in trouble.

"I'm not sure. I'll give you a call after the new year."

Harley didn't seem too surprised that Tripp had turned her away. "Okay, thanks. Hope you and your family have a Merry Christmas and a happy New Year." She turned to walk away then stopped and faced us again.

"For what it's worth, walking away from you was the hardest thing I've ever had to do and the biggest mistake of my life. One

I've regretted since the moment it happened. I hope you believe that."

Okay, that one tugged at my heart strings. *Tugged*...but didn't pull. It did pique my curiosity though. It actually sounded like she had no choice but to leave Tripp. I gave her a smile as I shut the door and said, "Have a good day, Harley, and tell your parents we said happy holidays."

Tripp stared with a dumbfounded look. "You totally shut the door in her face when she was saying something important."

"No, I didn't. She was turned slightly and had started to walk away."

"Waylynn, that was sort of mean!"

Grabbing my brother by the arms, I gave him a good shake. "Tripp Parker, don't you dare forget what that woman did to you. Just because she shows up looking all hot and grown up with breasts I would kill to have..."

He jerked his head back. "Gross...mental image alert."

"You have to be strong. Listen, Harley hurt you, and yes, she probably realized her mistake and her pride got in the way of crawling back to beg for forgiveness. That doesn't make what she did okay. She has to earn your trust, Tripp. She cheated on you... Don't forget that just because your dick wants to stand at attention when she's in proximity."

He nodded.

"I get that she was the love of your life, but take things slow. Let her know that she can't walk back into town and pick up where she left off. As a matter of fact, I think you need to go out on a few dates with other women. Let her know you haven't been pining away all these years."

"You think Mitchell would let me borrow Corina?"

Hitting him on the chest, I rolled my eyes. "Stop it! There are plenty of women in Oak Springs who would kill at the chance to date you."

"I've probably slept with most of them."

I rolled my eyes. "Come on. Let's go eat before Mom sends out a search party."

Tripp let out a sigh. "Maybe you're right. I need to proceed with caution."

"Of course I'm right. I'm always right and why you boys won't just admit it is beyond me."

As we walked into the dining room, Tripp chuckled and said, "Poor Jonathon."

CHAPTER 23

Waylynn

I walked back and forth, wringing my hands as I waited for the open house to begin.

"I have the refreshments set up in the lobby, and Paxton put out the information fliers."

Looking up, I forced a smile. Amelia returned one. "Don't be nervous."

"What if no one comes? What if this was all a bad idea, and I just dumped thousands of dollars into a dance studio that no one wants to bring their kids to?"

Placing my hands on my stomach, I moaned. "Oh God! What if this whole thing tanks?"

Amelia laughed. "Look at you freaking out! I don't think I've ever seen you freak out before, Waylynn."

"Well, take a good look 'cause this is what it looks like!"

She laughed. "Calm down. The place looks amazing. Jonathon did a great job."

I stopped walking and looked at her. For the first time today, I took a deep breath that actually settled my heartbeat.

"He did do a great job, didn't he?"

"Yes, he did. Please stop worrying because you're even making me nervous."

"Ugh! I can't help but be nervous. This is huge! Huge!" Spinning around, I walked to the large picture window and stared into the courtyard. Amelia placed her arm around me.

"I remember being little and waiting for you to finish your dance classes. I loved watching you through the windows."

"Why didn't you ever get more into dance? You certainly had to be dragged to enough dance recitals and classes."

She grinned. "I don't know. Maybe because it was your thing and you were so good at it. I remember hearing the other moms telling our mom how talented you were."

Facing my sister, I took her hands in mine. "You didn't dance because I danced?"

"No, I didn't dance because it wasn't my thing. Writing was. For as long as I can remember all I've ever wanted to do was write. You danced, and I wrote little stories in my journal while we waited for you."

Smiling, I squeezed her hands. "I'm so proud of you, Meli. I hope you know that. I don't think I say it nearly enough, but I am truly proud of the amazing young woman you've become. You reached for your dream and snagged it like the Parker woman you are."

She chuckled. "Thank you. That means a lot to me. And I'm proud of you and everything you've done to get to where you are today."

The light knock on the door had us both turning to see Jonathon standing in the doorframe. He was holding a giant bouquet of roses.

"Oh my gosh, you didn't have to do that, Jonathon," I said, making my way over to him.

"Jonathon, those are stunning!" Amelia gushed.

"I hope so. I tore up my hands cutting them from my mother's garden."

My heart melted. Everything seemed to be going so amazingly, especially since we had declared our love for each other last week at my parents' house.

"I love them." I reached up on my toes and kissed him gently on the lips. "Here, I'll put them in the vase I had the fake flowers in. These will look ten times better."

Jonathon handed the flowers to Amelia. "Thanks, Meli," I said.

The second she shut the door, Jonathon had me in his arms kissing me. I was instantly lost to him.

"I want you, Waylynn," he whispered against my lips.

"Here?" I gasped. "Now?"

His hand went up my skirt, slipped into my panties, causing me to let out a moan.

"We can be fast."

My body trembled. "Lock the door."

His smile nearly blew me away. It was sexy as hell: my weakness.

After locking the door, he picked me up and set me on top of my desk. Pulling out his phone, he started up some music.

"This is gonna be fast, baby."

The pull in my lower stomach grew by the second. I knew that the moment he slipped into me I was going to fall.

With shaking hands, I unbuckled his belt and unzipped his jeans. His dick sprang free, and I licked my lips. When he took himself in his hand, I let out another moan.

"Touch yourself, baby. Tell me when you're wet and ready."

I let out a nervous chuckle. "Oh, I'm pretty damn sure I'm wet and ready."

Doing as he asked, I slipped my fingers inside and closed my eyes. "Oh God."

The next thing I knew, he was pulling my hand away and slamming into me, causing me to let out a moan that I'm sure could be heard throughout the town square.

He buried his face in my neck. "Shh, you have to be quiet. Tripp and Cord are here."

My eyes snapped open. "What!"

He laughed and slammed back into me. The thrill of what we were doing sparked a flame inside.

With a hushed voice, I commanded him to give me more. "Harder!"

Gripping my ass, he did as I asked.

I was on edge, about to fall into a beautiful orgasm.

"Waylynn, baby, I can't hold off much longer."

"So. Close," I whispered. "Harder! Fuck me, Jonathon!"

He picked me up and carried me to the back of my office, against the wall. It was exactly like our first time and the irony hit me all at once as he had given me all that I asked for.

Dropping my head, I tried like hell to keep it all in while my orgasm hit me like a brick wall.

"You're fucking squeezing my cock."

That was it. I buried my face into his neck and whimpered as my body unleashed a pleasure I'd never experienced before in my life.

Jonathon let out a low moan as I felt him release into me. When he finally stopped moving, we stood there, still connected.

"Marry me, Waylynn."

Drawing back, I stared at him like he had lost his mind.

"What?" My chest heaved up and down from our fuckfest.

"Marry me."

"But we've just started dating!" I said, a small laugh slipping from my lips.

"I don't care. I want to spend the rest of my life making love to you."

Running my fingers through his dark hair, I smiled. "You know what we just did was pure fucking."

"And you loved it."

I nodded. "My God, I did! It was thrilling."

He laughed. "It was dangerous! For me!"

"Are you being serious, Jonathon?"

Slowly pulling out of me, he reached for the tissue box on my desk. Dropping to his knees, he lifted my leg and gently began wiping me clean, and I knew this man was the only one I ever wanted to kiss me. Touch me. Make love to me.

Once he was finished, he adjusted my panties and dress before getting himself tucked back into his pants.

"I've never been more serious about anything in my life. I knew the moment I laid eyes on you that you were the woman I've been waiting for. The one I want to grow old with in rocking chairs on our front porch."

Wrapping my arms around his neck, I buried my face against his body.

"We don't have to tell anyone. Let's just go do it."

Drawing back, I felt a tear slip from my eye. Jonathon wiped it away. "Will you do me the honor of taking my last name and spending the rest of your life being a pain in my ass?"

My teeth sank into my lip as I nodded and whispered, "Yes."

The knock on the door startled us both.

"You better not be getting it on in there, you bastard!" Cord shouted.

Jonathon's brows lifted, and I covered my mouth to keep from laughing. He quickly walked to the door and opened it. Cord walked in and looked around.

"I was trying to have a private dance with my girl."

My stomach dropped.

Jonathon Turner just asked me to marry him, and I said yes!

"Well, wrap it up, Waylynn," Cord said. "It's almost time. Mom and Dad just showed up."

The nerves came back. Jonathon's little fuckfest had helped me relax for all of two minutes.

Reaching for my hand, Jonathon guided me out of the office as Cord followed. Standing in the middle of the dance floor was my entire family: my parents, Aunt Vi, and every single one of my siblings. Tears fell like a dam had been broken as I covered my mouth and sobbed.

"Told ya she would cry!" Chloe yelled.

Pointing to my niece, I shook my head. "You little stinker!"

Steed put Chloe down, and she rushed over to me. She was dressed in her dance clothes and ready to go.

"I want to be your first student!"

My heart melted. "You'll be my favorite student."

When her arms wrapped around my neck, I closed my eyes and held her tight.

"I love you, Aunt Waylynn, and you're going to kick butt."

Squeezing her tighter, I replied, "I love you the most, kiddo."

I let go of her, and she ran over to the middle of the dance studio and started to run in circles.

"I can't believe y'all are here. Thank you!" I said as I made my way down the line of family, kissing and hugging each one.

When I got to Trevor, I laughed. "Just so you know, this is not the place to pick up women. They're pretty much all going to be married with kids."

Tossing his head back, Trevor laughed. "Damn, here I thought it was new meat!"

"Trevor Parker!" our mother said, hitting him on the back of the head.

"It's almost time! Okay, I need everyone to be in your spots."

"Spots?" I asked.

Amelia winked. "Yep. Everyone has a station. Steed and Paxton are in the ballet room with Gage and Chloe."

Chloe beamed. "I'm going to show them the ballet moves you've taught me."

I looked from Chloe to Amelia. "Oh, that's just brilliant."

"I minored in marketing. I've got this shit."

Laughing, I shook my head and motioned for her to keep talking.

"Mom and Dad are behind the lobby desk ready to sign people up. Cord, Mitchell, Corina, and Tripp are ready to give tours."

"And Trevor?" I asked, waiting to hear the response.

"His job is to flirt with the women."

I nodded. "Right. Just let him do what he does best!"

We both started laughing. "Good call." She said.

"What do you need me to do?" Jonathon asked.

"If you can help me keep the drinks and food stocked, I think that will be it."

"It's time! It's time!" my mother cried out.

I took in a deep breath and slowly blew it out. Jonathon pulled me into his arms.

"It's going to be great. Please, don't stress. When you stress, I stress. And if you break out into tears again, I'm afraid my man card will be stripped from me by your brothers 'cause I'm goin' to bawl, too."

Laughing, I buried my face into his chest before looking into his grey eyes.

"You've got this."

With another deep breath, I blew it out and replied, "I've got this. Even if we have five people sign up today, I'll be happy!"

He gave me another kiss and stepped out of my way.

"Okay, y'all! This is it!"

I raised the shades and was stunned at what I saw before me.

"Holy. Shit," Amelia and I said at the same time. There was a line of people standing outside the dance studio.

"Is that old lady Hopkins standing next to Mrs. Johnson?" I asked.

"Don't worry, Mrs. Johnson won't let her cause any trouble," Amelia added.

"Open the door, sweetheart!" my mother called out.

With shaking hands, I unlocked the door, forced a steady voice and welcomed everyone in.

I greeted them before Amelia and Jonathon took off and started telling them where to go, where the bathrooms were, and to help themselves to drinks and snacks.

My heart was racing as more and more families came in.

Old lady Hopkins stopped in front of me and gave me an indifferent look before she finally spoke. "I'm going to check this place from top to bottom!"

I motioned for her to come in. "You go right on ahead, old...I mean, Mrs. Hopkins."

Everything was going amazingly. Mom and Dad were busy the entire four hours of the open house. More people had signed up than I could have imagined. I was going to have to hire two more instructors before we officially opened in January.

Tripp walked into the lobby with a mom and her daughter. I had noticed he was with them earlier, giving a tour of the facility. I knew I had seen the mother before but couldn't put my finger on it. When Tripp's eyes caught mine, he smiled. I waved and watched him walk over to Mom and Dad as she signed her daughter up.

Amelia stood next to me and sighed. "Well, that was a very successful open house. Nearly everyone is gone, except for this mom and her daughter, and some friends of Steed and Paxton's. Their daughter goes to school with Chloe. They're in the ballet room talking."

I nodded. "Do you know who is with Tripp?"

"Yeah, she's new in town. She owns the boutique store that opened across the square."

"Oh, right. It opened right before Thanksgiving. We were in there on our girls' shopping trip. That's where I've seen her."

"She's been here for nearly two hours. Let me add that Tripp has been the only one to show her around. They were in the ballet room for the longest time talking while her daughter played with Chloe. She's a couple years younger than Chloe, from what Paxton told me."

My interest was piqued. "Huh, is she single?"

With a chuckle, Amelia replied, "Of course she is. Why else do you think our brother has been on her tail since the moment she walked in? I think he's smitten."

Turning to Amelia, I said, "Harley stopped by the house on decoration day. That's who was at the door. She wanted to talk to Tripp, have coffee with him after the holidays."

My sister's jaw dropped. "What?"

"I told Tripp not to be stupid and let her walk back into his life. I suggested he go on some dates."

We turned back to look at Tripp and the mom. "Well, let's hope he isn't using this lady as a means to make Harley jealous."

I shook my head. "Tripp isn't that way. He wouldn't do that. Look at how he stares at her. I think he's actually into this girl, and by *into* her, I mean more than just a one-night stand."

Crossing our arms over our chests at the same time, we both said, "This should be interesting."

CHAPTER 24

Jonathon

Waylynn rushed into the living room and shoved a fork in my face. "Taste this!"

Pulling back, I looked at the strange food on the end of it. "What is it?"

"It's lasagna!"

"It is?"

"Well, meatless lasagna."

My eyes lifted to look at her. "Why would you make meatless lasagna? That's gross."

"Because we're going to Mick and Wanda's house later today and Angie doesn't eat meat."

Mick and Wanda were Wade's aunt and uncle. Wade and Amelia tried to go often to visit them and the kids.

"A veggie eater, huh?"

She nodded. "Hence the veggie lasagna. Now, taste it and tell me if it's good."

Grimacing, I closed my eyes and opened my mouth. After a couple of bites, I lifted my brows and stared at Waylynn.

"Well?"

"It's actually really good."

She fist pumped. "Thank goodness. I've made two lasagnas since it will be fourteen of us."

"Fourteen!"

With a chuckle, she headed into the kitchen and I followed. "Remember all the Christmas presents we bought for the kids they foster?"

"Yeah, but I didn't realize they had that many kids. So, they have eight?"

She nodded. "When Amelia met them, they had twelve kids, but four were adopted. Wade said his aunt was heartbroken, but they went to amazing families."

"Wow, it's so amazing that they do that."

"I know."

I picked up a tomato that was in a giant salad and popped it into my mouth. "Do they have kids of their own?"

"I think two of them are theirs. A girl and a boy."

"That's pretty awesome."

She looked over her shoulder at me and grinned. "I think so too. To open their home and hearts like that to these kids…it warms my heart."

The doorbell rang and Waylynn motioned for me to answer it. "It's Amelia and Wade, I'm sure."

Opening the door, I smiled. "Hey, y'all. Come on in."

Wade shook my hand as he walked in. "Thanks so much for coming along with us to drop off all these gifts."

Waylynn had offered to help Amelia Christmas shop for the kids, and I don't think I'd ever had so much fun in a damn toy store.

"No problem at all. Waylynn and I had fun shopping for the kids."

Wade laughed. "Hell, don't get me started. Amelia spent a small fortune even after Wanda told her not to go crazy. I guess Amelia split the list with Waylynn."

"That was only for half the kids?" I asked.

"Yes! I'm not looking forward to the day we have children. My wife is going to spoil them."

Leading Wade into the living room, I pointed to the bar. "Want a drink?"

He shook his head as he sat on the sofa.

"Speaking of children, when are you Amelia going to pop out a baby or two?"

"I don't know. We talked about waiting another year, but we're open to changing our minds. It's hard to be around Chloe and Gage and not want one of your own."

"Tell me about it. Steed makes being a dad look damn easy too, and I know it's not."

"It should be fun to see Mitchell become a dad."

Laughing, I leaned forward. "Dude, Cord and Trevor? I can't wait until the day some woman knocks those two on their asses."

Wade agreed. "Hell, that is going to be fun."

"What's going to be fun?" Amelia asked, walking in and carrying a tote bag.

"When the love bug finally hits Cord and Trevor."

Amelia grinned. "Yes! That will be amazing."

Standing, Wade took the tote from Amelia. "Any more things to carry?"

"Two more bags. Waylynn said you already took the presents out to your truck?"

"Yeah, the back seat is piled high so I'm afraid we're going to have to take two vehicles."

Wade let out a gruff laugh. "Dude, you can't fit anything else into the backseat of my truck. This stuff is going to have to go on the floor."

Waylynn called out, "Okay! I've got everything packed up! Let's go! I'll lock up," she added over her shoulder as she grabbed her purse and another bag.

We were soon on the road and headed to San Antonio. I jumped when a crackling sound came from next to Waylynn.

"Testing. Testing one, two, three."

Waylynn giggled and grabbed a walkie-talkie from her purse.

"This is My Little Pony. I hear you coming in strong Princess Jasmine."

What in the fuck?

"My Little Pony?" I asked.

"Yeah, it's our code names. Yours is Flynn Rider, and Wade's is Kristoff. You know, from *Tangled* and *Frozen*."

"Oh, now wait a minute! Flynn Rider? Are you kiddi—"

I was interrupted by a loud scream. "Stop the truck!"

I didn't even think twice as I put the brakes on and pulled over.

"CODE GREEN!" Waylynn screamed into the walkie-talkie. "I repeat. Code green!"

She was out the door before I put the damn truck in park. Waylynn took off down the street, waving her hands for the other cars to watch out.

"What in the hell is she doing?" Wade asked, his face drained of all color. "You slammed on the brakes and then Waylynn's voice was screaming in my truck."

"You're lucky you didn't hit him, Wade!" Waylynn yelled.

Poor Wade. He looked lost. "You mean to tell me you haven't been on a turtle rescue mission with Waylynn yet?"

He stared at me like I was the one who had gone mad.

"Oh my God! He's peeing!" Amelia shouted.

Wade watched as Waylynn crossed the street with the turtle while her sister held up her hands to the car that had pulled to stop.

Amelia pointed to the cowboy sitting behind the wheel of the Ford truck. "That's right, mister. We are on a turtle lifesaving mission here."

"Are they fucking crazy?" Wade asked.

"They're Parker women. They give crazy a new meaning."

Waylynn set the turtle down, gave Amelia the thumbs up, and shouted, "All clear!" Waving the truck on, Amelia stepped out of the way. As Waylynn came walking back to us, she high-fived her sister.

"This is my sixth experience with this. After the second, I learned to put hand sanitizer in my truck."

Wade looked at me. "Good move."

I held the bottle of sanitizer up, and he laughed.

"You almost hit him, Wade!" Waylynn scolded as she walked up and took the hand sanitizer and then handed it to Amelia.

"Yuck, I forgot he peed."

"I nearly ran into the back of Jonathon!"

Waylynn shrugged and slapped Wade on the side of the arm. "Don't tailgate, buddy."

And just like that, she headed back to my truck.

"I'm taking the lead now!" Wade stated as he climbed into his truck. Amelia wore a huge grin as she looked at me.

"What?"

"Oh, nothing. Nothing at all."

She rounded the front of the truck and got in. Shaking my head, I ran my hand through my hair and mumbled, "Parker women."

Five hours later we were sitting on the back porch of Mick and Wanda's house. A few of the kids had gotten ready for bed and were in their rooms. The older ones were in the living room playing video games.

"Are all the kids living here now adopted by y'all?" I asked.

Wanda's face lit up. "Yes. The last adoption was finalized a few weeks ago."

"It must be rewarding to be able to give these kids a loving home."

"It's one of the greatest gifts God has given us, besides our own two children. We don't look at them any different. They are all so loved."

A warmth filled my chest. "It's obvious."

Wanda scrunched her nose up. "I'm glad." She clapped her hands as if giving the signal it was time to change the subject. "So, Waylynn, Amelia tells me you own your own dance studio and that you used to be a professional dancer."

I took Waylynn's hand and smiled. I was so proud and happy for her.

"I've danced since I was about two years old. Went off to college in New York and ended up with the New York City Ballet. It was an amazing experience. I knew deep down I wanted to open my own studio some day, and when I moved back to Oak Springs it seemed like the perfect time."

"And how is it going?" Mick asked.

"We had an open house a couple weeks back and had about seventy students sign up, which is amazing for a small town like Oak Springs. I'll teach ballet, tap, jazz, and hip hop along with three other teachers I've hired. I'm trying to talk a friend I went to college with in New York to move to small town Texas and teach acro-gymnastics floor work for me."

"How exciting!" Wanda said.

Waylynn nodded. "It is."

"What does the Parker family do on Christmas Eve?" Mick asked.

Amelia and Waylynn glanced at each other and grinned.

"Christmas in our house is sort of a huge affair. On Christmas Eve we open one gift from our parents and then have the big traditional meal. Christmas day is all about the breakfast."

Wade laughed. "What is it with you southern folks and your breakfast?"

Glancing at me and laughing, Waylynn asked, "What does your family do?"

"Not breakfast!" I laughed. "It's usually wake up and do presents and then a big lunch and football games after that."

Mick and Wade held up their hands for me to slap. "Yes!" Wade added.

"What about y'all, Wanda?"

"Christmas Eve is when we do the big family dinner. The kids get involved and each one has a job to do. After dinner, we clean up and watch movies. Mick and I pick one and the kids get to pick two."

Waylynn snuggled in next to me. "I love that tradition. What movie do you normally pick?"

"It changes each year. This year, it's *Miracle on 34th Street*."

"I love that movie!" Amelia squealed.

"I've never seen it," I said.

All eyes were on me.

"Jonathon Turner, you've never seen *Miracle on 34th Street*?" Waylynn asked in horror.

"No," I replied with a chuckle.

"Tomorrow night we're watching it at my folks' place. Mom and Dad will love that idea."

Kissing her on the forehead, I replied, "Sounds like the perfect Christmas Eve."

CHAPTER 25

Waylynn

Christmas Eve was blissful at my parents' house, and the evening ended with everyone watching *Miracle on 34th Street*. Christmas morning was even better. Waking up to the man I loved gently kissing me all over my body was like a present in itself.

When he slowly made love to me I declared it the best Christmas morning of my life.

"You about ready, Waylynn?" Jonathon called from the living room. I took one last look at myself in the mirror and grinned. The lace bodice I wore was white with delicate-looking snowflakes hanging from the body. The red, flared, satin skirt hugged my waist and fell to the floor. The small amount of stomach that peeked through would have Jonathon going crazy all day and the thought made me giddy with happiness.

"I'm almost ready! Just need earrings!"

Slipping on my white flats, I grabbed a pair of snowflake earrings and put them on as I walked down the hall. Jonathon was standing on the back porch, looking out over the hill country and talking on the phone.

I walked up to the partially open sliding glass door.

"I'm not sure why you're calling me, especially on Christmas morning."

Stopping short of the door, I paused.

Jonathon let out a frustrated sigh. "Listen, Bethany, I've already told you I'm not interested. I'm dating Waylynn, and I'm very much in love with her so no matter what you have to say, I'm not interested."

Ugh. I cannot believe that bitch is calling my boyfriend, and on Christmas day, too!

Tapping on the glass door, I waited for Jonathon to turn around. The moment he saw me, a wide grin appeared.

"I've got to go."

He pulled his phone from his ear and hit End. Slipping it into his pocket, his eyes traveled across my body. Oh, yeah, Bethany was not a threat at all.

"Holy Christmas hotness."

"You like? Mom likes it when we dress up, and I saw this in the new little boutique on Main. You know, the one that Mallory Monroe owns."

Jonathon lifted a brow and shook his head as he made his way over to me. Bending over, he kissed me on the forehead. "Don't tell me you went into that poor girl's store to spy on her."

I gasped like I was shocked. "What ever do you mean?"

Laughing, he pulled my body against his. "I mean, Tripp asked her to dinner and all of a sudden you're shopping in her store. Seems fishy."

"Do you not see the adorable dress I have on, Jonathon Turner?"

His eyes drifted over my body again. "I see it, and it does look amazing on you."

"Well, Mallory helped me pick it out. I may have her a question or two. She knows who I am and that I'm Tripp's older sister."

"And does she also know you had motives for shopping at her store other than just buying a dress?"

"I bought three dresses."

"Three?"

"What? I like her! A lot. And she's a single mom and all of that. I felt like it was my duty to buy a few dresses. She also caught on pretty quick that I was on a recon mission to find out about her. She ended up inviting me to get an ice cream cone with her and her adorable daughter, Anna."

"So, do you approve?"

I nodded as Jonathan guided me away from the sliding glass door and locked it.

"I like her, but she's not Harley. The opposite, actually." I pointed to the breakfast casserole I had put on the island. "Will you grab that?"

Jonathon picked up the dish and said, "Maybe Harley isn't what Tripp wants, or even needs."

Sighing, I laced my fingers with his. "Maybe. It will be interesting to see where this goes."

"Just keep out of it, Waylynn. You didn't like your brothers getting into our business. Don't do the same thing to them."

I crossed my heart. "I promise I won't meddle...much."

Jonathon chuckled. "Why do I feel like that is a half-hearted promise."

"I have two concerns. One is that Tripp might lead this girl on, and that wouldn't be cool. Not when she has a three-year-old who he might be a part of our world if things progress. And my second worry is that this girl is only looking for security."

"You think that?"

Pausing a few seconds, I replied, "No. She seems pretty independent, and it's clear she's smart and knows what she's doing. Her shop is the talk of Oak Springs."

"There's a but in there."

I nodded as we walked toward Jonathon's truck. "I get a weird feeling about her. Like she's hiding something. I mean, seriously, what would make a woman like that come to Oak Springs, Texas, and open a business?"

"The town is growing a lot and the more we grow, the more tourists will come."

Jonathon opened the passenger door and held my hand as I got into the truck. He carefully made sure that my dress was tucked in before handing me the dish.

"Are you sure you're not overthinking this, Waylynn?"

Shrugging my shoulders, I frowned. "There is a good possibility I am."

He tossed his head back and laughed. "This is why I love you."

Another quick kiss and he shut the door. My heart hammered while I watched him walk around the truck. It wasn't like I had never had a man tell me he loved me, but when Jonathon said the words, it was more than butterflies in my stomach. My whole body felt it, deep into my soul.

Once he got into the truck and we took off down the gravel road that led to my parents' house, he started talking again.

"I understand, though, what you mean by Hope. She contacted me about remodeling the kitchen and bathrooms in her house."

"Really?"

"Yep. At first I thought I was wasting my time. I couldn't possibly see how a single mom who just opened a business could afford to remodel her kitchen and three bathrooms, but she gave me a letter from the bank stating she had the funds to cover the expenses."

"You mean that she was approved for a loan?"

Jonathon looked at me. "No. She actually had the cash in the bank. I mean, I get that the same thing happened with you, but hell, I knew you were married to a millionaire. This girl doesn't look like someone who just left New York City with a lot of cash in pocket. The house isn't huge. Just one of the old historical ones a few blocks from where Corina's place is. It needs updating, so I'm sure she got it for a great price. But, still…I have to admit, it had me curious."

"Huh. Well, we could always have Bethany do a story on her."

Jonathon grunted. "Yeah, I'm sorry about that. I have no idea why she called me. I haven't been in contact with her at all."

I took his hand in mine. "It was a bitch move, but I'm not questioning you about it."

"She was a bit obsessed with me for awhile. I feel like I need to tell you that, since she called today. I promise she won't be an issue for us."

Kissing the back of his hand, I replied, "Jack won't be an issue either, but I can't control his moves, like you can't control Bethany's."

"Let's not talk about the exes on Christmas. Ugh."

Laughing, I agreed. "So, later we'll go to your folks' place?"

"If you want. I told my mom I wasn't a hundred percent certain we would stop by."

"I'd love to stop by. I'm dying to see how many trees she has up!"

Jonathon chuckled. "Well, I can tell you you're overdressed for my folks' place."

"I figured. We always do a family picture, hence the reason Mom likes everyone dressed up. Normally I bring a change of clothes for afterwards, but I felt sexy in this dress."

"You look like one of Santa's sexy elves."

"Well, maybe Santa's elf has a few gifts for you on this Christmas morning."

Jonathon stopped the truck and put it in park. "Really now? Do tell, because I cannot possibly pull up to your folks' place with a hard dick."

Licking my lips, I unbuckled. "I bet I know how to fix that."

His eyes lit up. "Do show me."

Reaching to unbuckle his belt, my hands slipped down his dress pants, unbuttoning and then pulling the zipper open. "Pull those britches down and let me show you."

Jonathon quickly did as I asked.

"Your dress, Waylynn."

"Is fine."

I cupped his balls as I took him into my mouth. He let out a long hiss of pleasure as I moved up and down his shaft, sucking and licking his dick like it was my favorite lollipop.

When I moaned, he jumped.

"Fucking hell. Waylynn, I'm going to come."

One more long suck and I felt his cum hitting the back of my throat. After licking him completely clean, I sat up and smiled. His head was leaned back against the headrest with his mouth parted slightly.

"Feel better?"

"I feel like I want to return the favor."

Giggling, I got myself seated with my skirt back in order. "Oh trust me, I have big plans for Christmas night. Don't you worry, Mr. Turner."

CHAPTER 26

Jonathan

Chloe sat on the floor with a pile of presents in front of her. After Amelia and Wade passed out all the gifts, it was time for everyone to open them. In our house, it was usually a free-for-all, but Steed and Paxton wanted Chloe to open her gifts and thank us one by one. When it took five minutes for each gift, Steed nixed the idea and let Chloe have at it with her presents. Much to his and Paxton's pleasant surprise, Chloe got up and thanked each person for her gifts as she opened them anyway.

Steed stood and handed Mitchell a box wrapped in pink paper and ribbons. "This is for you, bro."

Glancing at his brother as he took the gift box, Mitchell grinned. "Yeah? Pink paper, huh? You know something I don't?"

Everyone chuckled. My eyes scanned the room as I took everything in. I was used to being around a large family, and mine wasn't very different from the Parkers. A warmth settled into my chest as I enjoyed the activity. I'd known this family for so many years, been a part of so many family functions, but this time it felt different. I felt

195

whole and happy. Not the best friend looking in from the outside, but a man loved by the woman sitting next to him.

"What in the hell, Steed!"

Snapping my head to Mitchell, I laughed when he held up a bunch of *Playboy* magazines.

"Dude! I used to sneak into your room and read those!" Cord said with a full-on laugh. He pointed to me. "Do you remember, Jonathon?"

I nodded. "You were reading them, Cord?" Laughter erupted all around. "I do remember that. Then one day they disappeared."

"That's because I stole them from Mitchell. I thought he was going to cry!" Steed announced.

"Screw you, Steed."

"Is that a bad word, Daddy? Like hell, shit, fuck?" Chloe asked.

"Yes, pumpkin. Don't repeat that word or the other ones you can't seem to forget."

As everyone finished opening their gifts, Chloe walked around the Christmas tree. "I think Santa forgot one of my gifts."

"Really? Which one?" Paxton asked. Everyone waited for Chloe to answer. My eye caught Mitchell and Corina snuggled up next to each other on one of the sofas. Mitchell had his hand resting on Corina's stomach. I couldn't help but feel a twinge of jealousy.

"It's okay. Maybe he thought I wasn't ready yet."

"My curiosity is piqued," I whispered into Waylynn's ear.

"Long story, short version, Amelia told Chloe that Santa would bring her a horse. That's what she's looking for."

"Did she get one?" I asked.

Looking up at me from where she was sitting on the floor, Waylynn winked.

Steed stood. "Well, hold on. What's this way up at the top? Looks like Amelia missed this one."

Amelia huffed as she folded her arms but still wore a smile.

"What do we have here?" Steed pulled a small black box out of the top of the tree. "It has your name on it, Chloe."

Her little blue eyes lit up, and I couldn't wait to see her face when she opened it.

"It does?" she asked. Her voice full of wonder.

Steed handed his daughter the box and sat next to Paxton. Gage was in a chair that had a bunch of toys hanging down from it, keeping him entertained.

Ripping open the package, Chloe took a deep breath and closed her eyes. When she pulled the lid off, she pulled a toy horse out of the box.

"Hmm, I think I better communicate with Santa a little better next year," Chloe said as she stared at the toy. Everyone laughed.

Steed's phone rang and he answered. "Oh, hey, Trevor. What did you find? No way! Okay, we're heading that way now."

"Trevor said he found another present when he went to the barn to check on something."

I'd never seen Chloe jump up so fast. "What is it?"

"I don't know, pumpkin. He said to go out front, so let's go."

Chloe raced to the door as we all piled out to follow her.

"She's going to be so excited," Melanie said as she and John walked hand-in-hand behind Paxton and Steed. Waylynn scooped up Gage and was holding him as we watched the scene unfold.

Standing on the porch, Chloe looked back at her father. "Uncle Trevor's not out here, Daddy."

Just then, Trevor came walking around the corner holding a lead rope with a beautiful brown and white tobiano-patterned horse on the end. He was stunning.

What happened next I don't think anyone saw coming. Chloe burst into tears and ran up to the horse screaming, "THANK YOU, SANTA CLAUS!" My heart felt like it was going to explode, especially when I turned to see Steed wiping away his tears.

"Daddy! Mommy! He's beautiful!"

Paxton was crying as she watched the gelding lower his head for Chloe to wrap her arms around him. When he lifted her slightly off the ground, I lost my battle.

"Jonathon Turner, are you crying?" Waylynn asked.

I wiped my face. "No, it's dusty out here."

Cord stood on the other side of me. "Fuck that. I'm man enough to admit that that shit got to me right here." He slapped his chest a few times while shaking his head.

Even Trevor was attempting not to let a tear fall as he dabbed at the corners of his eyes and said, "Cedar must be makin' an appearance and blooming early."

John chuckled. "Man up to it, son. Just man up to it."

"I love him so much!" Chloe shouted. "I will forever take care of Rip!"

"Rip?" everyone asked, while Waylynn busted out laughing.

Facing everyone, Chloe wore a huge smile. "Rip Turner has moved to my number one position as my future husband because he's so handsome, and if he looks like his brother…" She pointed to me. "When he grows up, he's going to be beautiful. Like my new horse. So, I have to name him Rip!"

She walked around the horse, running her hand along him. I guessed she was copying either her father or one of the other guys when they looked over the horses.

"I can't wait to ride, Rip!"

"Why does that comment make me sick to my stomach?" Steed groaned as Paxton smacked him.

I rubbed the back of my neck. "I'm going to have to have a long talk with my baby brother," I mumbled as Wade laughed next to me.

Wade glanced at Steed. "Look at it this way, Steed. She's long forgotten about me."

"I'd rather her have a crush on you than a boy her own age! She named the horse after him, for Christ's sake! Hell, I need a drink. Turner, come on. We have some talking to do."

"Me? Why me?"

"It's your brother my daughter just named her horse after. Arrangements for her to go to an all-girl private school must start now . . . and I'm thinking you have to foot half the bill."

"Steed Parker, you stop that!" Paxton cried out as she giggled.

"Come on y'all! It's time for Christmas breakfast!" Melanie called out.

Waylynn and I were finally back at her place, and I couldn't wait to get into a pair of jeans and a T-shirt. Melanie must have made us pose for over an hour for family photos.

"It was a good call on my part to wear the flats. I knew my mother was going to have us walking all over the damn countryside for the perfect photo."

I chuckled. "I can't believe we ended up back at the barn where we started."

Slipping her skirt off, she sighed. "I can. When Melanie Parker gets an idea in her head, you might as well call it a day."

My eyes traveled over her perfect legs to her white lace boy shorts. "Huh. That sounds familiar."

"Ha ha."

"I'm just sayin', the apple don't fall far from the tree, sweetheart."

Waylynn pulled her shirt off to reveal a white lace bra that showed an insane amount of cleavage. "Do we have time to play?" she asked.

Walking over to me, she lifted my shirt over my head and tossed it to the floor.

"Define *play*."

The corners of her mouth rose into a sexy grin. "Let's see. You sit on that sofa right there, and I crawl on top of you."

Her fingers unbuttoned and unzipped my pants. I kicked my dress shoes off and let her pull my pants and boxers down.

"Hmm, I'm liking the sound of this. Keep going. What are the rest of the rules?"

After she finished stripping me, she placed her hands on my chest. The warmth from her touch spread across my body. Pushing me backwards, she spoke softly.

"After I crawl on top of you, I'm going to do dirty things to you."

"I like it when you do dirty things to me."

Her teeth sank down into her lip. "Is that why you want to marry me, Mr. Turner? Because I'm good in bed?"

When I looked up as if I was thinking and pondering the reasons, she laughed and pushed me onto the sofa.

"I want to marry you because I want you to be able to crawl on top of me anytime you damn well please."

"Is that the only reason?" she asked as she straddled me, putting her weight down on my rock hard dick.

Moaning, I dropped my head back onto the cushion. She still had her panties on, but I could feel the heat from her pussy.

"Wait. What was the question again?" I asked, taking a hold of her hips and lifting up into her.

"Oh God," she mumbled as she moved her hips in a circular motion. "I am addicted to you."

Burying my face in her neck, I kissed her soft skin. "I feel the same way."

She lifted to slide her panties out of the way when the doorbell rang and we froze.

"Who in the world could that be? We just left everyone!" Way-lynn exclaimed.

"Ignore it," I whispered, pulling her back onto me.

"What if it's important?"

"They are cockblocking me. There is nothing *that* important. Answering that door could endanger the life of whoever is on the other side!"

She giggled and kissed me. "Hold on. Let me pull up the security camera."

The doorbell rang again as Waylynn jumped off me and turned on the TV, changing it to the channel that had all of the ranch's security cameras.

"It's my dad!"

"What?" I yelled as I jumped up and grabbed my clothes and ran to the bathroom as fast as I could.

Waylynn followed and said, "Turn on the shower! Quick."

The doorbell rang again.

"You want to take a shower while your father is standing outside? Do you want a death wish on my head?"

Rolling her eyes, she pushed me into the bathroom and ran to her bedroom. I shut the bathroom door, turned on the shower and crawled into the corner, waiting for him to bust through the door and shoot my ass.

I could barely hear the muffled voices so I moved to the door and cracked it open.

"It doesn't need to be taken care of now, Daddy. Honestly."

"So, has Jonathon moved in?"

I swallowed hard.

"Well, he stays here and I stay at his place sometimes."

"So, does that mean y'all are living together?"

A loud bang from the kitchen caused Waylynn to let out a yelp and me to jump.

"I guess so. Do you have a problem with that? I know this is your house."

"You pay rent each month, Waylynn. Stop saying this is my house."

"You brought it up, so I'm assuming it bothers you."

"No. It doesn't bother me in the least. What bothers me is not knowing if you're going to be living here or back near the city."

Needing to hear her response, I pushed the door open farther. Then it happened. I started to slip. In water. That was now covering the floor.

"What in the fuck?" I spun around to see the showerhead had been spraying outside of the tub the whole time.

I tried to get back to the shower and started slipping on the marble.

"For fuck's sake! Who puts marble in a bathroom?!" I yelled while my feet went out from under me, and I went down. Reaching for the shower curtain, I grabbed it to save me from an untimely death...or a trip to the hospital for a concussion. It didn't work.

The noise of that damn rod hitting the tub was like a bomb going off.

"Jonathon, are you al...*shit*!" Waylynn shouted as she ran into the room, slipped on the wet floor, and landed on top of me. Her face landing right in my junk.

"As a father, there are some things you never want to see. This. This is one of them. The garbage disposal is fixed. Next time I'll call before I come over. Merry Christmas, you two."

It took me half a second to realize John Parker had just seen me naked. On the floor in his daughter's bathroom. With her face in my no-go zone. The only thing I couldn't figure out was why she didn't jump up. She laid there, face pressed against the boys.

"Shit!" I said, helping to lift Waylynn off of me. "Are you okay?"

"Is he gone?"

I laughed. "Yes, he's gone. Why didn't you try to get up?"

Rolling onto her side, her entire body was soaking wet, and the shower was still running.

"If I had moved and looked him in the face, I would have combusted into flames and died from embarrassment." Her hands covered her face, and she started laughing hysterically. I couldn't help but join in as I crawled to the shower and turned it off. We must have laughed for ten minutes before we came to our senses.

Reaching for two towels, I wrapped one around me and handed the other to Waylynn. We sat up against opposite walls in the bathroom.

I chuckled and said, "This is something to tell the kids someday."

Her smile grew bigger. "Do you think we're moving too fast? I mean, we're living together. We've told each other I love you. You asked me to marry you, and we're sitting in a soaked bathroom after my father just saw you naked and me face planted into your twig and berries…and now we are talking kids. Are you sure about this?"

I shook my head. "I've never been more sure about anything in my life. I knew the moment I first saw you I wanted to make you my forever. I'm unapologetically in love with you, Waylynn, and I don't care who thinks it's too fast or it's wrong. I know it's right."

"Me too," she whispered. "I've never felt this way before."

"Not with Jack?" I asked, knowing I needed to hear her response for my own peace of mind.

"Not even with him. This feels much deeper. More meaningful, if that makes any sense. Jack swept me off my feet and promised me the moon and stars. You've captured my heart with your touch, your kiss, and the sweet words you whisper in my ear when you make love to me. I realize now that the lifestyle in New York was just for show, his 'love' for me never compared to what you and I have. It's so much more and I know now that it was meant to be."

"What was meant to be?"

"Us. My dream of starting a family, but not with Jack. I can only imagine doing that with you, and I'd be lying if I didn't say that sort of blows my mind, because we've only just started dating!"

"Well, if you think about it, we've been flirting for a lot longer, so the attraction was certainly there."

She grinned. "So, is this sort of a love at first sight type of thing?"

"Before my father passed, he told me the moment he saw my mother he knew she was the one. It was at a football game, and he looked up into the stands of the opposing team and saw an angel sitting there. He went over to the sidelines and started asking the football players who she was. After the game, instead of running into the lockers, he ran into the bleachers and begged for her number."

Waylynn tucked her knees into her chest and rested her chin. "Did she give it to him?"

"Yes. They went out on a date to the drive-in movies in Uvalde the next night. That's where my mom was from, originally. He'd always told us that she was his forever love from that first smile. They got married the day after they graduated. Two months after they met."

"Wow! How romantic."

I nodded. "My father loved my mother so much. You saw it in the way he looked at her when she walked into a room. Or when he was leaving to work the fields, the way he would kiss her goodbye. It was magical. That's why Mom told Rip that he was sharing her heart, because a love like that doesn't disappear. I know that sounds corny."

"I don't think it does at all. I love that you noticed their love like that."

"That's the way I feel about you. I can't imagine my life without you, and to hell with anyone who thinks we're moving too fast or that our age gap makes a difference. I love you, Waylynn, and I don't plan on stopping."

Standing, she reached down for my hand, pulling me up. "We better get ready to head on over to your folks' place. It was too nice of them to do dinner this year instead of lunch so that we could be at my folks' place this morning."

I wrapped her up in my arms. "Mom didn't mind at all. She adores you." I kissed Waylynn gently on the lips before leading her into her bedroom.

With a wink, I added, "I think we've got a few minutes to spare."

CHAPTER 27

Waylynn

"Are you nervous?"

Glancing up from my desk, I smiled at Aunt Vi standing there with a large basket.

"About?"

"Tomorrow! The dance studio officially opens, and you'll have little girls running all over here in adorable pink and black dance outfits!"

I leaned back in my chair and chuckled. "Why, Aunt Vi, are you going soft on me?"

"Just because I never had kids doesn't mean I don't like them. After all, I used to like y'all when you were little." She looked up in thought. "Although, I was forced into having to like you because you were my brother's kids, so there is always that."

Rolling my eyes, I pointed to the basket. "Did you bring lunch?"

She glanced at the basket and laughed. "Hell no. Do you think I'm that domesticated?"

"What did you bring then?"

"Booze."

"Why?"

With a loud thump, she set the basket on my desk. "Because we're going to get drunk and dance around your studio naked. Now we're just waiting on Joyce and Carol and a couple others to join in."

I nearly choked. "Come again?"

"We need to baptize this place with some good juju."

"Good juju? And getting drunk and dancing around the studio naked with your friends will do that?"

She stared like I was asking a stupid question. "Yes. It's been proven time and time again. When Joyce was about to marry her husband, we got ourselves a few cheap bottles of wine and drank them around her daddy's fire pit and chanted that we needed good juju for the marriage. That night we snuck into the reception hall of the church and danced naked. It worked. She's been married almost forty years."

Standing, I looked around. "Where's Sandra Bullock? I feel like this is *Divine Secrets of the Ya-Ya Sisterhood*! You're shitting me, right?"

Again, she stared like I was the one who was acting insane. "I don't know what in the hell you're talking about, Waylynn Parker. Asking for good juju is not a joking matter."

I couldn't help but laugh. "You're serious, Aunt Vi?"

She lifted her chin. "Of course I am."

"You and your friends dance around naked?"

"Not always, Waylynn. Only when we need to."

"Are you like sisters of the ya-ya hood or something?"

"For fuck's sake, child, what in the hell are you talking about?"

I had to cover my mouth to keep from laughing. "Aunt Vi, you've never seen that movie with Sandra Bullock and all the older women who had a secret ya-ya sisterhood?"

"I said juju, you nit, not ya-ya. I don't know what in the hell a ya-ya sisterhood is."

"You know, y'all cut your hands and press them together and swear to protect each other over a fire out in the woods."

"Holy fuck, Waylynn, what kind of weird shit do you and your friends do?"

"I didn't say I did it! In the movie they did it and the friends were always there for one another."

She stared with a blank expression. *Why do I get the feeling Aunt Vi, Joyce, and Carol somewhere along the way pricked their fingers and said some sort of vow?*

Forcing myself not to laugh, I waved it off with my hand "Never mind. We are for sure going to watch that movie, though."

"This isn't a movie. This is spreading good vibes so that your dance studio is successful and thriving!"

With a heavy sigh, I ran my hands down my face. "Aunt Vi! Why can't we just drink a toast and be done with it? Why the dancing around naked?"

"We'll have sheer robes on. Mother Earth needs to see us in our raw."

"Because that visual makes me feel so much better."

"Don't be bitchy. You aren't appreciating the sacrifices we are making for your future."

Paxton, Amelia, and Corina appeared at the door. Amelia walked in and kissed our aunt on the cheek. "You asked, and we're here."

I laughed. "Holy shit, y'all agreed to do this? Have you hit your damn heads on a brick wall?"

Paxton sat on the small loveseat. "What do you mean? Aunt Vi said she wanted to celebrate the dance studio opening tomorrow."

I stood. "By getting drunk with her friends Joyce and Carol."

"Oh, I love Joyce!" Amelia piped. "She is a hoot!"

Aunt Vi smiled big.

Putting my hands on my hips, I continued. "*And* she wants us to get drunk and dance around the studio to give it good juju."

"I love this idea!" Corina said.

"Does that mean good vibes?" Paxton asked.

Aunt Vi pointed to Paxton and said, "I knew you were my favorite."

"I wasn't finished, there's an important detail she didn't mention. She wants us to be naked, wearing nothing but sheer robes so that Mother Earth connects with us."

"The fuck?" Amelia said with a laugh. "You can't be serious, Aunt Vi. Is that what you and your friends do at night around the fire pit?"

With a half shrug, Aunt Vi replied. "Maybe. Maybe we're just getting ready to have an orgy."

Paxton and Corina lost it laughing.

"Okay, while tweedle dee and tweedle dum laugh on the sofa, I'm being serious. This is insane."

"Depends on what type of alcohol you brought, Aunt Vi," Amelia said.

My mouth fell open as I stared at my sister. "You can't be serious?"

"What? I think it will be fun. Besides, Corina drove, so we have a ride home. Jonathon can come pick you up."

"And what about Aunt Vi and her ya-ya sisterhood friends?"

"Her what?" Amelia asked with her head tilted to the side.

Aunt Vi chuckled. "We have plans to get back to my house, Waylynn darling. The boys will be by later to pick us up."

"What boys?" I asked.

She winked. "Just some friends. Don't worry your pretty little head about it."

Joyce and Carol came barreling into the office. "We are here! Let the drinking start!"

Aunt Vi opened the basket and pulled out a root beer. "Corina, this was the closest thing we could think of for you."

Jumping off the sofa, Corina rushed for the root beer like she hadn't seen one in years.

The next thing I knew, wine, whiskey, tequila, and beer were lined up on my desk.

"Take your pick, ladies. Let's get hammered, and then let's get naked!"

Lifting my hands up, I said, "Wait! Why do you have to get drunk?"

Joyce placed her hand on the side of my face. "Oh, Waylynn, honey. I know you aren't afraid of getting a little... How shall we say this? Getting a little *daring,* but if I'm going to dance around naked in my mid-fifties, then I'm gonna need to be wasted."

I had nothing to say to that. It didn't take long for Paxton, Amelia, Joyce, and Carol to get toasted. Aunt Vi could certainly hold her liquor. Even Corina seemed to be two sheets to the wind, and she was only drinking root beer!

"Aren't you going to have another drink?" Corina asked as I watched my sister and sister-in-law start stripping out of their clothes.

"No."

"Oh, come on, Waylynn! Don't you want to do something crazy for once in your life?"

I turned to face Corina. "Dancing around naked in my studio that is opening tomorrow is not how I want to start this journey!"

Reaching for the tequila, I took a long drink. "I'm nervous enough as it is."

Corina lifted her brows. "That's all the more reason to do it!"

I took another drink and shook my head. Thirty minutes later, I put down the empty bottle and stripped out of my clothes. Corina was attempting to put the sheer robe on me, but we were laughing so hard, she had to rush to the bathroom to pee.

"Ladies! It is time to give our thanks to Mother Earth!" Carol shouted.

Amelia, Paxton, and I all started giggling as Aunt Vi pointed to us.

"Now, we have to bring in our new flock. Girls, approach your elders."

I stumbled forward and turned to Amelia. "They're going to prick our fingers and make us touch blood! Watch!"

Laughing, Amelia replied, "Gross!"

"I'm not doing that!" Paxton declared.

"Shut up, girls," Aunt Vi snapped.

"Wait! Wait for me!" Corina shouted as she ran up to stand next to us. "What did I miss?"

"Aunt Vi wants our blood!" Amelia cried.

"Umm, I think I'll sit this part out."

"Corina! I do not want your blood," Aunt Vi said as she swayed on her feet.

Leaning over to Paxton, I whispered, "Is she swaying or is that me?"

"I think…it's all of us."

I nodded. "Thought so."

"Now, girls. Spit on your palms and stand in a circle holding hands."

"I'd rather do the blood," Amelia whispered as we all giggled.

"Once you join hands, Carol will offer up the chant."

The bell to the front door of the dance studio jangled and I froze. I had locked the door before everyone started getting hammered. The only person who had a key was…Jonathon.

"Oh my God! Someone just came in!" I shouted.

"What?" six other voices cried out.

"Waylynn?"

"It's Jonathon!"

"Waylynn, what's going on?"

I screamed, "We're naked! Don't come in!"

"I wouldn't mind the boy seeing me naked," Aunt Vi said with a snicker.

Jonathon looked through the windows to find us completely naked except for the sheer robes. "Holy fuck balls! This can't be happening!"

Spinning around, Jonathon covered his eyes.

"Fuck! Fuck! Fuck! I'm going to get my ass kicked repeatedly!"

He ran out the front door so fast I didn't have time to stop him.

"Why did he say he was going to get his ass kicked?" Carol asked.

I couldn't contain my laughter. My boyfriend had just seen my baby sister and two of my brothers' wives naked.

"Okay, ladies, fun times are over," I said.

"Wait. Waylynn, we didn't do the chant."

Kissing my aunt on the cheek, I replied, "Aunt Vi, I don't believe in any of that. This was fun, but now it's time for everyone to get their naked asses dressed." I pointed to Paxton, Corina, and Amelia. "And you three, go home to your husbands."

"Party pooper!" Amelia cried out as I walked through the dance studio and collected my clothes. Once I was dressed, I made my way outside to find Jonathon sitting on one of the benches that lined the square.

I sat next to him and bumped his shoulder. "Hey."

He closed his eyes. "I'm seriously scared for my life."

"Steed, Mitchell, and Wade don't even have to know."

He looked at me. "Oh no? I already know my ass is getting beat. I can't *not* tell them what I walked in on. Rather I get it over with quick than go the rest of my life looking over my shoulder, wondering when the secret might come out."

I chuckled.

Jonathon trembled. "I'm talking about seeing your Aunt Vi and her friends naked! Do you know the redhead flashed me her breasts?"

I covered my mouth and tried not to laugh. "That was Carol. She's single."

He shook his head. "What in the hell where y'all doing, Waylynn?"

"Aunt Vi and her friends are like a little mini sex cult, I think."

"That's not making this any better, just so you know."

"They have done some silly chant since they were young to bring good luck. They were trying to do it for the dance studio."

I hiccupped and covered my mouth again.

"You're drunk."

"Yep, maybe just a little bit!"

"And you were naked too. You were going along with this?"

I shrugged. "I didn't at first, but then it looked kind of fun to be dancing around for Mother Earth."

"Mother Earth?"

Nodding, I replied, "Yep."

"I don't think I want to know anymore. The less I know, the better."

Pressing my lips together, I tried not to laugh. "You interrupted us before the chant started."

The front door of the dance studio opened and Aunt Vi, Joyce, and Carol came stumbling out. To say they were loud, drunk-ass women would be an understatement.

A black limo pulled up and a guy in his late twenties got out of the back.

"Who's that?" Jonathon asked.

Aunt Vi walked up to him and smashed her lips with his. He lifted her up while she wrapped her legs around him and called out, "Come on, girls. Let's go back to my place."

"I'm guessing that's the boy Aunt Vi said would be coming to take them all home safely."

Jonathon's jaw hung open.

"Bye, Aunt Vi!" I called out as she waved, laughing as the young guy tossed her into the back seat.

"Vi, we never did the chant! The juju!" Joyce cried out.

Aunt Vi pulled her friend into the limo. "Come on, Joyce, we'll do it at my house."

We watched as the young man climbed in after the three women and shut the limo door. It pulled off and headed toward the house Aunt Vi was renting from Amelia and Wade.

Turning to me, Jonathon asked, "Juju?"

"That's the good luck for the studio."

"Good Lord. I had no idea your aunt was into that sort of thing."

The door to the dance studio opened, and Paxton and Amelia staggered out. Corina was walking behind them trying to keep them in line.

"Can y'all help me get these two over to my car? Amelia is about to fall flat on her face."

Jonathon jumped up and grabbed Amelia before she fell. He carried her over to Corina's car.

"Paxton," I cried out. "Stop singing! People are looking this way!"

"Screw them! I'm happy, and I want to sing!"

I glanced around and prayed old lady Hopkins wasn't around to see any of this.

"Come on. Get in there, Paxton," I said, softly pushing her into the backseat of Corina's car.

"I already called Steed and Wade to warn them they had some pretty toasted wives heading their way," Corina said.

I sighed. "Thanks, Corina." I was suddenly feeling very sober as I watched Amelia fall over in the backseat and start snoring.

"Be careful driving, Corina," Jonathon said from beside me.

Waving, she laughed. "I will. It was fun!"

We watched as she pulled out onto Main and headed down the road. I turned to say something to Jonathon, but he was walking into the dance studio. When I looked down the street, Bethany was approaching with Kenzie Lewis.

"Did you have a little private party that got out of hand, Waylynn?" Bethany asked. "Hopefully that won't be a common thing in your dance studio after hours."

"Bethany, knock it off," Kenzie said as she hugged me. "Hey, how's it going?"

I forced a smile. "It's good, thanks."

"God. You smell of alcohol!"

Leaning forward, I gave Bethany a good smell. "Sorry, sweetheart, that stench is coming from you. Have a good evening, ladies."

I turned and walked into the dance studio, locking the door behind me. When I spun around, Jonathon was standing there, disappointment etched onto his face.

"What were y'all doing in here, Waylynn? Do you have any idea what it looked like for all those women to stagger out of your place drunk out of their damn minds?"

"I know, Jonathon. Aunt Vi was trying to help, and I have to admit I got caught up in it. It was fun, so just let it go."

"Let it go? Let's just hope Bethany didn't see the little stunt your aunt pulled with the guy young enough to be her son."

My hands went to my hips. "Excuse me? Are you saying their age difference is a factor here?"

He rolled his eyes. "For goodness sake, Waylynn. Your aunt is old enough to be his mother. We're not talking about a few years. The last thing you want is bad press about your dance studio."

"You don't think I know that? That I haven't worked my ass off to make all of this happen? It's not like anyone walked in and saw anything."

"I walked in."

"Are you done sitting on top of your high horse?"

He closed his eyes and took in deep breath before looking at me. "I'm sorry I said anything. I only want to see good things happen for you. I'll keep my mouth shut in the future."

"That's not what I want. It's been a long day, and I'm ready to go home."

Nodding, he rubbed the back of his neck. "Do you want me to give you a ride? I'm not sure how much you drank. You were buzzing when I first got here, but you seem to be okay now."

"I drank a lot. I don't want to drive. Do you mind taking me home? I can get Steed or Mitchell to bring me back in the morning if you have things you need to do."

"No, I arranged to have the day off to be here in case you needed anything."

My chest tightened at his thoughtfulness. "Thank you."

Jonathon smiled and took my hands. "Always."

Chewing on my lip, I had the overwhelming urge to ask him to take me right then and there, but that was the last thing I needed to do. Instead, I made my way to my office and collected my things and followed him back out to his truck. The sooner I put this crazy evening behind me, the better.

Tomorrow I started a new journey in my life, and I couldn't wait to see where it would lead me.

CHAPTER 28

jonathon

I walked into the dance studio trying to balance all of the coffees. Melanie sprang into action and grabbed one.

"Thanks, Melanie! I was positive I was going to drop them."

At the front desk, I set them down on the counter. "I hope I got everyone's order right. Waylynn gave it to me before I left."

Melanie's brows pulled down. "Waylynn's not with you?"

My head pulled back in surprise. "No. She left this morning to get here ahead of everyone, after Cord brought her car back."

"I opened up this morning," Maggie said.

"What?" my heart started to pound, and I felt sick to my stomach.

Trying to hide the panic in my voice, I asked, "Has anyone heard from Waylynn?"

John shook his head. "I don't have my phone, it's in the truck. Call Steed and see if Waylynn has been back to the ranch."

I pulled out my phone and hit Steed's number.

"Hey, how's it going?" he answered.

"Steed, do you know if Waylynn came back to the ranch this morning? She's not here at the dance studio."

"No, she didn't stop by the house. I can ride over to her place and…"

I heard a commotion on the other end of the line. Someone was yelling.

"Mitchell, I can't understand you. Slow down," Steed said.

All I heard were the words *accident*, *Waylynn*, and *airlifted*. I stumbled, and Melanie reached out to keep me from falling.

"Jonathon! What is it?"

"Steed…what's going on?" I asked, my voice cracking.

"Um, hold on." He covered the phone and talked to Mitchell. It seemed like an eternity before he came back on the line.

"Jonathon, Waylynn's been in a car accident."

Melanie's cell phone rang, and John took it from her hand. He could tell from the look on my face it wasn't good news. "Mitchell, talk to me," John said.

I focused back on Steed. "Wait. What did you say?"

He cleared his throat, and I could tell he was getting in his truck. "Waylynn's been airlifted to University Hospital in San Antonio."

My entire body went cold. "W-what? Is she…is she…"

"I don't know. The state trooper who arrived at the accident called Mitchell. He said he tried to call Dad's cell but there was no answer."

My head was spinning. "Is she okay?"

"I'm on my way to the dance studio to pick you up."

"No, I need to go now."

"Jonathon, don't drive."

I stood there, frozen to the spot. *Waylynn. Please, God. Please, don't do this to me.*

Someone took my phone out of my hand and guided me out of the dance studio. It seemed like everyone was talking all at once. I heard Melanie on my phone.

"Steed, your father is going to drive. No, we'll be okay. You just drive safely."

Then came Maggie, one of the dance instructors. "Samantha and I will take care of everything here. Go, It's fine."

John was mumbling about me getting in his truck and that Waylynn was going to be fine.

The next thing I knew, I was staring out the window as John sped toward San Antonio. Melanie had called everyone in the family and was even on the phone with my mother.

Closing my eyes, I prayed the hardest I'd ever prayed in my life and made a bargain with God that I'd do whatever He needed me to do, if He would only please not take Waylynn from me.

"Jonathon. Jonathon, sweetheart, we're here."

My eyes lifted to see Melanie, standing outside the truck, urging me to get out. "We're at the hospital."

I was numb, but somehow I managed to follow John and Melanie into the hospital.

"My daughter was brought in by airlift from Oak Springs. Waylynn Parker."

The nurse nodded. "Yes, she's in surgery. Let me have Lori bring you to the waiting room. I'll let the doctor know her parents are here."

"And her husband," Melanie added.

My head snapped to look at her.

"Okay, I'll let him know you're all here."

John took my arm and pulled me over to the elevators. "We'll be on the fourth floor if you'd like to let other family members know."

Melanie smiled. "Thank you, sweetheart."

Melanie gave me a look that helped explain why she told the nurse I was Waylynn's husband, so that they would talk to me in case John or Melanie wasn't there.

We made our way to the waiting room, and Steed jumped up as Melanie rushed over to him. "Have you heard anything?"

He shook his head. "I got here about five minutes before y'all. The nurse said someone would come out and let us know what was going on."

"Do we know what happened?" I asked, finally finding my voice.

"The state trooper isn't sure if she swerved to miss a deer, or if someone might have cut her off, but she caught the rough edge of the shoulder and her car ended up off the road. It rolled a few times and went through a fence."

Melanie covered her mouth and started to cry. "When they got there…" John's voice stopped.

"Was she breathing, was she awake? Why did they airlift her?" Melanie asked.

Steed shook his head. "I don't know. That's all Mitchell knew."

We sat in the chairs and waited for someone to come out. I went over the entire morning in my head. Why didn't I drive in with her? If I had been driving maybe this wouldn't have happened.

Scrubbing my hand down my face, I dropped my forearms to my knees and stared at the floor.

Steed's voice came from my right. "This isn't your fault."

I closed my eyes and forced the tears back. "I should have driven in with her."

"It was an accident, and we're not even sure what happened."

Lifting my head, I stared into his eyes. "She told me she had a surprise later today, and she couldn't wait to tell me about it."

Steed placed his hand on my shoulder and squeezed. "She's going to tell you."

"God, I hope so."

"Mr. and Mrs. Parker?"

Melanie and John stood.

The doctor looked at Steed and then me. "I'm Dr. Frank Andes."

Melanie put her hand on my arm. "This is Waylynn's husband, Jonathon Turner, and her brother, Steed Parker."

When my eyes met the doctor's, I couldn't help but notice how sad he was.

The doctor reached for my hand and shook it before shaking Steed's, then John's.

He took a deep breath before motioning for us to take a seat. He sat too, and looked between each of us. "I'm assisting Dr. Wright in the operating room. He's the lead surgeon and has asked me to give you an update."

"Your daughter, as you know, was in a car accident. The vehicle flipped a number of times and went through a fence."

Melanie tried to contain her emotions, but a sob slipped from her lips.

"She was conscious when the first responders got there, although no one knows what caused the accident."

He looked directly at me. "She was airlifted to our hospital because she had major trauma. A piece of the fence crashed into her lower stomach."

I felt like I was about to be sick. Steed put his hand on my back, and I tried not to let my worst fears come to life.

"We were able to remove the object, but it did major damage."

Melanie was sobbing.

"I'm sorry, Mr. Turner, but we've had to do a hysterectomy with a bilateral oophorectomy on your wife. There was no other way. Even if we hadn't removed her uterus, the damage would have been so severe she would have never have been able to become pregnant, let alone carry a child. It would have most likely led to other problems further down the road. One of her ovaries was so severely damaged it had to be removed. The other was covered in endometriosis. Dr. Wright had to make the decision to leave the one ovary or remove it. After consulting with a top gynecologist in San Antonio, they both agreed it would be better to do a complete hysterectomy."

"Would she have been able to still produce eggs had you left it in?" Melanie asked.

He shook his head. "Most likely the endometriosis would have impaired her fertility."

My entire world stopped. Tears fell freely as I let his words soak in. It was clear he knew I needed a few moments. I dropped my head and took in a few deep breaths as Steed grabbed my shoulder. The pain in my chest was unlike anything I'd ever experienced in my life. I instantly felt the loss of the children we had yet to even have together. When I was finally able to speak, I focused on the doctor.

"Does she…does she know? Does she know about the hysterectomy? Was she told before the surgery?"

"No, she doesn't know. She has been under for surgery so there was no way to discuss it with her. The decision was made once we saw the extent of the damage."

Closing my eyes, I forced the bile down my throat.

Melanie's voice caused me to refocus. "Oh my God, all she's ever wanted is to have children."

The doctor gazed sympathetically at Melanie. "There is always adoption, but this is something your daughter is going to need help with, I'm sure." He looked back at me. "We've got some amazing therapists we can recommend."

Steed placed his hand on my shoulder again. The simple gesture gave me the strength I needed in that moment.

"Thank you."

The doctor nodded then said, "I'm talking about for you too, Mr. Turner."

"Th-thank you, Dr. Andes. Is she…hurt anywhere else?"

"Her wrist is sprained badly, but no broken bones."

I sat there stunned. "Her wrist?"

He nodded solemnly. "Some scratches and bruises as well, but yes. The fence was the major reason she was airlifted and rushed into surgery. There is no other internal bleeding or damage. Had the object been any higher it would have done damage to her intestines and stomach and possibly killed her."

My hand pushed through my hair. "Thank God it wasn't higher," I mumbled. As much as it sickened me to lose the possibility of kids with Waylynn, it would have been so much worse to lose her.

"Thank God it wasn't more serious," John said as Melanie nodded her head.

"As much as I hate what had to be done, it could have been worse," Steed added.

"There was no trauma to her head which is very good news. She should be out of surgery in the next thirty minutes and then in recovery for a bit before they assign her a room."

"Thank you, Dr. Andes," John said as they both stood and shook hands.

After I thanked God for not letting Waylynn die, the anger came. "I'm glad God didn't take Waylynn from us." Shaking my head, I stared at the three of them. "What I don't understand is why would He take that away from her?"

Melanie stood. "Jonathon, why don't we take a walk and get some fresh air."

I faced Waylynn's mother. "It was the one dream she had left. We both wanted a child. Why would He take it from her?"

Tears rolled down her cheeks. She took my hand.

"Please excuse us."

Dr. Andes nodded as Melanie and I walked to the elevator.

Melanie's voice made me jump. "Is there an outside courtyard or somewhere private?"

We were standing at the information desk.

"Yes, if you go out these doors and follow the light green path, it will take you to the outdoor sanctuary."

"Thank you."

I allowed her to lead me down the path. My head was telling my heart to be strong. To be prepared to help Waylynn through this, but I also felt like God had ripped a dream from me, as well.

Walking around a corner, we came to a small garden with benches. Melanie let go of my hand and wandered over to the one next to the fountain.

"I don't understand why He would do this," I said again.

Melanie sat down next to me. "He has a reason and what you need to do is let the anger out now, Jonathon, before Waylynn sees it in your eyes. Because the first thing she is going to worry about is that now that she can't have kids, you'll leave."

It felt like someone had kicked me in the gut. "What? I would never leave her. Ever."

She took my hands. "Good. That is what I want to hear from you, and I want you to promise me that no matter how tough this gets, you don't let her push you away."

Furrowing my brows, I stared. "What?"

"She's going to push you away, and I need you to be prepared for that."

"Wh-why would she push me away?"

Melanie looked down and wiped her tears away. "Tell me why you love my daughter, Jonathon."

I sighed. "Where do I start? She loves me, she makes me feel whole, she's my entire world. The reason I feel like God put me on this Earth. She makes me laugh. Makes me happier than I've…than I've…"

Burying my face in my hands, I started to cry. Melanie wrapped her arms around me and held me tight.

"She makes me happier than I've ever been before. She scares the shit out of me."

We both chuckled.

"She is the only woman who will have my heart. There is nothing I wouldn't do to make her happy."

Withdrawing, she smiled. "I am one-hundred-percent positive she feels the same way, but the first thing she's going to think is that she can't give you a child."

"I don't care."

"Maybe not right now, but in her mind, you will at some point down the line. I want you to be ready for that when it happens and fight…fight harder than you've ever fought before."

I nodded. Deep down I knew we were both going to have to work through this. Right now, my only concern was Waylynn. Everything else would have to work itself out. I knew if we had each other, we would be able to make it through anything.

"We're going to be okay. We'll be here for her through all of this and do whatever it takes to help her heal physically and emotionally"

She gave me a weak smile just as the rest of the Parker family showed up.

They rushed over to us, and I whispered, "We'll be okay."

CHAPTER 29

Waylynn

Opening my eyes, I glanced around the room. Jonathon was sitting in a chair with his head back, eyes closed. I wasn't sure if he was awake or sleeping. To my left, my mother sat next to my bed, her head resting in her hand and her eyes closed.

Taking a deep breath, I looked at Jonathon again. "Jonathon…" I whispered.

His eyes opened, and he immediately came to my side.

"Hey, baby. I'm right here."

"What happened?" I asked, my mouth feeling so dry.

"Waylynn, my sweet baby!" my mother said, drawing my attention back to her.

"Momma."

"Let me go let the nurses know you're awake." She glanced at Jonathon and nodded.

"I'm so thirsty."

She stood and kissed my forehead. "I'll get some water, sweetheart."

Jonathon took my hand and kissed the back of it while I watched my mother walk through the door.

"Are you in any pain?" Jonathon asked.

I shook my head. "I don't think so. There were two turtles in the road. Another car was passing and I tried to move over to the side to avoid them, but the road was uneven and my tire must have caught. I lost control of the car. I went off the road and the next thing I remember...I was in the car and they were trying to get me out."

A tear slipped from his eye and rolled down his cheek. He wiped it away. "Your car flipped a few times, and you went through a fence. A tree stopped you from rolling down a hill."

Everything seemed to come back to me at once.

"Blood. There was blood all over my hands, and I felt a terrible pain in my stomach."

Jonathon swallowed hard. "You had to be airlifted to the hospital here in San Antonio and they did emergency surgery."

I lifted my left hand to see it bandaged up. "Did I break my wrist?"

"No. You sprained it pretty badly, but no other broken bones."

I stared at him. "Then why did I have to go into surgery?"

Tears filled his eyes, causing him to blink several times. He held onto my hand tighter. "A piece of the fence went through the car and impaled your lower stomach."

The memory of me looking down and seeing metal sticking out of my stomach hit me hard. I swore I felt the pain all over again.

"Oh my God. I saw it...I screamed when I felt it push into my stomach. Did they do any damage getting it out? Will I have a big scar?"

Jonathon's chin quivered as he pressed his lips together. "It did a lot of damage and they had to..." His voice shook and fear rushed through my veins.

"What? They had to what?"

I could see how hard he was fighting not to get upset. Pulling in a deep breath through his nose, he slowly blew it out.

"They had to do a h...hysterectomy."

The words didn't filter into my brain right away.

Jonathon cupped my face and kissed me. "I'm so sorry, baby. I'm so damn sorry I wasn't driving that morning."

Did he say hysterectomy?

"They did a hysterectomy? On me? They did one on me?" A sob pushed from my lips as I repeated myself. "On me, Jonathon? They did a hysterectomy on me?"

He slowly shook his head. "There was no other choice. I'm so sorry."

"No. No! Why did you let them do that? Why didn't you stop them?"

"Waylynn, I didn't get to the hospital in time. It was almost an hour after the accident before I even knew you were in one. I went into town on forty-six so I could pick up the coffee. I didn't see the accident."

"You let them take away my only chance for a baby! They took that away from me! You should have stopped them!"

My body shook as I sobbed, aching for her.

"Waylynn, honey, look at me."

It was my mother begging me to look at her. All I could do was stare at Jonathon.

"Why didn't you stop them?"

Sadness swept over his face, making me wish I could take back what I'd just said. But the only thing I could think about was that my dream of becoming a mother was fading into the blackness.

Jonathon leaned in closer. "Waylynn? Waylynn, baby, please stay with me!"

His voice faded as quickly as the light did. I slipped into a slumber of peace and prayed that when I woke back up, this would all turn out to be a bad dream.

I blinked as I tried to adjust to the sunlight shining through the window. The chair that Jonathon had been sitting in was empty. An ache formed in my chest and my throat felt sore as I attempted not to cry.

When I turned my head, I saw my mother. Her head was lying on my bed.

"Momma."

Popping up, she let out a sigh of relief. "Waylynn, sweetheart."

From the look in her eyes, I knew I hadn't been dreaming when Jonathon told me about the hysterectomy.

"Where's Jonathon?"

"Cord made him go to the hotel and shower and get some sleep. He hasn't left your side in three days."

"Three days?" I asked. "What happened?"

"You passed out and the doctors said you were in shock. We've been worried sick, and Jonathon has been holding your hand for hours, begging you to wake up."

I vaguely remembered his voice, muffled through the pain.

"It's true then. They did a hysterectomy?"

She nodded. "There was no other option. They did it to save your life, and even if Jonathon had been here in time, they would have still done it."

A tear slipped from my eye. "Is he angry with me?"

Her eyes widened in horror. "No! Of course he's not."

"I blamed him. I didn't mean to."

She took my hand and kissed the back of the bandage. "He knows that. He loves you so much."

I began to cry as I looked at the ceiling. "I can't give him…what he wants, Momma. I'm…I'm broken." My body shook as I cried.

"Oh, Waylynn, my sweet baby girl. Don't you say that. Jonathon loves you regardless of if you can carry a child or not."

I shook my head. "He wants kids. We talked about how we were going to tell them stories about the two of us before we had them."

Another round of sobs came, and my body hurt like hell, but I didn't care. I couldn't stop the tears if I tried. "He wants more than one. I can't even give him that now!"

I could hear someone walk into the room, and my mother spoke to them.

"Mitchell, call Jonathon and tell him Waylynn is awake and needs him. Have the nurse come in also."

The door shut again and I turned to her. "I can't face him."

"He needs to see you, and you need to see him. Now, I want you to take a deep breath and relax."

"Momma," I said, tears building so fast I could hardly see. "I can't give him a baby. I can't have a baby!"

The nurse walked into the room, and my mother stepped away from the bed. Her hand covered her mouth as I cried harder.

"I can't give him a baby!"

The nurse spoke to me in the calmest voice as she placed a needle into the IV. "It's okay, Waylynn. *Shhh*...this will help you relax."

"I don't want to go back to sleep. Please, don't make me go back to sleep."

A warmth spread through my body and I instantly began to relax.

I felt a hand brush my hair back, and I looked to the right. "Daddy," I whispered.

"I'm here, baby girl. Daddy's here."

Smiling, I closed my eyes. "Where's Jonathon, Daddy?"

"He's almost here, darlin'. He's almost here."

"I love him, Daddy. Please tell him for me."

The room felt charged as I felt someone kiss me on the forehead.

"I'm right here. I love you, too, Waylynn."

Opening my eyes, I smiled when I saw Jonathon. He hadn't shaved and his eyes looked so tired.

"I'm not leaving, I promise."

Emptiness swept over me. I knew he meant those words, but how long would he mean them?

Jonathon leaned over and gently kissed me. As if he could read my mind, he whispered, "I'm never leaving."

"How is she today?"

I rolled my eyes and sighed loudly. It had been five weeks since my accident, and my mother and Aunt Vi still walked on eggshells around me. "You know I can hear you. I had a hysterectomy, they didn't remove my ears."

The voices lowered, and retreated. The back door opened, and Corina stepped out onto the porch.

"Mind if I join you?"

My heart nearly broke in two as I looked at her stomach, a small little pooch.

I forced a smile. "Sure, I don't mind at all. How was the sonogram?"

She sat next to me. "It was good."

Facing her, I took her hand in mine. "Please don't be afraid to talk about the baby with me. I want to hear about my future niece or nephew."

The corners of her mouth rose slightly. "Everything looks good. We could see the baby moving."

I smiled. "That's good. Did you find out the sex?"

She shook her head. "We decided to be surprised."

"Well, that would have made a fun Valentine's gift to each other."

Corina chuckled. "I guess."

I glanced down at my hands and then back to her. "I'm not jealous or angry that you're having a baby. I won't lie and tell you it doesn't make me sad, but I'm so happy for y'all."

Tears gathered in her eyes. "I'd give anything to carry a child for you, Waylynn. Anything."

I pressed my lips together. "I know. Amelia and Paxton said the same thing. They even asked me if I somehow had my eggs stored."

Corina's eyes widened in hope.

"I didn't. I only went to a sperm bank."

"Oh."

I nodded. "Anyway, have you decided on how you'll decorate the baby's room?"

"I think we are going to do baby animals. Keep the color simple for either gender."

"That's smart if y'all are going to keep it a surprise." Looking away, it took everything in my power not to tear up. Not only dealing with the emotional toll of having a hysterectomy and both ovaries removed, I was also dealing with the hormonal changes of my body basically being thrust into menopause in my thirties. I was all over the place, up one minute and down the next.

"Do you want to talk about anything, Waylynn?"

Giving her a slight grin, I shook my head. "No. I'm tired of talking about it. The counselor has been a big help, but I'm ready to move on. I want to get to the dance studio, that's my main focus right now and the only thing that matters in my world."

"And Jonathon?"

Turning away, I stared out over the Texas hills. "Mom said he's been by every day for the last week, and you won't see him. He's not giving up on you, Waylynn."

My lips trembled. "I don't have anything left to give to him."

"What about your love?"

Snapping my head to look at her, I laughed. "It's different now. It can't be the same between us."

"Hey, how is my beautiful sister and wife?"

Mitchell walked up on the porch and kissed me on the forehead, before kissing Corina on the lips.

"Y'all have plans for Valentine's dinner?"

They looked at each other, and Corina blushed. "Oh, I get it. Some hanky panky planned. Tell me you're at least taking her to dinner first."

Mitchell laughed. "I am. We're heading into San Antonio and spending the night."

A slow, dull ache pulsed in my chest. Jonathon had begged me to let him make me dinner, but I told him I was spending the evening with my parents.

"Sounds romantic."

Mitchell wiggled his brows. "I hope so."

I flashed them both a big smile. "Well, I guess I should go for my daily walk. The doctor says walking helps me heal faster."

"You're getting around good."

"Yep. Parker willpower and all."

"Tell Jonathon I said hi," Corina said as I made my way down the steps.

I lifted my hand. "I will the next time I see him."

"You're not seeing him tonight?" Mitchell called out.

I ignored him. "Have fun, y'all."

I made my daily walk down to the main barn to see Cooper. He was waiting for me when I walked inside. Letting out a laugh, I grabbed a handful of oats and made my way over to him. The other horses called out for the oats, making me laugh a little more.

"They're all jealous of your daily snack, buddy."

Cooper bobbed his head up and down. "I should be able to ride you soon."

My hand ran across his neck as he ate his oats. Leaning my head against his neck, I felt the tears build. I held them back, refusing to cry yet again.

"Jonathon called me earlier. I didn't answer."

Cooper let out a bray.

"I know. You don't have to lecture me about it. I know I need to talk to him. It's hard, though. When he's around I have to pretend I'm okay, and it's exhausting. I know he can see right through it and it makes it even worse when I see his sadness. He thinks he can't help me."

Cooper bobbed his head again, as if he understood what I was saying.

"Maybe I should call him. He asked me to marry him again a couple of weeks ago. He wanted to do it on Valentine's Day. Today. He wanted to surprise my family and plan an intimate ceremony on our ranch. I just couldn't do it."

Leaning my forehead against my horse, I let the tears fall. "I don't know what to do, Cooper. I love him so much and I feel so empty when he's not here. But I want him to be happy, and I feel broken."

A soft whine came from my horse as he took a few steps away. His eyes piercing mine.

"I can't hide out in here forever, can I?"

He took his foot and dug at the dirt.

"I'll take that as a yes."

He kept going, hitting the ground harder and faster.

"Okay! Okay! I get it. I'm leaving, but it's on you if I don't come back tomorrow for your snack."

Making my way out of the barn, I caught a glimpse of Steed coming down in the Mule with Jonathon sitting next to him. I slipped back into the barn and into Cooper's stall. I slowly slid down and sat in the corner. I knew Cooper would ignore me; I'd slept in his stall on more than one occasion.

"Corina said she was walking down here, and Mitchell said she comes down here everyday."

I could hear Jonathon sigh. "Tell me what I'm doing wrong, Steed. I'm trying to give her space, but I don't want to give her too much space. I'm trying to figure out what she needs, but every time I talk to her she acts like she's fine and tells me she's just tired. I'm going out of my goddamn mind. I go to hug her or kiss her, and she fucking flinches. God, I don't know what to do!"

Burying my face in my hands, I tried like hell not to cry.

"Jonathon, I wish I had some magical, fix-everything words for you, but I'm the worst person to give advice. I think it's clear to all of us how much you love Waylynn, and I know she loves you. My parents are beside themselves trying to figure out what to do, too. She refuses to talk to anyone, and my mom said any time your name is brought up, Waylynn starts to talk about the studio."

"She's going back to work tomorrow. The doctor gave her clearance."

"You went with her?" Steed asked. Guilt pulled in my stomach.

"Yes, but I had to find out from her mom when her appointment was. I showed up and asked to wait in the room, so she wouldn't tell me to leave."

Steed laughed. "I bet she was pissed when she saw you in there."

"That's putting it mildly. I think that's why she refused to let me cook her dinner tonight. I know she's staying back at her house now. I've been sitting outside until two in the morning, until I see her turn off her bedroom lights."

I wiped my tears away and leaned my chin on my knees, trying to breathe slowly. I wanted to stand and tell them I was there, but it was too late. I'd already eavesdropped on the conversation too much. I could hear the hurt and confusion in Jonathon's voice and it killed me. I had only one option and that was to break up with Jonathon.

Steed let out a sigh. "Damn, I wish I knew what to tell you."

"Yeah, so do I. Let's head on out. She's probably walking one of the trails. I'll try to give her a call later."

I lifted my head and strained to hear as they walked out of the barn. Once I heard the Mule start, I stood and gave Cooper a pat.

"Thanks for not outing me, boy."

He turned his back and neighed.

"Men. You all stick together, don't you?" And as I walked out of the stall, and out of the barn, I made the decision that I had to walk out of Jonathon's life for good.

CHAPTER 30

Waylynn

Dropping my phone on my desk, I glanced at my calendar. It had been seven weeks since the accident. I was back at work full-time, not teaching yet, but at least I was there. I'd missed the first month and a half of my dance studio being open and that pissed me off more than I wanted to admit. Maggie and Samantha had done an amazing job, and much to my surprise, Carrie Mills, my best friend from college, agreed to come teach gymnastics for me. She had also picked up the two and three-year-old classes since I wasn't able to teach just yet.

I heard a sound in the courtyard. Jonathon was out there with Hope. She was showing him a spin she had learned, and he was trying to duplicate it. They had stopped by to pick up her backpack for school she'd left the night before. I knew it should have made me smile, but all it did was tear another piece off my heart.

"Hey, didn't you hear me knocking?"

I discreetly wiped my tears away and faced my sister, Amelia. Plastering on a fake smile, I hugged her.

"Hi! How are you doing? To what do I owe this honor?"

Her eyes drifted past me to Jonathon and his sister, then back to me.

"Was going to see if you wanted to have lunch with me at Cord's Place."

"Umm…"

"I already asked Maggie if you had students coming, and she said there was only one class left and Carrie was teaching it."

Damn Maggie. I was going to have to have a talk with her about letting people, even family, walk back to my office.

"I've got some paperwork to do."

I could see the disappointment on her face.

"But sure, lunch sounds good."

Reaching for my purse, I peeked out the window. Jonathon and Hope had left. My stomach dropped when I realized Jonathon hadn't even come in to say hello. But I had no right to be disappointed when all I'd done for the past seven weeks was dismiss him. I followed my sister out of the dance studio and across the square to the other side.

"So, is that Irish place still planning on opening?" Amelia asked as we walked.

"Yep. There is a city council meeting tomorrow. I'm dying to watch Cord's face when he realizes the girl he bumped into that night at the bar is the new owner. It sounds like it's going to be more of a restaurant, but Tripp keeps feeding Cord stories about 'an Irish Pub' and how excited he is to have another bar on the square. He said Cord tells him to fuck off each time."

We both laughed.

Amelia pulled open the door to Cord's Place. "So, how have you been feeling?"

"Good. I'm feeling like my old self again," I lied.

She stared, and I knew she could read right through it.

As we walked into the bar I noticed the place was empty except for our entire family sitting at a table. Stopping, I looked at Amelia.

"What's going on?"

My mother stood and walked over to me with her hands out for mine.

"Waylynn, darling, we wanted to all be together as a family."

I took a step back as I let my eyes drift across everyone. The only person who wasn't sitting at the table was Jonathon.

"Why? What's going on?" I asked, knowing damn well this was about me.

"Waylynn, you never were a good liar."

I let out a gruff laugh. "Is that right?"

"You're hurting and in pain. You need to talk about it, and if you won't talk to Jonathon, you're going to talk to your family."

Swallowing hard, I faced Amelia. "You tricked me."

"You're putting off the pain, Waylynn, and we want to help you. You only went to the counselor a few times, and you need to get it out. It's eating you up inside."

"But tricking me into talking?"

"Waylynn…" Tripp started.

Putting my hand up to stop him from talking, I shook my head. "No. Y'all don't get to decide when I talk about this. I can't have kids and you all know that was my dream. What else is there to talk about?"

"What about Jonathon?" Cord asked.

I laughed and looked away. "He'll come to his senses and see he's better off with someone who can give him a family."

"He wants you, Waylynn!" Amelia practically shouted.

Tears slipped from my eyes. "I can't, Amelia. I'm not the person he fell in love with. I can't give him the things he wants…the things we both wanted so badly." I turned as a sob escaped my throat.

"Bullshit!" Trevor said, standing and walking over to me. "All he wants is you. You can have kids together. Maybe not the traditional way you wanted, but you still can."

My hand covered my mouth to muffle the sobs. "You don't understand, Trevor."

"Then tell me, goddammit. Explain it to me."

I turned away and buried my face in my hands. My mother wrapped me in her arms and whispered, "Let it out, sweetheart. You have to let the anger and hurt out."

Pulling away, I wiped the tears and glared at everyone.

"You want me to explain it to you? I can't have fucking kids, Trevor!" Pointing to the entire table, I kept going, my voice void of any steadiness as I forced the words out. "All of you can sit there and tell me it's okay, but it's not okay!" I screamed.

"Oh my God, nothing about this is okay! I cannot have kids! Ever! I will never be able to see a baby bump growing, or feel a child move inside of me. Never have my husband lovingly put his hand over my stomach and talk to our child."

Tears flowed now and I didn't care. I was actually surprised I had any left. It gutted me to see the hurt on their faces. The *pity*. My brothers wiped tears away as my father wrapped his arm around my mother. They were hurting as well...but not nearly as much as I was.

"I'll never experience what giving birth is like or the excitement of finding out I'm pregnant. It's all...it's all been taken away from me. So, don't sit there and tell me I need to fucking move on! I don't want to move on! I don't want to sit here and watch all of you have what I can't have." I was crying so hard now I could hardly talk between sobs. "I don't...want to watch...Jonathon...look...at other women's bellies and wish...wish that was me."

I started to feel my legs give out, and Trevor was right there to catch me. Slowly dropping to the ground, I buried my face in his chest. His arms wrapped around me tightly.

"It was all I ever...wanted. And I wanted it with him."

Slowly rocking us on the floor, Trevor whispered against my head. "I know, honey. But you can't push him away any longer."

It felt like I cried forever into my brother's chest. I gripped his T-shirt so hard I was surprised it didn't rip.

My mother rubbed her hand down my back. Over and over she said, "Let it out, baby. Let it all out."

Pulling back, I looked at Trevor. "Will you take me home? I just want to be alone."

"Are you sure?" he asked. "I don't think you should be alone."

My chin trembled. "I just want to sleep."

He stood and picked me up in his arms. I didn't want to look back at anyone. If I did, I would see the pity in their eyes.

"Come on, let's get you home," Trevor said as he walked past Amelia and my mother.

"Trev, call once you get her home."

I didn't remember anything. Not Trevor putting me in his truck, not the drive back to the ranch, not even Trevor carrying me into my bedroom and laying me on the bed.

"Waylynn, I've got a water and some Advil here for you."

I had my back to him as I stared out the large window in my bedroom. "Thanks, Trev."

He placed his hand on my shoulder, pulling me to face him. "Take it for me. I know that drop to the floor had to hurt your stomach."

I slowly sat up and took the water and pills. After popping them into my mouth, I took a long drink.

"Where is everyone?" I asked.

"After we left, Mom and Dad came back to the ranch and everyone else stayed at the bar for a bit."

Nodding, I took in a deep breath. "I didn't mean to break down like that."

"I'm glad you did, and I'm glad you said what you said."

"Corina is probably afraid to even look at me now."

He shook his head. "Hardly. She's coming over later to bring you some food."

I rubbed the side of my head and let out a breath. "I have a headache."

"Rest for a bit. I'm going to be in the living room if you need anything."

Chewing my lip, I felt my eyes burn with the threat of more tears. "You don't have to babysit me, Trev. I'm not going to do anything."

He laughed. "Hell, I know that. I want to be here. I'm waiting for my relief."

With a roll of my eyes, I groaned. "Oh great, now y'all think I need to be monitored."

Kissing me on the forehead, he chuckled. "Hardly. Get some sleep."

I stared out the window. My mind kept drifting back to one thing...and it wasn't the fact that I couldn't have kids. It was Jonathon. I'd ignored him so much the last few weeks. When he was with me, I hardly spoken two words to him. The fact that he had swung by the dance studio earlier and not bothered to even stop and say hi scared me shitless. What if I had pushed him away enough that he was beginning to see the light? I was unable to give him a child, or the love he deserved. This was what I wanted after all, wasn't it?

My eyes closed, and I laid there silently crying.

"Jonathon," I whispered as I felt the entire room fill with warmth. I didn't even have to look to know he was there.

The bed moved, and I held my breath.

"When I walk into any room with you in it, I am engulfed by your presence. It's the most beautiful thing I've ever experienced."

Unable to keep the sobs at bay, I turned to face him.

"What are you doing here?" I managed to ask as I sat up.

"Do you realize you have ignited a spark so deep inside of me, that no matter how much you push me away, it only burns deeper?

You can try and disappear, but I swear to God, Waylynn Parker, I will wait for you a thousand years if I have to. There will never be anyone I love like I love you."

My hand covered my mouth as I listened to him speak.

"You think you're broken, but I don't. What I see is the most amazing woman I've ever known, and I cannot wait to start my life with you. I promise you that I will always come to your rescue time and time again. You can pull me in and push me away, but I will always be right here. I love you, Waylynn Parker, and if you told me you would marry me today, I would marry you and happily spend the rest of my life with you."

I rubbed the back of my hand across my snotty nose. "Wh-what about kids?"

He gave me the most beautiful smile I'd ever seen. "We can still have kids. Maybe not the way we thought, but we can have as many kids are you want. I'll make it happen."

Crawling out from the covers, I threw myself into his body as he wrapped his arms around me.

"I love you so much. So very much."

Burying his face into me, he replied, "And I love you. More than you'll ever know."

Drawing back, we gazed into each other's eyes. Jonathon lifted his hands and wiped my tears away with his thumbs. "No more crying, okay? We're going to talk about this any time you feel like you need to, right?"

I nodded. "I promise you. I'm so sorry I pushed you away when I should have relied on your love to get us through this."

Tilting my chin up, he kissed me gently on the lips. I knew he didn't blame me, and I loved him for not giving up on us.

When he broke the kiss, I instantly realized how much I had missed him these last few weeks.

"Please, tell me Trevor is gone."

He laughed. "Yes, I was his relief. I had to bring Hope back to school after we had lunch together. Trevor called to let me know what happened and that he was at the house waiting for me to get here."

"I sort of broke down."

"Sometimes we need to let the hurt bring us to our knees before we can start healing."

Staring into his eyes, I took a shaky breath. "I'm still hurting, and I'm not sure if I'll ever stop."

Jonathon brushed a piece of hair from my face. "There is nothing wrong with admitting that. But when the pain gets to be too much, I'm here for you."

"The same goes for me. I know I'm not the only one who lost something, and I haven't been here for you at all. I'm so sorry."

He shook his head. "You're incredible, do you know that?"

"Yes."

Laughing, he cupped my face with his hands. "May I please make love to you?"

My lips pressed together to keep my emotions in check. Once I felt like I could talk and not cry, I responded.

"I was wondering when you would ask."

We spent the rest of the afternoon in bed together. Jonathon was so tender. When he kissed my scar, I cried again, but my tears soon dried as he slowly made love to me. Whispering in my ear how much he loved me. Loved my body. It was in that moment I knew whatever God had in store for me, I was ready. All my well laid-out plans over the years, He had to prove again and again to me that I wasn't actually the one in control…He was. And whatever plans He had for us, I was ready to face them, good and bad. Not only because this experience made me stronger, but because I had Jonathon Turner by my side and together we would be able to face anything.

CHAPTER 31

Jonathon

"Holy shit. I don't think I've ever remembered it being so cold."

I glanced up to see Mitchell wrapped in a winter coat and scarf, walking through the door.

Cord laughed. "Dude, you look like a pussy with that scarf wrapped around your face. It's February. It's supposed to be cold."

"Fuck you, Cord. I'm warm, and that's all that matters."

Tripp walked up to his brother and laughed. "You look like you just came down off a mountain." He pulled the knitted hat off Mitchell's head.

"You know what, you two work inside. I don't! I've been out chasing down a damn fucking rogue cow who refused to leave the damn pasture."

"A rogue cow?" I asked, trying not to laugh.

Mitchell pointed to me. "You keep your mouth shut."

I lifted my hands. "Hey, I get staying warm. They did the same thing to me when I walked in."

Cord laughed. "Jonathon here is wearing some fancy leggings."

245

I groaned. "They are not leggings! They're long underwear."

"They look like something a girl would wear to yoga class."

Tripp jumped into the conversation. "Hey, wait. I've been going to yoga with Mallory, and it's not all that bad."

"How are things going with you and Mallory?" Cord asked.

With a smile, Tripp replied, "Pretty good. We hang out every now and then. Nothing serious, but I do like her. The sex is hot as hell."

"Have you talked to Harley?" Mitchell asked. "I saw Doc Harris, and he said she was supposed to take over mid-January, but her move from Dallas got delayed and she only started a couple weeks ago."

Tripp shrugged. "Yeah, I guess she's moved back for good."

"Alone?" Cord asked.

"From what I hear," Tripp answered. "Karen has been trying to get all the gossip from Harley's folks, and I have to keep telling her to mind her own business."

Mitchell sat down next to me and turned to Tripp. "You're not the least bit interested to know what happened with the dickhead she left you for?"

"I can always count on you to remind me of that fact."

"Hey, I'm just asking and stating the obvious."

Tripp rolled his eyes then let out a sigh. "I overheard Karen say that Harley had dated some guy named Al for a couple of years. Moved to Dallas with him and as far as she could find out, they broke up a few years back."

"Al? What in the fuck kind of name is Al?" Cord asked with a chuckle.

"Hey, I have an Al who works for me. He's a nice guy."

Cord turned my way. "And how old is he?"

"Um...well...he's around fifty-five."

"There ya have it. Al is an old man's name."

Mitchell, Cord, and I all looked at each other. "How does it make you feel to have her back in town for good?" I asked.

"I don't know. I'm not sure what she expects or why she is so insistent on us talking."

"Maybe she wants to say she's sorry, or she wants to date again."

Tripp lost it laughing as he rubbed the back of his neck. It was a scared shitless laugh. What if she did want to try again? Would Tripp open up his heart like that again?

"You know what pisses me off? I finally meet a girl I like and connect with after all these years, and Harley walks back into town like she never left."

"Does Mallory know about Harley?" Mitchell asked.

"I told her all about her. I figured I at least owed it to her to be honest. I'm not sure I'm ready to settle down with anyone. And with Mallory having a little girl, we want to be careful with how much I'm around and that sort of thing. We went out to dinner right after Christmas and ran into Harley and her folks. It was awkward to say the least, and Mallory picked up on the history almost instantly."

Mitchell nodded his head. "Women are good about that kind of shit. It's some sort of internal radar."

I agreed. "Yep."

Tripp slapped me on the side of the arm. "Enough of me. We're here to talk about Jonathon fucking Turner. The man who is going marry our big sister. Are you sure you're going to be able to handle a Parker woman, Turner?"

It was my turn to rub the back of my neck in a nervous manner. "Hell, I think so. I have a feeling she'll keep me on my toes."

They all chuckled. "Ask Wade. I'm sure he can fill your head with all kinds of tales."

Cord's eyes met mine and his smile faded. "Seriously, though, thank you for being so patient with Waylynn and not leaving her side. I know it has to be hard for you. I know how much you were looking forward to having kids."

My chest tightened slightly. "We'll have kids, not in the traditional way, but I know we will."

"Adoption?" Mitchell asked.

"That's one option," I answered.

Tripp sat down on a barstool. "Is there another option?"

"One I'm not too keen on at all, but Waylynn brought it up. I guess women donate their eggs and Waylynn suggested we use my juice to fertilize it."

All three of them frowned. "Would you consider that?" Cord questioned.

"No. Donated egg or not, it's not Waylynn's. It would be like having a baby with another woman. I'm not interested in that."

"But it would be your biological baby and a part of you," Tripp added.

Shaking my head, I blew out a breath. "I don't think I could do that."

"I get you, I really do, but if Waylynn brought it up, it might be something she's interested in, so I wouldn't push it to the side altogether. I suggest y'all have some long conversations about it," Tripp advised.

Cord cleared his throat. "I'm with Jonathon. I think you try adoption first, and if that doesn't work out then you go with the other option."

"Who would carry the baby if you had a donor egg?" Mitchell asked.

With a half shrug, I replied, "I'm not sure. Waylynn mentioned it. I told her it wasn't an option right now, and we dropped the subject. Everything is still pretty raw, and at this point I just want to marry her and be her husband."

They all nodded. "That's understandable...and the reason we're here."

I chuckled. "I don't need a bachelor party."

"Dude! Yes, you do! It's an excuse to shut the bar down for a private event and have strippers!"

"What?" Mitchell and I said at the same time.

"Hell no to that!" Mitchell added.

Cord groaned. "Come on, Mitchell. Just because you're married with a kid on the way doesn't mean we all have to suffer."

"I'm not down for the strippers either," Tripp said. "I'm pretty sure that's all you and Trevor."

Rolling his eyes, Cord went into full-on pout mode. "You've got to be fucking kidding me. You too?"

"Cord, I'm about to announce that I'm running for mayor, and you want me to get freaky with a bunch of strippers? Hell, no. It's not happening."

"Buzz kills. All of you."

"Why don't we just do something out at the ranch?" I asked. "A combined party for both me and Waylynn. Invite some friends, have some drinks, and just chill."

Cord stared like I'd lost my damn mind. "Where in the hell did my best friend go? All I see is a damn seventy-year-old man standing here. Should we play bingo? Maybe set up a shuffleboard court on the back forty? Should I start calling you Al?"

"Dude, I actually won a hundred bucks at bingo the other night," Mitchell announced.

Stumbling and clutching his chest, Cord gasped. "Da fuck did you just say? You went to bingo? With whom?"

"Paxton, Amelia, Corina, and Wade. It was fun. Steed was pissed he couldn't make it, but Mom and Dad couldn't watch the kids."

Cord spun around and went behind the bar. He grabbed a bottle of whiskey and poured a few shots. "Drink that."

Mitchell drew his head back in question. "Why?"

"So I know you've not turned into a pussy. Hopefully that shit is strong enough to make your balls drop back into place." Then he pointed to me.

"You, Handy Smurf, if you tell me you've been to bingo I will take your damn Man Card and make Dustin my new best friend."

Facing Tripp, I asked, "Did he just call me Handy Smurf?"

He laughed and nodded his head.

"Why the hell did you call me Handy Smurf?"

"How come I can't be Handy Smurf? Why does Jonathon get to be him?" Mitchell asked.

"You're Tracker Smurf. The whole cop thing," Tripp stated.

"Yes!" Mitchell said, pointing to Tripp. "That makes sense. Dude, you're Brainy Smurf, all the way."

"Hell yeah, I am. Wait…was there a Mayor Smurf?"

"Papa Smurf, but that's Dad for sure."

My gaze bounced between all three of them. Cord seemed stunned as Mitchell and Tripp got excited about their Smurf names. I had seriously just fallen into the Twilight Zone.

Shaking my head, I headed to the door, but not before grabbing my jacket, hat, and gloves. I glanced back over my shoulder to find Cord drinking out of the whiskey bottle while Tripp and Mitchell argued about which Smurf Cord might be.

I jammed my hat on my head, mumbling, "What in the hell kind of family am I marrying into?"

"How do I look?"

Lifting my gaze from the paperwork I was doing at the kitchen bar, I nearly fell off the stool. Waylynn stood before me in a long skirt, cowboy boots, and a baby-blue shirt that showed a little more cleavage than I usually liked. But damn, did she look hot as hell.

"Holy shit. You look amazing."

Waylynn grinned and lifted the sides of her skirt. "I know how you like easy access."

I wiggled my brows. "That I do. I'm sure we can sneak off for a little one on one later."

Her teeth sank into her lip. "I would like that."

I placed my hands on her hips and drew her to me. "How are you feeling?"

"Better. I think the meds are starting to work. Hopefully I won't have any issues."

"Do you like the patch better?"

She nodded. "I like it a lot. It seems to be keeping my hormones in balance now so no chance of me going bat ass crazy on you."

I kissed the tip of her nose. "Thank God."

Hitting me on the chest, Waylynn wrapped her arms around my neck. "You're sure about this?"

"Yep. Are you?"

"I have never been more sure. My poor mother. She's probably wondering where she went wrong with her children and why one of them can't just have a normal wedding."

"Well, there are still three left."

"Ha! I think her only hope is Tripp. He'll have a huge wedding just because he'll probably be mayor when he gets married."

I chuckled. "Probably. Hey, have you met Meabh yet?"

"May?"

"Maebh. It's like May with a V sound on the end."

"Who is that?"

"She's opening the new restaurant a few doors down from Cord. She contacted me about remodeling the place. I guess her contractor hasn't been by in over two months."

"What?"

"Yeah, I feel bad for her. The asshole totally ripped her off. She was in Tripp's office earlier today to see if he would take the case.

She's not sure about her legal rights. She's only been in America for a year. Her mother was from Leaky, Texas. She and her father came over from Ireland to bury her in her hometown, and Maebh loved it here. Said she felt closer to her mother."

"Wow. She's from Ireland, so how can she be opening up a place? Aren't there rules or something for that?"

"She was born here in America and kept her American citizenship, but she's lived in Cork her whole life."

"What does Cord think about Meabh? I'm assuming he met her at the council meeting."

I chuckled. "From what Tripp said, Cord couldn't keep his eyes off her the entire time and couldn't understand her accent. He spent the whole time asking Tripp what she had said and missed half of everything. Tripp keeps playing it off like it's a bar. A chick running a bar."

Waylynn rolled her eyes. "I swear, my brothers live for tormenting each other. I'm surprised you haven't caved and told poor Cord."

"Nope. He thinks it's her father who's running the show."

"You're not a very good best friend for not telling him."

"Oh, Tripp, Trevor, and I have a plan on when Cord will find out."

She lifted a brow. "Do I want to know?"

"Probably not."

"Just don't do anything before we get married. I want you to be able to stand to say the vows and not be sitting in a wheelchair because my brother broke both your legs."

My head dropped back as I let out a round of laughter. "Man, oh man, I do love screwing with Cord."

She hit me on the chest. "Are you finished working? Can we leave now?"

"Are you excited about our combined bachelor and bachelorette parties?"

"If it means no strippers grinding on your cock, yes."

"Damn, girl, you have a foul mouth."

She winked. "And you like it. Now, let's go, I'm sure everyone is waiting on us."

Waylynn grabbed her purse and coat as I put on my cowboy hat and grabbed a sweatshirt. It had warmed up, but it was still chilly out. The way Waylynn's gaze moved over my body, it was clear the last place she wanted to go was this party.

"You like what you see, baby?"

Pulling her lip between her teeth, she nodded. "Mmm...hmm. Maybe we could be a little late for this party."

My dick jumped in my pants, and I was about to agree when someone banged on the front door.

"Are you sure you want to live here on my folks' ranch? I'm thinking your place sounds better and better."

I chuckled as we made our way to the front door. The doorbell started ringing, followed by more pounding.

"Holy shit! Hold onto your panties!"

Throwing open the door, Amelia stood there panting like she had just run a marathon.

"Okay, we're not *that* late, Amelia."

She held up her hand and took in a deep breath. "Something has happened. Something...that could...change your life!"

CHAPTER 32

Waylynn

Amelia always was overly dramatic. Pushing past her, I turned and locked the door after Jonathon walked out.

"Mmm, let's see. Change our lives, huh? Did Mom forget to order the food?"

"Hardly!" Amelia gasped.

"Exactly why are you gasping?"

"Got a flat…down the drive…ran up here."

I gazed down the long drive that went from my house to the main road that went around the entire ranch.

"How in the hell did you get a flat? And why didn't you just call me?"

She bent over, her hands on her knees. "Patches. Ate. Phone."

"Great, the goat's eating phones now." Spinning on my heels, I pointed to Jonathon. "He's *not* invited to the wedding. I'm saying that right now and don't you let Chloe bat her little eyes at you, Jonathon Turner!"

Jonathon nodded but kept looking back at Amelia. "Amelia, are you okay?"

She stood up and waved her hand in the air. "I think I might actually…have exercise…induced asthma or…something."

"For Christ's sake, Meli, you didn't even run a quarter of a mile. Come on, you can drive back with us."

"No, wait!"

"No can do, little sister," I said, walking around to the passenger side of Jonathon's truck. "We're late, so whatever life-changing thing you want to tell us, you'll have to do it on the way."

"Wait! We need to act now!"

I scoffed. "You know what this means, don't you?" I said to Jonathon as we both got into the truck. "The boys did something. Probably rigged up something to come down and hit you in the face."

"What!"

"No! That's not it!" Amelia dragged in a deep breath as she climbed into the backseat. "I need water!"

Looking around, I picked up a bottle off the floor of the truck. "Is this yours, Jonathon?"

Amelia grabbed it. She downed it while I stared at her with a disgusted look on my face. "That is just gross. You have no idea whose lips have been on that."

"I'm pretty sure it's mine," Jonathon stated.

"It's still gross," I replied.

"There's a baby!"

Jonathon and I both turned to face Amelia. My heart started to beat harder as I forced the next words out. I had no idea what my sister was talking about, but that word caused a strange flame of hope in my chest.

"What do you mean *there's a baby*?" I asked.

Amelia took a few deep breaths and then she launched into it.

"Wanda and Mick called. They were contacted by a friend of theirs. He is trying to set up a private adoption and asked if they knew anyone who would be willing to adopt the baby, as well as pay for the delivery. The girl is only twenty, and she is not going to be able to provide for the baby. The father has given up all rights and wants nothing to do with her or the baby."

I sucked in a breath. "That poor thing."

"She didn't want to go through an adoption agency because she's due in the next few weeks. She thought she would be able to manage the money, but when she got the call from the hospital and they told her how much the delivery was, she knew it was beyond her means."

Jonathon closed his eyes before looking at me and then Amelia. "So, you mean this poor girl is giving up her child because she can't afford to pay for the delivery?"

"Among other things. She's trying to get through college and she has no support at home. Her parents aren't in the picture. She loves the baby and feels like in order to give her a better chance at life, she needs to let her go."

I covered my mouth, tears pooling. I blinked several times to keep them at bay.

"It's a girl?" Jonathon asked.

"Oh, she doesn't know. She calls the baby 'she' but she hasn't found out the sex yet."

Spinning around, I pushed the door to the truck open and got out. I started to pace, and before I knew it, Jonathon was standing in front of me, gripping my arms.

"Talk to me, baby."

Lifting my head, I captured his gaze with mine.

Amelia went on. "I know this is soon after everything happened, but Wanda said when their friend called, she told him she thought she knew a couple who might be interested. Strings will have to be pulled to get the adoption to go through fast, but Mick said they could make it work."

"Waylynn, please. Say something."

My head should have been spinning. My heart should have been aching, but instead, I was making plans in my head to prepare for a baby. Which was insane. The girl might not even like us. Jonathon probably wasn't ready for this step yet.

"Do you want this? Now? I mean, we're not even married, and we'd have to put a few things on hold, like the wedding and the honeymoon. I mean, this might not even work, and we could have our hearts broken if things didn't work out."

Cupping my face in his hands, he looked deep into my eyes. "I'm ready. The question is…are you ready to take this leap with the knowledge that it might not work in our favor?"

A tear slipped from behind my lashes as I nodded. "I want to try. If it doesn't work out, we keep moving on. Our situation would be no different than it is right now if it falls through. It's just part of the journey."

His lips pressed against mine.

"Umm…not to interrupt this amazing moment, but Wanda is waiting to hear back from us, and I need a cell phone."

Jonathon broke our kiss and handed Amelia his phone. "Shit! Yes. Call her back."

Amelia took the phone and stared at it.

"Meli, what's wrong?"

Chewing on her lip, she looked over at us. "I don't remember their number. It was programmed into my phone."

"The goat ate your phone," I groaned and pushed her toward Jonathon's truck. "We need to get to Wade. Where is he, anyway?"

"Chasing Patches. I told him I had to leave and come find you."

We piled into the truck, and Jonathon started down the driveway driving like a bat out of hell. "Jonathon, why don't you have Wade's number?" Amelia shouted.

"That's my work phone! My regular cell is at my house. I forgot it."

"Christ Almighty! Who forgets their phone!" Amelia cried out as she tried to remember Wade's number.

"Wait, you don't know your own husband's phone number?" I asked.

"No! Do you know Jonathon's?"

"Of course, I do."

"Screw you, Waylynn. He's in my favorites and I just tell Siri to call him!"

Jonathon snapped his fingers. "Cord! Call Cord, he's on that phone."

"Oh! Good!" Amelia said as she looked for Cord's number. "Found it!"

Punching Jonathon on the arm, I yelled, "Go faster!"

"I'm trying! Do you not see all the cows up ahead?"

"Answer, damn it! Answer!" Amelia shouted.

"Why are we freaking out?" Jonathon asked. "Surely they understand we would need a bit of time to think about this?"

"I want that baby, Jonathon Turner!" Amelia shouted. "I mean, I want that baby for y'all."

Jonathon looked at me with wide eyes, and I couldn't help but giggle.

"Cord!" Amelia shouted. "Find Wade! I need to talk to him. No, I don't care that he and Daddy are setting up a game. I need to talk to him now!"

Chewing on my nail, we waited for Cord to get Wade.

"Wade! I need you to call Wanda or Mick and tell them that Waylynn and Jonathon want the baby. Yes! Okay, we're almost there, but call them right after I hang up."

Amelia hit End and then looked at me. We both stared at each other.

"Oh. My. God. What did we just do?" I asked.

"Not we…you…y'all," she said, pointing between me and Jonathon with a huge grin. "Y'all just signed up for a baby."

Jonathon paced while I sat in the chair with my hands folded in my lap. When the door opened, I stood. A young girl with beautiful dark hair walked into the room. Her warm smile brought tears to my eyes. I couldn't imagine how hard this must be for her.

"Liberty, this is Waylynn Parker and Jonathon Turner. This is the couple who is interested in adopting your child."

She glanced over to her lawyer and then at the two of us. "Y'all aren't married? I thought your paperwork said you were married."

"Not yet, but we were about to have a civil ceremony tomorrow and had planned on a beach wedding later this year, but then this came up so we've put that on hold."

"Oh. Okay."

Sitting down in a seat, Jonathon and I sat at the opposite end of the table.

Liberty's lawyer sat and set a few folders on the table. Our lawyer cleared his throat.

"Good afternoon, my name is Dereck Winters, and I'm the counsel for Ms. Parker and Mr. Turner."

Liberty's lawyer stood back up again. "Rider Flynn, and I'm Ms. Wilson's attorney."

I couldn't help it, but I giggled and so did Jonathon. We both tried to hide it. I prayed like hell no one caught the slip.

"It seems to me, Mr. Wilson, that this is cut and dry. Your client will terminate her parental rights, and my clients will petition for adoption. My clients understand that their petition will not be finalized until the child has been in their care for six months, at which time they will present the court with a social study as well as a genetic history. We have already presented the criminal history and will submit an updated report at said time."

I cleared my throat. "We'd also like to ask Ms. Wilson if she would be interested in an open adoption."

Liberty looked at her lawyer. It was clear she didn't understand what that meant. Sitting down, he said, "An open adoption is where the adoptive parents and the birth parents, or parent in this case, would have contact with one another after the child is born."

Liberty's mouth opened some before closing abruptly. "You mean, you'd let me see the baby after she's born?"

Jonathon took my hand in his. I tried to slow my breathing and speak with a calm voice.

"Yes, if you would like."

When Liberty's chin trembled, I had to look away. "Mr. Wilson, Mr. Winters, may I please speak with Waylynn and Jonathon alone?"

Both lawyers looked at each other and then to us. Jonathon and I nodded.

"We'll be outside the door," Dereck said with an unsure smile.

Once the door shut, Liberty covered her mouth and let a sob slip through. I instantly got up and made my way to her. Sitting next to her, I took her hand in mine.

"Are you okay, sweetheart?"

She nodded and attempted to get her emotions in check. "Why would you do that? Let me see the baby?"

Lifting my eyes to Jonathon, we smiled. Focusing back on Liberty, I spoke softly. "I won't pretend to understand how you feel, because I can't imagine it. I know you read my medical records and you know I had an accident—and a hysterectomy. It was very emotional to find out that I would never be able to carry my own child. So, for you to carry your child, and then give her up...I know it cannot be easy to do. We just want you to know that the open adoption is an option if you choose us as the parents of your child. I don't have all the details of how we would handle it, or how you would want to handle it, but I feel strongly that we needed to ask you."

Liberty wiped her tears away and smiled. "I want to go to medical school."

"That's amazing, Liberty," Jonathon said, sitting down on the other side of her. "Your parents must be very proud of you."

Her smile faded. "My parents disowned me when they found out I'd gotten pregnant."

My hand covered my mouth in an attempt to hide an angry gasp.

"Your parents disowned you?" Jonathon asked.

She nodded and sighed. Then she looked at me. "You own a dance studio?"

I grinned. "I do. I used to be a dancer in New York City."

"Wow, that's pretty neat. The paperwork didn't mention *that*."

We all chuckled.

Turning to face Jonathon, she asked, "You own your own construction company?"

"Yes, I do."

"Caring for your child will not be a problem, Liberty. She or he will have every opportunity we can give them."

With a slight grin, she glanced at her hands. Her cheeks turned pink. "I have to admit, my lawyer told me who your momma and daddy are, Waylynn, and I Googled them. You come from a very wealthy family. It makes me feel good knowing that you're both driven and have family support. I know you can provide her with the things I can't. At least not in the near future. Once I go to school and get my medical degree, I'll be more...ready. For lack of better words."

The only thing I could do was nod. "I think what you're doing is very brave, Liberty. And it's nothing to be ashamed of."

She scoffed. "My momma and daddy don't think so. They said I deserve to suffer with the baby since I was careless enough to get pregnant. He's a good guy, the baby's father. He's just scared. He's on a scholarship for football with Texas A&M."

Liberty wasn't supposed to tell us anything about herself. "That's where I go to school."

Jonathon's face broke out into a smile. "That's where I went."

"I saw that!" she said.

Wringing her hands together, she seemed like she wanted to ask us something else.

"You can ask anything you want," I said.

"Y'all are getting married?"

Jonathon and I looked at each other and smiled. "Yes."

"And I can see the baby?"

I squeezed her hand. "Yes."

"Can we tell her that I'm a family friend?"

"If that's what you want. But Jonathon and I have already spoken about this, and we plan on telling the baby when she is older that she is adopted. And we'd love for you to stay a part of her world."

Tears streamed down her face. "You mean, you'd tell her I'm her momma? And why I had to give her up so that she knows I did it for her?"

My eyes stung as I fought to hold my tears back. "Of course. If that is okay with you."

Liberty stood and threw her arms around me. "I knew God would bring me the right couple to love and take care of my baby. I just never dreamed he'd bring me angels."

CHAPTER 33

Waylynn

Jonathon and I parked next to the line of cars outside my parents' house.

"My folks are here," Jonathon said with a chuckle.

I took a few deep breaths and faced him.

"I wish we could have more time to let this all soak in. I feel like we just found out we won the lottery, and everyone wants a piece of the pie!"

Chuckling, Jonathon nodded. "It's a lot to take in. I know everyone is anxious. A lot has happened the last couple of months."

"Does it feel like it's too good to be true? That we're going to wake up, and it's all been a dream?"

He took my hand in his. "Yes. A little bit. But it's not a dream, and I feel like this all happened for a reason. I mean, I hate that the option for you to carry a child has been taken from us, but if it hadn't…"

"We'd have never met Liberty. And she would have given up her child to a couple who would probably never let her see the baby again."

"Exactly. It's meant to be."

A tear trailed down my cheek. Jonathon brushed it away with his thumb. "You're the most amazing woman I've ever met. When you told me you wanted Liberty to stay a part of the baby's life, I had to fight to hold back tears. That's such an unselfish gift."

"She's the one giving us the most amazing gift. If one mother is good...two has to be better, right?"

His hand slipped behind my neck, pulling me closer to him.

"I love you so damn much."

My hand covered his. "I love you too."

The knock on the window made both of us scream.

Amelia and Wade stood outside the truck. Well, Wade was standing there and my sister was jumping up and down like a crazy person.

We took a deep breath, exhaled, and said at the same time, "Let's do this."

I opened the door, and Amelia nearly pulled my arm out of socket.

"What happened? Why are y'all sitting out here in the car? What was the mother like? Did she like y'all? Are you getting the baby? Oh my God, why are you not talking?"

I replied, "Cool your tits, Meli. Christ Almighty, I can't talk because you won't let me get a word in."

Wade shook Jonathon's hand. "How did it go?"

We glanced at each other and smiled.

Amelia threw her hands in my face. "No! Wait! Don't say it yet. I want you to say it in front of everyone!"

Grabbing my hand, she started pulling me behind her as she ran up the porch stairs.

"Jonathon's folks are here, too, as well as Evie, Hollie, Dalton, Hope, and Rip."

"Rip? Oh, man. How's Steed handling that?" Jonathon asked with a chuckle.

Wade answered. "Let's just say he's not handling it well. Especially since he and Chloe are sitting on the porch swing talking away."

"Oh hell, my poor little brother. The Parker woman spell is already upon him."

Everyone greeted us the moment we walked into the house. Hope came running up and jumped into Jonathon's arms while my mother engulfed me in a hug. Kristin, Jonathon's mother, followed.

"Jonathon, Cord promised to take me horseback riding!" Hope exclaimed. Her crush on Cord was beyond cute.

Kissing his sister on the forehead, Jonathon replied, "How fun, Squirt! Maybe I can come too?"

She frowned and then shrugged. "I guess. If you want."

"How did it go? I want to know everything!" My mother gushed as she guided me to the family room. When we walked into the room, my father kissed my cheek. Moving his mouth to my ear, he asked, "Overwhelmed?"

With a giggle, I replied, "A little."

He gave me a wink before turning around. "Alright! Everyone take a few steps back and let's give Jonathon and Waylynn some breathing room."

"What's 'breathing room'?" Chloe asked.

When I looked down and found her holding hands with Rip Jr., I nearly lost it laughing. The look on Steed's face was priceless.

He hit Paxton on the arm. "They're holding hands! Make them stop!"

She hit him back. "Hush up, Steed Parker!"

Glancing around, I saw Corina holding Gage. I smiled. "How are you feeling?"

She looked confused at first, but flashed me that beautiful smile. "I'm feeling amazing. "

Kissing my nephew on the head, I faced everyone. Jonathon made his way over to us.

"So...how did the meeting go? Did she like y'all?" Amelia asked again.

Taking my hand in his, Jonathon gave me a slight squeeze. I opened my mouth, but nothing came out. I was overwhelmed with emotion, so Jonathon spoke.

"We met the mother. Her name is Liberty Wilson. She's a college student right now and wants to go to medical school."

"Oh my," Kristin said with a smile.

"Good for her!" my mother added.

"She asked to speak with us alone. Once the legal people left, we got to know her. We talked about an open adoption and asked for her to be a part of the baby's life. We told her that we could work out visiting times when the child is old enough."

You could hear sniffling, and I reached up and wiped a tear away. I wasn't surprised when I saw my handsome future husband doing the same thing.

"Um, anyway, after talking to Liberty for over an hour, the lawyers came back, and we signed the paperwork. Liberty signed over her parental rights, and we are on the road to adopting a baby."

Cheers erupted in the room, and between my family and Jonathon's filling the family room, it felt like we were at a sports event.

The sound of a cork popping drew everyone's attention over to Jonathon's stepdad, Rip. "Time to celebrate!"

And celebrate we did. When I finally needed a break, I made my way to the quiet of the front porch. I sat on the swing, leaned my head back, and let out a contented moan.

"Would you like to be alone?"

I jumped at the sound of my Aunt Vi's voice. Lifting my head, she stood in front of me, two small shot glasses in her hands.

"Is that whiskey?" I asked.

"Why, yes, it is."

"Please, tell me they're both for me."

She winked and handed me one and then the other.

"I always knew you were my favorite for a reason."

I laughed. "Aunt Vi, why is life so crazy? I don't know if I should be crying or celebrating. I mean, I'm still upset about the hysterectomy, yet I'm thrilled to be adopting this baby. It's like I don't know how I'm supposed to feel. A part of me feels guilty that I moved on so quickly, yet deep down inside, I still hurt."

Sighing, I buried my face into my hands and groaned. "Ah, shit, I don't know!" My hands dropped into my lap.

"Have you ever wondered why I've never had kids?"

I stared at her. "Yes. I've even asked Daddy, and he said that was your story to tell."

She nodded. "He was right, and I haven't told it in years."

Lacing her arm with mine, she pushed off the porch and we started rocking.

"I remember when your momma was pregnant with you. Lord, did she ever look cute as a button, that Melanie. I was so happy for them. Then came Tripp and my brother got the boy he wanted so badly."

"He was hoping for a boy with me?" I exclaimed.

"Oh, yes, he had been calling you Waylon for months, but I know for a fact that you had him wrapped around your little finger from the first moment he laid eyes on you."

With a contented sigh, I leaned my head on her shoulder.

"The day I found out your momma was pregnant again I was living in California. I had just left the doctor's office and had been told I would never be able to have kids."

My head snapped up. "What?"

She forced a smile. "It was a tough day, for damn sure. When I got home, your daddy had left me a message with the news. Twins. I thought for sure God was playing some cruel joke. I let myself cry for a good two hours then I plastered on a smile and called your folks back and told them how happy I was for them. And I was, don't get me wrong. I was over the moon, but when you're feeling so overwhelmingly sad, your head plays tricks on you. From that point on, I told myself I was going to just live my life like I was going zero to ninety without a damn care in the world. I went through men like candy and used sex to cover up my hurt."

She turned to look at me. "Now don't get me wrong, I do love sex. The best times of my life have been when a dick has been slipped inside my pink pocket. And let me tell you, I've had some pretty nice ones."

My mouth dropped. "For fuck's sake, Aunt Vi! The visual. I didn't need that."

She let out a roar of laughter.

"Why didn't you ever adopt?" I asked, once she stopped laughing.

"I don't know. I guess I got a bit lost in myself and didn't really think about it. I'm so very proud of you. But I know the emotions you must be feeling."

"It's a little crazy. I mean, you go from thinking your life is going to go one way, to it not going that way, to oh, wait…it's going that way after all! Just not the exact way you thought it would."

She placed her hand over my leg and gave it a squeeze. "Do you love Jonathon?"

Drawing my head back, I pinched my brows together. "Of course! Why are you even asking me that?"

"Just double-checking. I figured you did with how you look at him all puppy dog eyes."

"I do not look at him like that."

She rolled her eyes. "Yeah, okay, keep telling yourself that. Come on, stop hiding out. If you're going to hide anywhere, hide where the damn booze is, for Pete's sake."

I watched my aunt head to the front door. Even though my life had been a rollercoaster of emotions, it hit me how blessed I truly was. No, I'd never be able to have my own biological child, and that would always make my heart ache, but I was surrounded by the most amazing family a woman could ask for. And I had a beautiful adopted baby coming as well as a man who loved me unconditionally and who had taught me how to love again.

Life was about to get good…no doubt about it.

CHAPTER 34

Jonathon

"Jesus, dude, could you move any slower? My father moves faster than you," Trevor shouted.

"Well, for fuck's sake, I'm not driving the damn stack cruiser like Tripp, Mitchell, and Steed! Why are we doing this by hand?"

Wade laughed. "They're breaking you in. Think of it as a welcome to the family."

Removing my cowboy hat, I wiped the sweat off my forehead. "It's sixty degrees out, and I'm fucking sweating my ass off! And what do you mean breaking me in? How long is the break-in process? You've been married to Amelia since last summer and it's March!"

"Less talking, keep stacking, assholes," Trevor said.

Wade laughed again. I had a feeling I was the one he was laughing at.

Another thirty minutes went by, and we had the ranch truck and trailer completely stacked with square bales of hay.

Leaning against the truck, I lifted a bottle of water to my lips and drank the whole thing.

"Thirsty, Turner?" Wade asked.

"I bet I lost ten pounds from sweating."

Wade and Trevor chuckled as they drank. "Shit's hard work, but every now and then a little bit of hard work is good for you."

I stared at Trevor. "I work hard every day, asshole. Just because I'm not in a field doesn't mean I don't work my ass off."

Trevor lifted his hands in defense. "I wasn't saying you don't. For the record, we're bringing this hay to the barn in the south pasture, so we need to unload it, as well."

I was pretty sure my jaw hit the ground.

"I hate you right now, Trevor."

A honking horn made us look down the road at John's truck, flying toward us.

"Man, does your dad always drive like a bat out of hell?"

Trevor put his cowboy hat back on and pushed off the truck. "No, he doesn't. Something must be wrong."

Wade was the next to push off the truck. "Shit, I hope the girls are all okay."

I saw Waylynn sitting in the front seat of her daddy's truck. The closer they got, the better I could see her…and the huge smile on her face.

"Dude, I think you're fixin' to be a father," Trevor said, slapping my back. My heart felt like it dropped to the ground.

The truck came to a halt and Waylynn jumped out. "Jonathon! Why aren't you answering my text messages?"

I pulled my phone out. I had twenty missed calls and five texts.

"Shit, it was on silent."

"Liberty is having the baby! She called thirty minutes ago and said she was on the way to the hospital."

"What?" I nearly shouted. "Holy shit!"

Waylynn ran over and jumped into my arms. "We're having a baby!"

"Come on, kids, we need to get going. You want to be there when the big event happens."

I turned to Trevor. "Bummer, I'm not gonna be able to help y'all unload all this hay now."

Trevor gave me a shit-eating grin followed by the middle finger. "Just go and keep us up to date. I want to meet my new niece or nephew."

I reached out and shook Trevor and Wade's hands. "We'll let y'all know."

Wade pulled me in for a hug. "Good luck. I'm happy for y'all."

The lump in my throat kept me from talking. I nodded before jumping into the backseat of John's truck.

John swung back by the house and picked up Melanie, and we were on our way to San Antonio.

"Daddy, don't get a ticket," Waylynn said as she gripped my hand tighter.

"Baby, you're gonna cut off the circulation in my hand," I said.

She glanced down at our interlocked hands. "Oh. Sorry."

The drive into San Antonio seemed to take forever.

"Will the lawyers be there?" Melanie asked.

"No, but I've texted Wanda and Mick. They've hired Liberty to work for them part-time and told her during the summers she can go full-time. She's got a lot of academic scholarships, but with her parents cutting her off, she'll still need to pay for some of school. My heart hurts for her, but the fact that Mick and Wanda are helping her just shows you the amazing couple they are."

"What a wonderful thing for them to do. How sweet," my mother said glancing back at Waylynn.

"Yeah, once we told them her story and how her parents had stopped talking to her, they took her under their wing. She's able to work from her dorm, so it's perfect for her."

John turned into the hospital, and my heart rate must have spiked tenfold. "I'll drop y'all off and park. Just let me know where you'll be."

Waylynn jumped out of the truck before John came to a stop.

"Goodness, that girl never could wait for a vehicle to stop before she jumped out in excitement."

We power-walked to the information desk and a sweet, older woman greeted us with a friendly hello.

"Hello, there! You look like you're on a mission."

"Labor and delivery, please," Waylynn said with the twinge of excitement in her voice.

She pointed to our right and said, "Take the elevators to the fourth floor and check in. They'll be able to direct you from there."

"Thank you!" Waylynn said as she took off.

"I'll text John. That is, if I can text and jog!" Melanie said as we both tried to keep up with Waylynn.

Stepping onto the elevator, I tried to take a few deep breaths.

"Are you nervous?" Waylynn asked.

"Hell yes, I'm nervous. Aren't you?"

She giggled. "I am, but I think I'm more excited."

The elevator doors opened onto the fourth floor, and I took Waylynn's hand in mine. Then we just stood there. Melanie pushed us from behind, forcing us to get off the elevator.

The young lady at the desk giggled as we stumbled out.

Melanie walked up to her. "Hello, these are the scared-to-death, future parents of Liberty Wilson's baby."

The girl's eyes lit up. "Oh! Liberty told me the baby's adoptive parents were on their way. I'll let the nurse know she can bring them back to the room."

"Room?" Waylynn and I both said at once.

"Yes. For the delivery."

"Yes, of course," Melanie said as she took Waylynn's hand, as well as mine. When she squeezed the shit out of it, I snapped out of my daze.

"Ouch! Momma, what in the hell?" Waylynn whispered as the girl walked toward the nurses' station.

"You two need to snap out of it. Liberty wants you in the room when the baby is born. That's an honor."

I stumbled a few steps. "What?"

"Ohmygawd! Do you think so?" Waylynn asked as she jumped up and down.

"Settle down, Waylynn Parker. You're not five. And, yes, that is my best guess."

The next thing I knew we were walking into Liberty's room. We already knew from the tour we did last week that this was a one-and-done room: labor, delivery and recovery. Waylynn had also hired a doula to be Liberty's birthing companion after she saw Liberty looking at the information.

The moment she saw Waylynn, Liberty started crying. Waylynn rushed to Liberty side and took her hand.

"I…I was worried you wouldn't make it!" Liberty said as she cried.

"Oh my sweet girl, it's okay! We're here."

I walked to the other side and looked at everything hooked up to Liberty.

"It monitors my contractions…which are getting pretty intense."

"Have you taken anything for the pain?" I asked.

"I wanted to wait for you to see if it was okay."

Waylynn and I looked at each other in horror.

"Liberty! This is your delivery. You do what you need to do to make it as easy as you can."

Relief washed over her face. "Okay, 'cause I could really use an epidural."

The nurse chuckled. "I'll let the doctor know you're asking for one."

"Do you need anything?" I asked.

She shook her head. "No, thank you. Wanda and Mick left to go get lunch. I'm so blessed to have them in my life."

"They are pretty amazing," I added.

After a few minutes, the doctor we'd met last week walked into the room.

"Wonderful! Everyone's here. Let's take a look and see how you're progressing, and if we can call the anesthesiologist for that epidural."

"Should I step outside?" I asked.

The doctor glanced to Liberty. "Only if Liberty wants you to. You can't see anything if you stand where you are.

"It's totally fine," she said.

After examining Liberty, the doctor stood. "You're about six centimeters dilated so I see no need to hold off on getting you that epidural."

Both Liberty and Waylynn sighed. Once the epidural took affect, Liberty dozed.

"How long until she is ready to push?" I asked Waylynn.

"I talked to Paxton about it. She said with Gage she was stuck at five centimeters for a few hours with no forward progress, but once things got moving, they got moving fast."

I swallowed hard. My nerves were on edge. If that had been Waylynn lying there, I'd have gone out of my mind with worry. "I'm glad she is resting. Maybe we should head down and grab a bite to eat while she's sleeping."

Waylynn agreed. After meeting up with her parents and Wanda and Mick in the waiting room, we headed down to the cafeteria. We grabbed some sandwiches and coffee, then headed back to the waiting room. The nurse walked up with a huge smile on her face.

"We're ready to push."

Waylynn jumped up. "What? Already?"

She motioned for us to follow her back to Liberty's room. Waylynn spun around and looked at her parents. "This is it. Oh my God! Can you call everyone?"

Melanie stood. "Of course, darling. Now, go! Give Liberty a kiss for me."

I took Waylynn's hand, and we walked quickly back to Liberty's delivery room.

When I opened the door, the doctor was examining her so I looked away and headed to the side of the bed.

"We are at ten centimeters, people, and this little one is ready to make an appearance."

"She was feeling sick, so I let her smell some peppermint oil," Darcy, the doula Waylynn had hired, said.

"Are you feeling better, sweetie?" Waylynn asked as she pushed Liberty's hair away from her eyes.

She nodded. Darcy had been amazing during this whole process. Before we'd gotten there, she'd massaged Liberty through the contractions.

"This is it? Are y'all ready?" Liberty asked, her eyes filled with something I wasn't sure how to read. My biggest fear was that she was going to back out and Waylynn's heart would be broken all over again.

"The question is, are you ready?" Waylynn asked her as she took her hand.

Liberty's gaze bounced back and forth between me and Waylynn. "I'm ready, and as much as I love the baby, I know I'm doing the right thing. I want y'all to be her parents. I know you can give her the life I'm not able to right now."

Relief swept over me as Waylynn leaned forward and kissed Liberty on the forehead.

"Alright, let's get this show on the road, shall we?"

After Darcy explained how to hold Liberty's legs, the doctor went over what to expect. I would be cutting the umbilical cord. Liberty declined to hold the baby first, feeling it was important for Waylynn to be the first to hold the baby, skin to skin, so they had an immediate bond. I couldn't imagine what that must have felt like for Liberty to do that. Waylynn started to argue, but Liberty insisted it be done that way, and Waylynn quickly backed down.

Then it happened. The baby's head appeared, and I nearly broke down in tears. Waylynn coached Liberty through the pushes as the doctor and I stared at the little bit of dark hair that appeared.

"Oh. My. God," I whispered. One of the nurses walked up to me.

"Mr. Turner, are you feeling okay?"

I pointed in the mirror. "That's...that's a head. That's a head right there!"

She chuckled. "That's your baby's head, yes."

There was something so magical about what was happening. This was a baby. A sweet, innocent child coming into this world, and I was going to be his or her father. Tears fell down my cheek as I held Liberty's legs, and she let out a loud grunt when the doctor told her to push one more time.

The nurse told Waylynn to sit in the recliner. They took her shirt off and gave her a gown. My heart was beating so hard I was positive everyone in the room heard it. Waylynn's tears nearly brought me to my knees.

The doctor's voice pulled me out of my trance. "Come on, Liberty. Push down, sweetie, your baby is not pulling back in. You've got this. I only need one more."

My gaze drifted to Liberty. She was so young and had such an amazing future, and she was giving us this gift. I would forever be grateful to this young woman, and she would remain a part of our family no matter how big or small she wanted that part to be.

"Here the baby comes!" The doctor announced. I looked back to Waylynn who was watching the baby being born in the mirror. Her hands covered her mouth as she cried.

I held my breath as I watched our child come blazing into this world.

"It's a girl!" the doctor announced, causing both Liberty and Waylynn to cry harder.

"Okay, Mr. Turner, are you ready to cut the cord?"

Our baby's cry filled the room, and it was the most amazing song I'd ever heard in my life.

Liberty didn't take her eyes off of the baby while tears flowed. She smiled big and bright as the nurse made her way to Waylynn. I focused in on Waylynn and when they placed our child in her arms, everything in my world changed. Nothing else mattered but the two beautiful women I would forever be able to call mine.

CHAPTER 35

Waylynn

I sat in the chair in awe as I watched Liberty do one last push. The baby came out and I covered my mouth to hide my sobbing.

One quick glance at Jonathon and my heart nearly burst as he wiped his tears away. I loved this man, and I loved that he was on board with this crazy, beautiful idea.

"It's a girl!" the doctor cried out. When I heard Liberty start to cry, I cried harder.

A girl.

A little girl to dress up with and have tea parties. A little girl to teach the perfect way to do an arabesque and how to ride a horse.

"Okay, Mr. Turner, are you ready to cut the cord?"

I watched Jonathon's shaking hands cut the cord. I could see the love in his eyes, and it filled my heart with such joy. I thought I'd never be this happy again in my life. I was proven wrong when the nurse carried our daughter over to me.

"Are you ready to meet your little girl?" she whispered.

Nodding, I reached for her. The moment the nurse placed her in my arms and adjusted my gown so that I could place her on my chest, I knew I was right this time: this would always be the happiest moment of my life.

My chest was about to burst with love. My dream had finally come true and even though I hadn't carried this beautiful baby for nine months or brought her into this world, I knew with all my heart she was mine. She was my child, and I would forever love her with every ounce of my being.

Jonathon made his way over to me, and we gazed down at our little girl.

"She's beautiful," he whispered as he wiped the tears from my face.

"Yes, she is. The most beautiful little girl in the world."

My gaze lifted to see Liberty watching us. She wore a bright, beautiful yet teary smile and my heart felt both happiness and sadness. When she had said she wanted me to hold the baby first, I'd nearly broken down. This girl had no idea the gift she had given us, and I was hell bent on making sure she knew.

"Liberty…" I said with a sob.

She nodded and reached a hand for mine as she whispered, "She's beautiful."

"She is, just like her mother," I stated.

"You're her mother now, Waylynn. She'll always have a piece of my heart, and I will love her until the day I die, but you're her mother."

Closing my eyes, I tried not to cry harder than I already was.

Jonathon moved to my other side, causing me to open my eyes. He leaned over and kissed Liberty on the forehead. "You were amazing. Thank you for giving us this gift. We are so blessed to have you in our life."

Liberty wiped her tears away. "Thank you, Jonathon."

Moving back to my side, Jonathon sat in the chair one of the nurses had brought in. I repositioned the baby so that I was looking straight down at her.

"Do we have a name for the baby?" the nurse asked as she gazed upon us with a huge smile.

Jonathon and I looked at one another and then to Liberty as we answered the nurse.

"Yes. Liberty Grace Turner."

Her hand covered her mouth, and she closed her eyes as she said, "Thank you. I love it so much."

The doctor stood before all of us. "Looks like everything is finished up here. Liberty, once that epidural runs out, I want you up and walking around, but only with the help of someone, okay?"

She nodded. "Yes. I understand."

I lovingly gazed back to my daughter. Her little blue eyes opened as she captured mine.

"Hello there, sweet baby girl. It's Mommy and Daddy," I said. Jonathon ran a finger down the side of her cheek.

"Welcome to the world, Liberty. Wait until you meet Patches."

I started to laugh and wipe more tears away before handing our daughter to Jonathon. He took her like he was a pro at holding newborns. The way the two of them looked at each other had my chest radiating. It was the most precious moment I'd ever witnessed.

"Daddy loves you so much already. My beautiful baby girl."

Just when I thought I couldn't love Jonathon any more, he proved me wrong.

After the room had cleared and only one nurse was left, I turned to see Liberty sleeping. I had already fed our Liberty and Jonathon was holding her in his arms.

"I want Liberty to hold her before we take her to the nursery."

The baby was staying until tomorrow and then we would be able to take her home.

Standing, Jonathon walked over to her bed side while I gently roused her awake.

She opened her eyes and smiled. The doula had been so helpful and had somehow gotten Liberty to rest and fall asleep.

"Do you want to hold her before we have to leave?"

Sitting up straighter, she chewed on her lip. "I don't know. Would you mind?"

I smiled. "Of course not."

Jonathon placed little Liberty in her mother's arms. Her breath caught and her chin trembled.

"Liberty, we're going to give you a few minutes alone. If you need us, we are right outside."

"What?" Liberty asked in a shocked voice.

"If you don't want us to go, we won't," Jonathon added.

"You wouldn't mind?"

With a grin, I leaned over and kissed her forehead. "Not at all. We'll be right outside."

Jonathon placed his hand on my lower back and guided me from the room. One peek over my shoulder, and I smiled when I saw Liberty looking at the baby's toes.

Once we were out of the room, I faced Jonathon.

"I thought it would be hard to leave her with the baby, but it felt like the most natural thing."

He nodded. "I can't imagine how she feels."

My arms wrapped around my chest as I tried to picture giving little Liberty up. It was unimaginable. The heaviness I felt for poor Liberty nearly suffocated me.

Ten minutes passed before Liberty called for us. As we walked into the room, I was taken at the sight in front of me.

A young mother, holding the child she had given up so that they would both have a better life. The child that was now mine and Jonathon's. Our child. A little girl who would learn about the amazing young woman her birth mother was, who loved her baby so much she blessed us with becoming her parents.

"Thank you so much for giving me that time with her. It helped in more ways than you'll ever know."

I scooped the baby into my arms. "It was the least we could do."

Her smile was tight and her eyes filled with tears. "You better head on out. I'm fine."

A part of me didn't want to leave. I wanted to stay in that room…just the four of us. But I knew it was time.

"Thank you, Liberty. You'll call us when you've decided on what you want to do?"

She nodded. "I promise, I will."

I leaned over and kissed her on the cheek and whispered, "Thank you."

Stepping back, Jonathon kissed her forehead. "You let us know if you need anything. Or you tell Wanda and Mick, okay?"

"Yes, I promise. Thank you both."

As we turned to leave, I felt both excited and scared with a bit of sadness mixed in.

A nurse waited for us outside the room with a bassinet for Liberty. I placed her in it and followed the nurse as she showed us to where our baby would stay for the usual tests. She would be released after the pediatrician came by tomorrow to check her out.

"Y'all are more than welcome to come into the nursery any time you want. I believe your mother said you are staying at the hotel across the street."

"Thanks," Jonathon said as he wrapped his arm around my waist.

"Yes, thank you, but I'm pretty sure we'll crash in the waiting room all night," I said with a chuckle.

"There are a few tests we still need to do. Why don't y'all go get some rest or something to eat."

"Sounds like a good idea. I'm sure your folks will want to sneak into the nursery as well and hold her."

The nurse brought our daughter into the nursery and placed her next to a baby boy named Mark Loach. Our baby's name was slipped into the name holder on the bassinet. Jonathon laced his fingers with mine as I read it out loud.

"Liberty Grace Turner. It's beautiful."

"Of course, it is. A beautiful name for a beautiful baby."

My fingers came up to the glass. "I just want to hold her and never let her go."

"Same here. Look at how she's already eyeing up ol' Mark. Good Lord."

I laughed and shook my head. "I have a feeling you'll be asking Steed for a lot of advice."

He let out a gruff laugh. "No kidding."

Jonathon turned me to face him. Cupping my face in his hands, his grey eyes searched my face. "Happy Mother's Day."

There was no way I could stop the tears that came with those three simple words.

"Happy Father's Day."

His thumbs swept over my cheeks to wipe away my tears. "Do we have any idea what we're doing?"

Laughing, I replied, "Not a damn clue."

He kissed me gently before drawing back. "This is going to be fun."

Sinking my teeth in my lip, I replied, "And expensive. I want that round crib we saw in that magazine."

Jonathon's arms dropped to his side, a moan slipping out. "I can make that for half the cost!"

Draping his arm over my shoulder, we headed to the waiting room.

"It will take too long!"

"Next you're going to tell me you want her to have her own goat."

"Oh, hell no. You think I've lost my mind? I was thinking more along the lines of a puppy!"

"Good Lord. What have I gotten myself into?"

I stood back and looked at my handiwork as I smiled.

"Look at that, Liberty. The finishing touches on your room. Pink curtains."

Glancing at my three-day-old daughter, I nodded. "I know. I know. It was a compromise between your daddy and me. I could put up pink curtains, but they had to have little hammers on them. Don't ask me how he got them made so fast or who in the heck made them. I have a feeling your Uncle Cord was in on it."

Liberty stared from her bouncer. Dropping on the floor, I got up close.

"Mommy loves you so much, my sweet baby. How about we do a little dancing?"

Standing, I reached for the bouncer and carried it out into the living room. We both sat on the floor as I went through my music.

"Hmm...looks like Daddy has brought over all his music." I started flipping through the CDs. "Foreigner, Boston, Daughtry, Def Leppard, AC/DC."

Snarling, I shook my head. "We are not starting you out on AC/DC. Let's look at Mommy's."

I smiled as I went through my playlist on my phone. "This is more like it, Liberty Grace. Let's see what we have to pick from. Shania Twain, Rascal Flatts, Keith Urban, Miranda Lambert." When I saw the song, I felt a warm sensation in my chest. It was perfect.

"This is our song." I pushed on Rascal Flatt's "The Day Before You" and unbuckled Liberty. I lifted her up and held her against my chest.

"Let's dance, baby girl."

Holding my daughter in my arms, I rocked her as the music played. Every single word of the song seemed to be coming from my heart. I closed my eyes and started to sing the words to her.

I felt Jonathon before I saw him. My eyes stung as I forced my tears back. I watched him wipe his cheeks dry.

"Want to join us?" I asked.

"It would be my honor."

Jonathon made his way over to me. Kissing me softly, he leaned down and kissed Liberty on the forehead.

"I love you both so much."

"And we love you, too, Daddy. Don't we, baby girl?"

Jonathon pulled me closer as we danced in the middle of the living room with our little Liberty.

"Hey, you never did tell me about that surprise you had for me the day of the accident."

Gazing up at him, I smiled.

"I'll be sure to wear it tonight."

Jonathon's eyes smoldered with desire. "And I didn't think this day could get any better. I do believe I'm in heaven."

"Heaven on Earth," I said softly as he pulled us closer. I closed my eyes and thought back over the last four months. The ups and downs. The laughter and tears.

All of it was preparing us for this moment.

And what a beautiful moment it was.

It's not The End...
the journey is only beginning.
Sneak Peek at *Blind Love*

Tripp

My phone buzzed on my desk.

"Yes, Karen?"

"There's, um, someone here to see you, Mr. Parker."

"Do they have an appointment?"

"No, she doesn't."

I smiled.

"Is it Mallory?"

There was a slight pause. "It's not Mallory. It's Harley Carba-jal."

Sitting back in my chair, I cursed under my breath. She was back for good in Oak Springs. With a sigh, I stood up and made my way to the lobby.

When I walked out and saw her, I had to catch my breath. She was beautiful. Even dressed in scrubs covered in cat and dog fur. Her hair was pulled into a ponytail, and she looked...panicked.

"Harley, is there something I can help you with?"

She looked nervously at Karen and then back to me. "I know you don't want to talk to me, but I need your help, and it's sort of an emergency."

Glancing at my watch, I knew Mallory would be walking through the door any minute for our lunch date.

"I'm meeting someone for lunch. I have about five minutes, so why don't we head into my office."

I could feel the heat of Karen's stare as I let Harley walk by. When I looked at her, Karen lifted a brow and crossed her arms.

Pointing to her, I muttered, "Stop giving me that look."

"What look? The one that says you're taking your ex into your office when your current girlfriend will be here any moment?"

"Hush!" I whispered as I followed Harley into my office and shut the door.

"What's going on?"

She stood there wringing her hands, staring down at the floor.

"Harley? What's going on? What's so important that you need-ed to see me?"

When she started pacing, I grew more worried. Something was wrong for sure.

"Harley! I don't have all day, for Christ's sake. What's the emergency?"

Stopping in front of me, she took a shaky breath and blew it out.

"I think he's found me."

Blind Love coming . . . July 2018

Contains Spoilers

Imagine Dragons – "Demons"
Waylynn's inner struggles

Shania Twain – "Poor Me"
Waylynn seeing the picture of Jonathon in Vegas

Taylor Swift – "Ready For It"
Before Waylynn and Jonathon's first date

Shania Twain – "We Got Something They Don't"
Waylynn overcoming her fear of her age difference

Shania Twain – "I'm Alright"
After Jack's visit to Waylynn

Rascall Flatts – "Let It Hurt"
Amelia talking to Waylynn after the accident

Lady Antebellum – "Hurt"
Jonathon telling Waylynn he will never give up on them

Miranda Lambert – "Well Rested"
Waylynn breaking down in front of her family

Amy Grant – "Love Has A Hold On Me"
The birth of Liberty <3

Rascal Flatts – "The Day Before You"
Waylynn, Jonathon, and Liberty's song

Taylor Swift – "This Love"
This entire book!

With each book there is a list of people to thank. I know I always forget people!

Darrin and Lauren – I love you both to the moon and back.

Kristin, Laura, and Tanya – Thank you for reading this book when none of it makes any sense! You are the best and I couldn't do this without you.

Julie – You make the books so beautiful…just like your soul. You are crazy talented and I'm blessed to call you a friend.

Danielle – Thank you for always being the voice of reason and not letting me lose my shit when that's all I really want to do. You keep my crazy world in check and I couldn't do this without you

Elaine, Cory, and AmyRose – Thank you for making my words better! We are half way done with this family and that makes me so sad!

The readers – Your endless support and words of encouragement mean the world to me. Thank you for letting me share my stories with you. It truly is an honor.

Thank you to the Lord above. Who without his blessings and guiding hand I couldn't do any of this. Give mom a hug for me.